I0717860

# The Derbyshire Set:

## Omnibus Edition 1

## Regency Historical Romance

# Arietta Richmond

# Books by
# Arietta Richmond

## The Derbyshire Set

A Gift of Love (Prequel short story)

A Devil's Bargain (Prequel short story - coming soon)

The Earl's Unexpected Bride

The Captain's Compromised Heiress

The Viscount's Unsuitable Affair

The Count's Impetuous Seduction

The Rake's Unlikely Redemption

The Marquess' Scandalous Mistress

A Remembered Face (Bonus short story – coming soon)

The Marchioness' Second Chance (coming soon)

A Viscount's Reluctant Passion (coming soon)

The Duke's Improper Love (coming soon)

## Other Books

The Scottish Governess (coming soon)

The Earl's Reluctant Fiancee (coming soon)

The Crew of the Seadragon's Soul Series, (coming soon
- a set of 10 linked novels)

The Derbyshire Set - Book 1
Regency Historical Romance
The Earl's
Unexpected Bride
2nd Edition - Revised and Expanded
BEST
NUMBER 1
SELLER
Bestselling Author
Arietta Richmond

# The Derbyshire Set ~ Book 1

# Regency Historical Romance

# (Second Edition ~ Revised and Expanded)

# The Earls Unexpected Bride

# Arietta Richmond

ARIETTA RICHMOND

# Dedication

For everyone who had the grace to be patient while this book, and the ones that follow were coming into existence, who provided cups of tea, and food, when the writing would not let me go, and endured countless times being asked for opinions. And for all the writers of Regency Historical Romance, whose books I read, who inspired me to write in this fascinating period.

For the reviewers and beta readers, whose valuable opinions helped me know what was needed to make the story much, much better, in this revised and expanded edition.

As the water closed over her head, the events of the last few minutes replayed themselves in Catherine's mind, with the intense clarity that sometimes comes in dreams. But this was all too horribly real.

The water was such a cold shock after the warm sun of the bright May morning, and part of her believed that she would drown, even while she flailed against it.

*

She had been walking along the road from Lavenham to Harteston, returning from a visit to her mother's friend, Mrs Brown, when she first heard the sound of a horse's hooves.

Not those of just any horse she might have heard, picking its steady way along the hard-packed earth of the road, but a powerful, fast horse, obviously in some considerable hurry, hooves pounding out the urgency of its pace. It stopped her right in her tracks for a moment, so out of place was that rush on this quiet road.

The thudding rhythm, the pounding of its progress - she heard it coming up ahead of her, on the other side of the bridge, although she could not yet see it, for the trees and the high bank on the side of the road quite obscured what might lie around the corner.

She was, for no sensible reason, filled with a sudden dread - not a horrible sense of fear, or a real worry for her safety, but a dread nonetheless, at what was approaching, at the source of that clamour, coming towards her from around the corner. Then, taking her first few steps onto the bridge over the Shimpling stream, she saw him.

He came clattering onto the wooden slats of the bridge, apparently unconcerned by the prospect of any passer-by. The first thing that struck her, in that first instant that she saw him, was the rider, his thighs, to be precise, inappropriate as that may be. He sat the horse with the confidence of long years riding, and controlled the stallion without apparent effort. His powerful thighs, flexing as they held him effortlessly in place, spoke eloquently of power and authority.

She was embarrassed by her thoughts, and a flush of colour came to her cheeks, but she could not drag her eyes away.

His breeches, creamy white and tight as skin, clung to him, giving definition to every muscle and sinew.

His boots were almost as magnificent, well-worn black leather, the same colour as the horse's glistening hide. Everything about him spoke of wealth and power.

He sat atop his animal with an easy grace, casual almost in his manner, unencumbered by a glove or a hat. From the other end of the bridge, she could take in all of his magnificence, the broad strong chest, the shoulders that seemed to span the entire width of the road, the chin that jutted forward. His face was strong, robust and masculine, with chiselled cheek-bones below dark eyes.

And on top of it all, above the square manliness of his face, and the rather wild look of his eyes, was a rich mane of dark hair, shot through with red and gold tones, that glinted in the sun, tousled, swept aside by the onrushing wind and lent buoyancy by an irrepressible energy that could be felt the moment you saw him. She suspected that hair was not easily controlled. So focussed was she on the sight in front of her, that she had simply stopped walking, unaware that she had done so.

The horse did not stop as it came towards her. Its rider seemed not to see the small and simply dressed young woman on the the bridge, who also had cause to cross the green expanse of the Shimpling stream, late this Thursday afternoon in May.

He spurred his mount on, charging over the rickety structure, as if he were master of all he surveyed.

She realised, with a gasp, that he was not going to stop for her, and, with a cry, threw herself to the side. Almost brushing the stallion's flank, she hurled herself against the side rail, but could not stop herself from toppling, tumbling over the rickety rail and into the stream.

With an almighty splash, and a roaring in her ears, she was in the water. She could feel the slimy grasp of the reeds, feel the weight of all the water on top of her as she flailed about. She panicked.

She had never learned to swim. The mill pond at the back of her village school had always seemed too terrifying to enter, and she had never learned. The thoughts rushed through her mind, replaying, over and over, the last few minutes, as she desperately fought the water, all to no effect.

She grasped around for the bank, for something to cling onto, but nothing presented itself to her flailing hands. She could barely see in all the darkness of the stream, and could feel her dress and petticoats soaking up the water, weighing her down, pulling her to the rocky bed of the stream. Every moment she became more certain that she was about to drown.

But then she felt something, a firm hand, a grasp from above, a man's grip. She was dragged up until she broke the surface of the water, spluttering uncontrollably. Some heroic force hauled her onto the river bank, onto the dry grass just above the shore. She was held in a standing position, only by the strength of her saviour's grip – he legs as yet refused to support her.

She looked up, still panting for breath. It was him. Of course it was him. Her assailant had become her saviour. He held her close, waiting to see if she could stand, if she would pull away.

Looking past his shoulder, she could see that the stallion was tied to a tree in the background, pawing at the grass, obviously wishing to be away and running again. She looked up into those dark devilish eyes and could not help but smile, even though her teeth chattered from the chill of the water.

"Are you quite all right?" he asked, with an uncertainty to his voice that betrayed his concern.

"Yes, yes quite all right." Her voice was shaky, and she was still short of breath, nerves still jangling from her watery encounter. She suspected, strongly, that she sounded unconvincing. Her eyes met his and she drank him in – he was just as good to look upon close up, as he had been from a distance.

"I must thank you kind sir, by your hand I appear to have been rescued from a watery grave."

"It was only because of me that you found yourself in such a predicament to begin with" he said, without hesitation.

His tone was that of man used to making declarations, to ordering the world around him. She realised that he held her slight frame in his embrace still, and could not but feel a shiver at the sensation. She knew that she should pull away, should put distance between them, that this was highly inappropriate, yet she did not want to. It was pleasant, every once in a while to have a saviour this handsome.

She was not used to anyone else taking care of her, except her mother.

"I must apologise for my haste in crossing the bridge," he continued.

"It appears to have compromised your passage somewhat. I was, unfortunately, rather distracted – after a trying morning, I just wanted to ride, and ignore the world."

"Oh, not at all sir" she replied, (although it was patently obvious that he spoke the truth).

She was still shaky, and unable to find anything sensible to say - she had often struggled to maintain her composure around handsome gentlemen – in fact, she had very little experience with gentlemen at all. Regardless of the fact that he had caused her fall into the stream, her gratitude to him for saving her was immense, for surely, without him, she would have drowned.

"Please!" he cried, cutting her off. "Do not deny it, the fault was entirely mine." He released her, apparently having finally noticed that they were in a rather inappropriate proximity to each other, and stepped back cautiously, watching to make sure that she could stand on her own.

His immaculately tailored coat of bottle green superfine clung to his shoulders, quite as beautifully tailored as those breeches, and showing of his devastatingly well-made body.

She was horrified to see that the fabric was marred by splashes of water, and that the pristine whiteness of his breeches had rather suffered from the muddiness of the stream.

Yet she was shocked to realise that she felt a desire to be back in the embrace of those arms, it had made her feel safe, to be held so, and she could not but consider what might follow such an embrace.

Her breath hitched at the thought, and, as he looked at her, patiently waiting to see what she would do, his eyes still full of concern, she became conscious of her wetness, of how it must make her face red and shiny, of how her hair was clinging unflatteringly to the side of her head and of how her bodice was clinging rather revealingly to her body, the cloth made somewhat translucent by the water.

The light stays that she wore, and the somewhat old and thin state of the fabric of her gown, did little to conceal her figure, once totally soaked in the water of the stream. It brought a blush to her cheeks, but he did not look concerned.

"I must regretfully confess, I can often become rather distracted when I take my afternoon ride." As he spoke was looking over at the horse, gesturing.

She looked down, blushing, and ashamed of her state, and realised that he was wet up to his knees, his beautiful Hessians undoubtedly ruined.

He had waded into the stream to save her, compromised his own dignity for her safety - how remarkably unlike most of the noble gentlemen that she had met before (admittedly, there were not many). This, she allowed herself to think, was quite an unusual man.

That, she thought, following the line of his hand to the horse, was quite some animal. It would take a remarkable man to tame it.

She could not ride – a humble village girl had no chance or reason to learn – her feet, or the innkeepers cart, had always been enough for her. Yet she knew a quality horse when she saw one.

"I recently acquired this splendid mount" he waved to the horse once more "at an auction at Tattersalls. I was informed by my dealer, Mr. Redgrave, that he was bred in the stables of the Maharajah of Nackulpande, renowned as the greatest horse breeder in all of His Majesty's colonies".

He fixed his gaze back on her. "His studs are renowned for their power and virility. Thaddeus here came at a not inconsiderable expense, but I believe such extravagance to have been worthwhile."

She nodded, unfamiliar with such matters – she could tell that the horse was quality, but of what type, or to what extent, she had no idea. She had never once ridden a horse herself.

"He is as powerful as he is headstrong. I see plenty of my own self in him – That is probably why we suit."

He looked back, when she made no response. She could think of nothing to say, she was too caught up in watching him, in the obvious energy that he brought to everything he did. It was compelling, and exciting.

He mistook her silence for disinterest.

"I pray I have not bored you with all of this discussion of the stallion. As an unmarried man, I am not often called upon to converse with ladies outside the confines of the drawing room and the ballroom. But where are my manners – here I am rambling on about my horse, and you are standing there, dripping wet and cold. Come, let me help you up the bank to the road."

He offered his hand. She clasped it, and felt a quaking in her breast, a quivering in the bottom of her stomach. He was unmarried! And so handsome and wealthy! How was it even possible? This chance encounter appeared to offer one of the great excitements of her life, and she could already feel her mind brimming with new passions, new hopes, new desires.

Village girls dreamed of things like this, of accidental meetings with handsome, wealthy noblemen, and, of course, those dreams always had a happy ending, with the couple falling in love.

She shook herself, mentally – this was reality, no dream, and the chances of anything happening were remote, to say the least.

"I thank you sir" she said, a little shakily, as she reached the top of the bank, and stepped on to the edge of the road. "And I must say that it is not at all tiresome to hear so eloquent an insight, on a subject with which I was not previously familiar."

"You flatter me" he said, with an ironic smile. "But I know enough of young ladies to have some awareness that the subject of stallions and auction houses does not generally greatly excite their interest."

He smiled and she could not help herself but smile warmly back. He had revealed another side, the tiniest hint of softness, of charm.

"Tell me miss, what is your name?" he enquired, with a renewed gravity. His warmth was hidden again, tantalising her in the background. She examined her feet humbly before she could look him once more in the eyes.

"My name is Catherine Thornberry."

"A charming name. The sweetness in the wilderness. I have always had a fondness for it."

She blushed at this spontaneously poetic response.

"Allow me to introduce myself; I am Charles Rockingham, Earl of Stanningfield. I must confess that I am surprised to have stumbled upon you. I had presumed myself to be familiar with every pretty young lady in the county, but it appears that at least one had slipped my notice - and barely a mile from my own estate. Amusing is it not, how these things can pass us by?"

"Oh yes sir, indeed it is!" she said, in a rush, excited by his flattery.  The Earl of Stanningfield, here on Shimpling bridge, plucking her, Miss Catherine Thornberry, from the stream as if it were the most natural thing on earth!  Catherine had a horrible suspicion that she was gushing, that she was making a fool of herself, but this man had an odd effect on her - she found that she struggled to think sensibly in his presence.

She was awestruck. Having never seen the Earl before, but having heard, from her friends and from her mother, much of his exploits, she had not anticipated that he should be so young, so handsome, so gallant in his readiness to help a young lady in distress.

The tales she had heard painted him as a rake, as a man with a great deal of life experience.  She had expected an older man, heavy of body from overindulgence, and jaded in his attitude to life.  Nothing could be further from the man who stood before her. She tried, as hard as she could, not to allow another red blush to flush her face, but it was all too much. It was all unreal, as if in a dream.

"Do not look so thunder-struck Miss Thornberry." He spoke forcefully - "You may have formed some idea of my reputation on the basis of idle parish gossip, but I must assure you that the overwhelming bulk of it is hearsay."

"I'm sure that it is sir, undoubtedly!" She was gushing again - it had always been a profound concern of hers that she came across as too enthusiastic in the presence of gentlemen. She checked herself.

"I have been at great pains to impress upon the county my courteous nature, but regrettably, I have an unfortunate past that seems to stalk me like a wolf."

She nodded gravely. She had heard some such stories, and always suspected that there might be some truth to them. Nevertheless, being of a kind and trusting nature, she had always wanted to believe that they were false, or at least, misrepresented. She found that she did not want to believe this man capable of terrible things.

"We shall speak no more of such unpleasantness. Please, allow me to escort you homeward. It would be the least kindness I could offer after our unfortunate interaction on the bridge."

"Oh sir, that will not be necessary. I am quite capable of completing my journey unaccompanied."

"I insist" he said, not as a politeness, but a declaration. "You are shaking like a willow in a gale and as wet as a hunting dog, and all on my account. It would be most improper of me to abandon you here." His expression was serious as he spoke, and, again, she felt that the concern in his eyes was genuine.

"I will not have it said of me that I abandoned a fair and defenceless lady, drenched, on the side of the road. And besides" he added, with a glimmer in the corner of his rich brown eyes "what on earth would your neighbours say if I did?" they shared a chuckle at his little joke.

"Thaddeus awaits!" laughing, he took her hand, tugging her towards the horse.

"But sir!" Catherine exclaimed "I regret to confess, I have never ridden before, and I do not know how!"

"Good heavens above!" he seemed genuinely shocked "Not ridden a horse? Why it is one of life's greatest pleasures! I would not wish to deny the thrill of a good, vigorous ride to my worst enemy. Allow me..." before Catherine even had time to make an objection, he had scooped her up. She clasped his thick, muscular shoulders and found suddenly that her face was close to his, so close, in fact, that she could see every bristling hair, every tendon in his neck.

Close inspection did him justice. His scent came to her, an earthy mixture of horse, leather, and an undertone of some more exotic scent, some cologne of citrus and spices. It was like nothing she had smelled before. She found it stimulating, and extremely pleasant.

"Time I think, for your first ride!" he chortled, before depositing her unceremoniously to sit sideways across Thaddeus' saddle. She felt the animal shifting beneath her, full of vigorous life. She clung to the abundant mane that drifted back over her hands, holding on as if for dear life, anxious that the horse might suddenly take off without warning, or that it would deposit her once again into the stream.

It had a will of its own and a powerful body after all, but her saviour, the Earl, held firmly to its reins.

He gently stroked the horse's nose to calm it, putting it under his spell, before firmly commanding it to stand.

Then in a single, graceful movement, he swung up into the saddle, lifting her to sit, still sideways, across his knees, his arms either side of her shaking body, and took charge of his stallion.

"Hold on tight" he declared, and she obeyed willingly. There was a moment where she hesitated, aware that her soaking clothes were already shedding even more water onto his attire, before a movement of the horse convinced her that she was quite happy to sacrifice his clothing for her safety.  She wrapped her white arms, still cold and wet, about his splendid torso, as tightly as she dared, her head resting against his shoulder. The shape and definition of his firm abdominal muscles could be made out beneath his coat and shirt.  The sensation quite took her breath away.

"Now where would you like me to take you, Miss Thornberry?" he asked, after a moment.

"To Hawthorn Cottage in Harteston" she replied. "Do you know it?"

"I know Harteston, but not the exact location of Hawthorn Cottage" he said. "A fine village indeed - do you live there alone?" As he spoke, without warning her, he had shifted Thaddeus into motion, and already they were crossing the bridge at a gentle canter. She was, again, impressed at his gallantry, as he was now heading the opposite way to his own original route.

With the unfamiliar rocking motion of the horse, and the stress of its forward motion pressing her ever more tightly against the body of her saviour, she could feel something thrilling stirring within her.

A new sensation, pleasurable, dangerous, was creeping up her inner thighs and into her bosom. She bit the back of her lip. It was entirely inappropriate for her to be thinking such thoughts about this man.  He was far above her, he was courteous enough to have saved her from drowning, and here she was thinking like a wanton.  Well, she thought that's what it was – actually, she had no idea, no idea beyond the fact that her body was reacting to its proximity to his – and she was scandalously enjoying it.

"Or…" he continued with a roguish chuckle "have you a sweetheart in Harteston perhaps?" This time she was wise to him. This time she played the game.

"I am unmarried, my Lord. However…" she added, with a slight laugh of her own "I must confess that the innkeeper's son and I have developed something of a rapport in recent times. He is a most handsome young man."

"Oh undeniably" replied the Earl, rising to her challenge. "Indeed I have often thought to myself, on visiting that very fine inn, that he would make a most attractive catch for a young girl in the village. Nevertheless", He paused in his speech a moment, as if considering the right words to use. Thaddeus was picking up speed. Her lower body was assailed with a new vigour, rocked against the Earl's thighs, and the front of his body, in a rather intimate fashion. The warmth of his body was penetrating the chill of her wet clothes – it made her want to press herself even closer against him.

Having obviously chosen his words carefully, he continued "Are his manners and breeding not a little coarse, for a young lady of distinction, such as yourself?"

Catherine did not allow herself to laugh, but she was overwhelmed. This man was clever. He knew the workings of the female heart. Moreover, by asking this question, which she now, perforce, had to answer, he had coaxed a difficult admission out of her, concerning their relative status.

"I am but a humble schoolmistress, sir" she said reluctantly. "I have education and, I flatter myself, a little breeding – but certainly not any significant status in the world."

"Stuff! I could tell the moment that I saw you, that here is a lady who carries herself well, evident poverty notwithstanding."

"You are indeed, courteous, my Lord. Nevertheless, I could never make any claims to be a noble lady. My mother, with whom I share Hawthorn Cottage, has long maintained that we are descended from the de Quincy family, who came over with William the Conqueror no less, but I fear, from what little she is willing to tell me of the detail, that lineage may be rather obscure now, to say the least."

"The de Quincys?" he came back, not bothering to disguise how impressed he was. "Not bad at all. Tell me, how does a girl with such a fine pedigree find herself reciting the alphabet to ungrateful village brats?"

"I suppose some ancestor of ours must have fallen on hard times" she said, keeping her poise.

Thaddeus was going at quite a speed now, and it was necessary to raise her voice. She tried as hard as she dared to disguise the quaking in her body that the movement of the ride, and the sensation of his body against hers, was giving her.

"Mother has mentioned a gambler, in my great grandmother's generation, who may have lost us our estates. That is long ago, and of no relevance to our lives now. I am unused to luxury, and the life of a humble schoolmistress is easy enough to bear."

He had exposed a quiet sadness in her, a longing. For years she had ignored her mother's pining after their heritage, her obsession with the importance of ancestors on their family tree, but now, in the presence of a real gentleman, she was, for the first time, embarrassed by her circumstances. She had no land, no money, no prospects of a higher match.

All she had ever hoped for was to make an honest living and to marry one of the boys in the village, but now, something else had stirred in her, passion, ambition, a reaching for something more. Thaddeus' movement seemed to fill her with a greater lust for more in life, as well as most interesting sensations in her body, with every galloping stride.

"I suppose someone's got to force some knowledge into 'em" he laughed, urging the horse along. The countryside sped by. She took in long, drooping willows, plump cows chomping in the fields, water mills churning, as they had for hundreds of years. It was not such bad country, Suffolk, especially as it had such charming people in it. The speed at which the road went by amazed her, so used was she to the time it took to walk this distance.

"Still, it is a terrible shame for a great and noble family to have fallen on hard times. Alright, I suppose, if you're happy enough looking after other people's infants, and cavorting with innkeepers' sons, then I can think of worse fates."

"Why yes sir. I suppose I am happy enough." She knew, even as the words came out, that she was lying to him. Had someone asked her the question yesterday, then that answer would have been truthful, but today, she was alarmed to discover, something in her had changed.  She was no longer satisfied with what she had.

"Well, jolly good then." He appeared to focus his concentration on riding now, for the first time taking his attention away from her. She could not help but feel a small pang of disappointment.

Thaddeus thundered on, down a shallow hill, and then splashed across a ford. Before she knew it, having never ridden upon a horse or experienced just quite how fast these noble animals could move, she was in the village of Harteston, shaken by the journey, quivering and awake deep in her body, and intensely aware of his body where it pressed against her.

"Here we are" he declared confidently. "Harteston - where I suppose I shall leave you."

"Yes. I must thank you my Lord, your kindness has saved me much effort, and possibly even preserved my life. For surely, had I not drowned, by now I would have taken a terrible chill on the road home."

"No need to thank me Miss Catherine, I am sure that you would have done the same were our roles to be reversed."

"I suppose I would have. Thank you again."

She released her grip on his body, regretfully, and he lifted her gently, supporting her as she slid down the side of the horse to land on her feet.

She hesitated, unsure of what to do now, part of her not wishing this moment to end, but unable to see any reason for it to continue.  Then, not wishing to betray the feelings that he had stirred in her, and holding her crumpled bonnet high upon her head, she dipped him a curtsey, and set off for home.

The Earl however, had never been the kind to let a pretty young lady get away from him, so coldly and suddenly. As she had silently, privately hoped, he swung out of his saddle and came straight after her, catching her in just a few steps. Grasping her fragile waist, he turned her suddenly towards him. She gasped, her eyes wide open. He pulled her against him, and the heat of his body against hers felt like fire rushing through her veins.

"Not so fast" he whispered, close against her ear. "We haven't even said a proper goodbye" and then, just like that, he kissed her, fully, without apology, on the lips. He gripped her for a moment that felt like it should last forever, a moment deserving of a painting or a symphony to capture it and preserve it. She felt his strong tongue, his hot mouth and his firm lips. Their bodies pressed together, seeming moulded just for that, and she could sense the longing they shared could feel the hardness of his desire, tangible through their damp clothing. Her body throbbed, with the sensation of the kiss, and the vitality imparted by the ride.

Just as suddenly as he had captured her, he pulled back, looking a little shocked himself, at what he had just done. He mumbled goodbye, and swung back into the saddle, heading for home. Catherine stood a moment, dazed, watching him go. She had never felt such a thrill in all of her twenty-four years on God's earth.

Charles Rockingham, Earl of Stanningfield, was bemused. He rather feared that he had just made a fool of himself, in front of a young lady.  Not something that he had ever been prone to doing. *That is,* an insidious thought reminded him, *except for the colossal fool he had made of himself, at 17, with Monique.* He pushed the thought aside.  That was old history, beyond being changed.  Today, he should be focussing on his current problems.  And what problems.

He groaned as it all forced itself back to the surface of his mind, now that he no longer had a ready distraction to hand. He chose to shove the thoughts away again, an act made easy by the fact that his clothes were uncomfortably damp, and his toes squished alarmingly in his boots, which were, he suspected, full of water.

They were certainly coated in mud. The condition of his attire would draw the wrath of his valet, and he expected that Johnson would be effective at making his disapproval known, without ever saying a word.

Still, even if he had rather made a fool of himself, it was, he decided, worth it.  He had been in such a temper when he had left the house.  His morning, reading through applications for the role of Theodora's Governess, had been enough to drive anyone to despair.

They were, universally, terrible.  The sort of women he would definitely never want in his house – the sort who would turn a bright, if sometimes difficult, girl into a prudish, boring society Miss, incapable of conversing on any topic except the weather.

He knew that the best solution to such a mood was a good hard ride, on a quality horse. And Thaddeus was quite the best horse that he had ever owned. But it had been spectacularly unwise of him to ride, at that pace, along the road – over the fields would have been a far better choice.

Well too late to change anything now. And…. Would he want to?

The girl was beautiful – and, it seemed, completely unaware of that fact.  He had not seen her, not until it was too late.  He had been so wrapped in his thoughts that the world around him had been barely registering.

He might not have seen her, but the thump against his leg as he rode across the bridge, followed by the scream, and the huge splash, had certainly attracted his attention.

At that point he had no idea who or what he had just caused to fall into the Shimpling Stream, beyond the fact that it was almost certainly a person, as nothing else screamed quite like that. Unwilling to leave anyone floundering due to his inattention, he had hauled Thaddeus around (somewhat against the stallions wishes at the time!) and gone back to investigate.

What he dragged from the water was a delectable surprise. A girl, or young woman rather, her shape thoroughly displayed by the unfortunate saturation of her gown, her piercing blue eyes shocking in her pale, water soaked face, her sodden hair seemingly a golden brown colour – although the mud made it hard to tell.  She had blushed charmingly as he held her, waiting for her to be steady on her feet again.

She held herself well – there was obviously some breeding there, or at least some education, but the gown was, as far as he could tell after its dip in the stream, rather worn.  It had been good quality once, but the hems showed signs of it having been turned, and the fabric was thin from wear.  Thinness he deeply appreciated, as it ensured that the water had made it almost translucent.  It had taken all his concentration to avoid staring at her breasts rather than her face.

Apart from the sodden gown, and its exposure of her attractions, there was something about her that took his breath away, in that first look.

It took only a moment to realise what – her shape, the turn of her cheek, the fall of her hair, even sodden, brought to mind, just for a second, Monique.

He had pushed that recognition away, and focussed on her more mundane attractions. He had been a rake for too many years not to appreciate a woman's body when he was given an unexpected viewing. But, it seemed he was rather out of practice.

The sight of her body had robbed him of sensible, coherent conversation, and he had made a complete ass of himself, prattling on at her about the horse, of all things. Women, in his experience, did not give a damn about horses, so long as they transported them where they wanted to go. He was depressingly sure that he could not have made a bigger fool of himself if he had tried.

And then, to top it off, he had taken her home. What else could a gentleman do? He certainly couldn't leave her to walk four miles in a soddenly transparent dress, when she was already shivering from the cold! What if she had met some oaf along the way, who thought to take advantage of her? *Like you wanted to,* said that insidious voice in his thoughts. She was schoolmistress at the parish school – the school that his family funded, had funded for 50 years now, for the good of their tenants and the villagers. A less suitable woman for him to find tempting he couldn't imagine.

The feel of her body against him, of her arms around him and her soft breasts pressed against his chest, rubbing against him with the movement of the horse, the feel of her rounded derriere, rubbing against his thighs, pressing against his manhood, had been enough to drive a saint wild. The wet fabric of her gown was no barrier, and the water soon transferred to his breeches as well. They might as well have been skin to skin, he could feel the detail of her body so clearly.

His cock had hardened in response, making the ride an exquisite agony.  She must be an innocent, for she had appeared to genuinely not notice, even though Thaddeus' every stride had thrust the evidence of his arousal against her nether regions.

Which made his behaviour at the end of the ride all the more despicable.

Not only had he flirted with her, in a rather suggestively inappropriate way, but he had, at the end, kissed her…. Hard…. Full on the lips.

He had not intended to, but, when she turned away, all stiff and unsure, after that ever so wobbly curtsey, and simply began to walk off, her ridiculously crushed and sodden bonnet perched on her equally sodden hair, he had not been able to stop himself – he wanted a reaction, wanted more than just a departure.

He did not know why - he was, obviously, simply a fool.  But he had gone after her, grabbed her and pulled her to him.  In the middle of the damned village street, for pity's sake! And she had tasted divine.  Her innocent response had been to press into the kiss, and the feel of her body fitting so perfectly against his had roused his passion like no woman had for years.

Had the chiming of the town clock not interrupted, he might almost have taken her there, on the street. He was, most definitely, a fool.

And, he was no further ahead with solving the governess problem.

He was just as frustrated by that as before, but now, he was frustrated in an entirely different way, and sodden as well. He sighed, and steeled himself for Johnson's response to his maltreatment of his attire.

# Chapter Three

"Well of course there's not a single chance he'll marry you".

"Mother!"

"Don't speak out of turn child! I know gentlemen and their ways. He just wants to use you, as he uses that horse you seem to be so very taken with."

"But I'd never ridden before."

"No you had not, and quite right too – you've no need of riding and horses – where would you go? And considering what I've heard about the Earl's predilections, you would have been better off nowhere near riding with him!"

Catherine's mother paused for a moment, to stir the copper pot that was perched above the fire.

They would eat the same type of food as they ate every night- a mealy stew with perhaps a little bacon or fatty pork, supplemented by some vegetables grown in their garden and some bread.

An old weaving of the de Quincey family tree might hang above the fireplace, upon the blackened brickwork, but that was history, and now, in the present, they could not afford to dine on anything more extravagant than this.

"I may be old, but I know gentlemen" her mother continued, repeating herself as she often did lately. "A fellow like him's nothing more than a cad, a bounder. He sniffs out a pretty young girl who may be of noble heritage, but is poor and unimportant, as far as he is concerned, and he thinks only to have his way with her."

"Mother!"

"I only speak the truth, Cathy dear. I only have your best interests at heart. No good will come of this, I tell you." Catherine thought to reply, but she could not muster the courage. Deep-down, she knew that her mother might be right. Her mother's words were giving voice to a fear that she herself had felt, ever since the Earl first plucked her out of the stream. Maybe he was a bad man. Maybe all the rumours one heard about him were true.

"He did at least have the decency to stop and save me" she said at last, in a reedy voice that sounded a little desperate, a fact that annoyed her, even as she spoke. "You must at least concede that that was an act of considerable kindness?"

"Oh yes, of course" her mother replied, in a voice with a tone perilously close to a whine.

"I suppose yes, he was good enough not to just let you drown, after it was by his actions that you were deposited into the Shimpley stream in the first place. Yes, I suppose the fact that he's not actively a murderer is one small positive we can mark down in the ledger."

"Oh mother, I wish you wouldn't use that tone!"

"What tone?"

"That sarcastic, bitter tone you always like to use, whenever we speak about young gentlemen. It's almost as if….. as if you don't even want me to fall in love and get married! As if you want to talk me out of leading my own life and keep me here by the hearth with you forever, supping at stew and getting old by myself!"

"Now, now!" her mother replied, suddenly kinder. "Why on Earth would make you an assumption like that about your own dear mother, eh?"

She had come over, and placed her arm around Catherine's shoulder.

Unlike the Earl's, Mother Thornberry's arms were thin and frail. Catherine could feel them, all skin and bone wrapped in a scratchy shawl. It was a comfort to have her mother's embrace there, but not always a warming one.

She worried at how thin her mother seemed to be getting – she was not, when Catherine added it up, really very old at all, so it must be the result of their poverty, of eating so little, over so many years.  It distressed her to realise that she could not do more for her mother, who had done so much for her.

"All I'm saying" her mother said, softly, "is that a young lady like you has to be careful. You don't want to end up embroiled in some short-lived affair that strips you of your honour, but leaves you with nothing, save perhaps, an illegitimate child. Take it from me…"

She stared now into the middle distance, out of the little window of their cottage, towards the far fields, her expression sad and longing.

There was pain and sadness in her voice, pain that came from hard-won experience. Catherine knew. She had grown up knowing. Her mother had made this very same mistake herself.

Catherine herself was the illegitimate issue of a sudden affair, carried on beneath a haystack.

She knew little more of it than that, as her mother always refused to speak of it further, beyond the warning for Catherine not to be foolish enough to repeat her mother's errors in life.

She wished that she did know more, that there was some way to ease the sadness that her mother had carried for so many years.

"Men can be wonderful of course. Handsome, dashing, strong and charming, all at once, as if they are the most perfect creatures in all of creation. But they can also be brutes. Something stirs within them, some spirit, or instinct and all they can think about is a woman's body, her femininity. They have no care for a woman's feelings, or her life beyond the moment when she satisfies their desires."

"Mother, I am aware of the simple biology of it all."

"Are you child? Are you? I have tried to teach you more than is considered proper for a young lady to know, to protect you, and, as a result, I fear that you do believe that you know, but take it from me, you don't. I don't think you entirely understand the risks that you run in becoming involved with a man. I certainly didn't at your age."

"Then what would you have me do mother?" Catherine had risen from her chair by the fireside, throwing off her mother's embrace, and was standing now on her own feet, the very same feet that had, earlier that day, dangled down the side of The Earl's prize stallion, while her body was pressed so arousingly against his. Turing to face her mother, she asked the question that had kept her mind in turmoil ever since she had arrived home.

"What should I do?"

Her question, asked imploringly, drew a wry smile from her mother's lips.

The little wrinkles around her eyes tightened and she seemed to be forming new wisdom behind her eyes, even as Catherine watched, hoping against hope that there was an easy answer to an impossible question.

"You must be clever Cathy, that is all." The words were a long time coming, and Catherine had begun to wonder if her mother would answer her at all.. "You must anticipate what the Earl will do, and act accordingly. Bear in mind, at all times, that he lusts after you, and formulate a strategy on that basis. Consider also…" and she turned around to point straight at the family tree.

The illustration was beautiful, with the de Quincey coat of arms - a rampant Panther with a crown around its neck – surmounting the detailed listing of those who were her forebears. Frustratingly, the illustration had been created more than eighty years ago, and the link between herself, and her mother, and those listed on it, was not at all clear to Catherine..

"...that yours is amongst the highest heritages in all the land. The blood of Jocelyn de Quincey, and his noble ancestors, flows in your veins. We may not have money, titles or estates, but we do have that, and can never be stripped of it. If you can remind the Earl of that, he will be impressed by you, and may consider you a possible match. It all falls to you now, my Cathy, only you can revive the fortunes of our once great family. Don't squander this one chance."

Catherine looked up at the coat of arms. It was a proud image, but had been battered by time and obscurity, faded on the page. Her heart swelled with the thought of it, the possibilities that her mother's words brought to mind, but she trembled at the pressure that those same words placed on her. Could she do it? Could she really find herself married to the Earl of Stanningfield?

"I believe in you, Catherine Thornberry" her mother said, gravely. "But don't you go making any foolish mistakes. You're still only a girl, after all."

She was still only a girl, a maid even. It was true, her mother was right, even if she didn't like to admit it. She had to be clever, and careful, but her heart sang for him, for that kiss they had shared on the outskirts of the village.

With the thought of that, she was filled with a new warmth. Oh, it was all so exciting! She felt young and pretty and on the cusp of a great love affair! In her mind, she already thought of him as Charles, however lacking in propriety such forwardness might be, and the desire to see him again ran through her, bringing a flush to her face at the thought.

"Now child," her mother said, "if you are to become the great seducer of the county of Suffolk, I think you'd best keep your strength up. Come and have a bowl of this stew." The words were spoken lightly, with a true sense of humour in them, yet they were underlain with an aching desire for what might come. Catherine smiled, sat down willingly, and ate her fill.

Charles handed Thaddeus to his groom, and took himself into the house through the servant's door, in an attempt to minimise the spread of mud.  That was a failure.

Wilton eyed him expressively as he made his way up the stairs, and Johnson greeted him in silence, with an expression of outright horror on his face. A hot bath was called for, his maltreated clothing and boots were stripped away, and he was left to soak in silence. If only his thoughts were as silent and peaceful as the room around him.

He was in turmoil – he did not know what to do about any of his current problems.

The last three years he had been, comparatively, respectably behaved.

He had taken no new mistress, and had kept those short affairs that he indulged in to a strictly business basis – and exchange of the satisfaction of physical needs, with nothing emotional, and nothing exposed to the critical eyes of the *ton*. It had been a most considerable change from his previous approach to life.

Three years of 'good behaviour' had not completely dispelled the rumour and gossip that his previous life had generated, but it was fading. He could hope that, in time, they would forget. He had chosen to change, not for himself, but for Theodora's sake. From the day that she had been delivered into his care, at the age of eleven, he had vowed to provide her the love and care that her mother was no longer there to provide.

For the sake of her reputation, and eventual acceptance by the *ton*, when she reached a suitable age for her come-out, he had pushed aside many of his own desires, and to his mother's delight, begun to behave 'as an Earl should'. It had not been easy at first, but had become more so with time.

He had, six months ago, when old Mrs Walsh died, finally acquiesced to his mother's wishes, and agreed to make the long standing agreement between the families formal, with his betrothal to Lady Blanchette Cavendish. He did not love her, but, in the ranks of the ton, love between husband and wife was rare - marriages were for dynastic reasons, nothing more.

He knew that he needed an heir, and that Theodora needed another woman to help her grow up, now that Mrs Walsh was gone. He had hoped that lady Blanchette might be that woman. It was, it seemed, a vain hope, for Theodora had taken her in strong dislike, and, in her strong willed way, made that abundantly clear.

But by then, it was too late – the betrothal had been made public, and it was his duty to go through with it.

Lady Blanchette had been rather a surprise – whilst she was rather cold and harsh on the surface at times, she had proven to have a hidden core of passion.  Once they were betrothed, their parents had seen no harm in allowing them a walk in the grounds, some time alone together – time which had resulted in a passionate kiss, which he had begun, in exploration of what he might live with for the rest of his life, and she had taken further, with a response that had taken his breath, and all of his control, away.

After more than two years of minimal physical release, and that with women who were as jaded as he had become, Lady Blanchette's relatively innocent passion had been too much to handle – he had, to his later regret, pulled her into a nearby outbuilding, and taken her there, with little care for her experience – a fact of which he was still somewhat ashamed.

She had seemed somewhat shocked by his demanding and forceful actions, but she had responded with some strength of passion as well.  He had found her confusing, then, and did still, to this day. He excused his actions to himself, only by the fact that they were to marry.

She had, since that time, once more given him her body, for reasons that he could not determine, but otherwise she had been rather haughty, and not always pleasant.

He wondered if she lacked confidence, and acted this way to appear stronger than she was, or if she was simply of mercurial temperament. If the latter, he was, perhaps, in for a difficult life.

Now, he had a marriage to Blanchette to deal with in a scant month or so's time and the need to find a Governess for Theodora, who might have the strength of mind to manage her, enough education to teach her, and enough gentility in her breeding to know at least some of what Theodora would need to know, to behave appropriately as a young lady of the *ton.*

The marriage arrangements were in his mother's control – a fact which was both a relief, and terrifying. The Governess situation was all his problem, and he had no answer.

But today had tried his patience sorely, and he was now struggling not only with the need to find a Governess, but with the fact that a certain Miss Catherine Thornberry was taking over his thoughts. He could not wipe from his mind the image of her, standing before him on the bank of the Shimpling Stream, saturated, looking more like a water nymph from some erotic fantasy than a respectable young woman.

His thoughts became heated as he remembered the press of her body against his, and the delicious pain of his hardened cock being rubbed against her body by every stride of his horse, as he delivered her home. He was hard again now, lying back in his bathtub, just from the memory.

He wanted her. There was no denying it.

Why her, he wondered, why now, when he was soon to marry, and she was by far too below his station to be marry (even had he been able to), and of by far too respectable a family and position for him to simply use. Not that, he realised, he would wish to do such a thing now. Perhaps in his youth, but no longer. But he wanted her. More, he realised, than he had wanted any woman, since Monique.

It was insane to feel so, yet he did.  Resolutely, he tried to push her from his mind again, and focus on solving the Governess problem.  The bath water had cooled, but his body had not.  He still ached with need – perhaps if he eased that, by his own hand, he could stop thinking of the damn woman, and deal with everything else.

His release came hard, and fast, his mind imagining her beneath him as he came, but his thoughts were no clearer afterwards. He dragged himself out of the tub, and scrubbed himself dry with unnecessary force, then called for Johnson to dress him for dinner. Staring vacantly ahead, ignoring Johnson's still offended attitude, he thought once again about the qualifications he wanted in the Governess.

He was not sure such a woman existed, as most governesses were daughters of the lesser families of the *ton*, fallen on hard times.  Few had much education themselves, and even fewer had any idea how to either teach, or command respect – so how could he ever hope that they could deal with Theodora effectively?

Something about that last thought made him pause – there was something there, something that he was missing.

He worried away at it, mentally, as Johnson, poked and prodded, brushed and combed him into his clothes and into a well turned out presentation.  Then it came to him, in a flash of inspiration. The answer had been right before him this afternoon, he just had been so distracted by the 'packaging' that he had not realised.

Miss Catherine Thornberry fulfilled all of his requirements in a Governess, exactly.

She was quite well educated, she had practice teaching, and getting her students to respect her – the village children were not an easy lot to manage!  And she was of at least reasonable breeding, although sunken to poverty.  She knew how to curtsey and had at least the minimum of socially acceptable graces.  It was inconvenient that she also had the ability to drive him to distraction just at the sight of her figure, but he was sure that he could learn to manage his reactions – Theodora's need for a Governess came first.

He startled out of his thoughts, as Johnson spoke, for what must have been the third time.

"I believe you are ready, my Lord – will that be all? I fear I must return to the…. resurrection…. of your clothing, if you need nothing more from me now?" Johnson's tone left his opinion of the treatment of the clothing in no doubt.

"Thank you Johnson, yes, that will be all." Charles turned, as Johnson left the room, with a pleased smile on his face. He resolved to visit the village tomorrow, and speak to Miss Thornberry, to offer her the role of Governess to Theodora.

Perhaps today was not such a loss after all. Except for his favourite pair of Hessians.

The next day Catherine could barely focus, at all, on her work at the school. How on earth could she be expected to? The curtain was coming up on the great drama of her life and it had all of her energy, all of her attention (internally, she admitted that, perhaps this was melodramatic and overly optimistic, based on one meeting, but that did not stop her feeling that way). In the morning she stumbled her way through basic arithmetic.

The children looked confused, and seemed to be struggling to follow. She would lose track of her thoughts as they came to her, and frequently needed to sit down. Whilst talking them through one particular sum, she started giggling remembering him telling her all about the horse.

One of them asked her: "Miss, why are you laughing?" and all she could think to say was "Oh, nothing, it's none of your concern".

After the children had had their lunch, she had become grave and serious, thinking constantly of the consequences and the risks of her affair, should she be able to make it become so, in truth.

She tried to tell them about the exploits of Henry VIII but Charles Rockingham filled her thoughts. She even referred to Thomas Cromwell as 'Charles' once, an embarrassing mistake which caused all of the children to laugh.

"Who is Charles Miss?" one of the girls asked in a strong Suffolk accent. "Is he your sweetheart?"

"No, no of course not" she stuttered in reply. "I was merely thinking of Charles I, the king during the Civil War" - she did not sound very convincing. "That was all. I was thinking ahead. We'll be studying him next week" the girl eyed her suspiciously.

"Do you even have a sweetheart, Miss?"

"Jemimah, you will stop asking improper questions if you know what is good for you!" Catherine found a tiny reserve of strength and managed to implement some discipline. Jemimah Blenkinsop however, would not be silent.

"You're pretty enough to have a sweetheart Miss!" she declared. "All of the young fellows in the county should be asking for your hand!"

"Well that is very kind of you to say, young mistress Jemimah" Catherine replied, blushing.

"But please, if we could concentrate our attention on history for the present time, we are here to receive education, not to indulge in girlish gossip."

Despite her best efforts though, it was no use. She could not focus at all on teaching the children, her mind was on Charles, on his robust strong face, his broad, broad shoulders, his muscled thighs, his devilish wry smile, and of course, that kiss.

The kiss that they had shared already felt like the most significant moment in all of her life. She desperately wanted another, a chance to find out what more might happen, if such a kiss continued.

Later in the afternoon, shortly before the children were to be released for the day, Catherine was just directing the their attention towards the practice of writing, and spelling, when she heard a tap at the window.

Surprised, she turned to face it, and was both shocked, and delighted in equal measure, to see that it was the Earl himself, this time in a splendid jacket of rich dark crimson, as beautifully tailored as his coat of green, holding a riding crop and grinning through the grimy window pane. What a sight!

She gasped in astonishment, and was filled at once with questions, anxieties, warmth and longing. He was here! How on earth could he be here, what was he doing? It was so improper, for an earl to lower himself to come to the village school like this, interrupting her working day, so sudden, so (she dared to hope...) romantic! Or was something wrong?

Still he was smiling, waving at her to come out and greet him.

The children stared at the window, clearly confused at the sight of this unfamiliar and well-dressed man beckoning their schoolmistress so unexpectedly.

It could never have made any sense to them she thought, if she had tried to explain her reaction, and truly there was nothing she could say to explain his presence.  The power of her feelings and the dark beauty of that man waiting for her, made her shake with nervousness as she turned towards the door.

This was an unusual school, the result of the charity of the Earl's family, and some other local nobility, and of the enterprise of the local vicar – who, unlike many 'so called' churchmen, actually cared for his flock, and believed that even girls should be educated.

The donations of the nobility, plus the fees paid by the families who could afford to contribute, were just enough to pay Catherine's wages, and to buy some supplies for her to teach with.  She was dedicated to her work, and genuinely cared that the children should have a chance to learn, no matter what their status in life.

"I'm terribly sorry children" she improvised "I'm afraid I should have given you prior warning. That gentleman is here on urgent parish business. I shall have to speak with him, I shouldn't be more than a few moments. In the meantime…" she was already halfway to the door, rushing towards what she hoped would be the Earl's powerful embrace, "finish your exercises on the slates".

Without a moment's further hesitation she burst outside to greet him.

He had moved away from the window, and was standing with his legs wide apart, tapping the riding crop against his brown leather gloves. He was taller than she remembered, and even more magnificently attired.

Next to the deep red of his coat, the unblemished cream of his breeches, the glint of the richly polished leather of his boots and the perfectly executed cravat that topped it all off, she felt perfectly plain in her simple grey-blue dress and petticoats.

She wished, suddenly, that she had had more time to think about what she would wear today, wished that she had money for a maid, whose opinion she could consult, who could curl her hair and advise her on the angles that best suited her face. Charles outshone her this afternoon, indeed he would probably have outshone all of Suffolk, and beyond. She had never seen a man this handsome in her entire life.

"I hope I'm not disrupting the children's studies" he said, his lip curving slightly at the edge, into a half smile. "I wouldn't want the parish to be turning out dullards after all."

"Oh no, not at all!" she spluttered unthinkingly. She was filled with a desire to move into his arms, to kiss him wildly, but she knew that this would be beyond improper. She blushed at her own thoughts.

Apart from being improper, it would most definitely be liable to startle him and show her feelings, too suddenly, all at once. Besides, the children might see, or worse the vicar... This planning to seduce the man into wanting her was somewhat more complicated a thing than it had seemed, when she was talking to her mother!

"What were you teaching the children?"

"Just a little writing and spelling, nothing too taxing or important."

"Writing and Spelling is quite enough.  I was forced to learng grammar too - I could never stand the subject myself, awfully dry" he said, casting his thoughts back to his school days with an enchanting grin. "But then, I never was much of a scholar really – my tutors despaired of me. I was always too interested in riding and hunting."

He gestured vaguely towards an old oak tree, to which he had tied Thaddeus.

The memory of that invigorating ride came to Catherine, and she could feel the same stirring in her loins, hot and damp, a strange aching in her lower body, the like of which she had not felt before yesterday.

Yesterday, surely it was longer ago than that, since these over-powering feelings had first come to her? She felt as if she ached for this man for a lifetime, as if it had always been her destiny to unlock the secrets of womanhood, and of men.

Her eyes met his and they held each other's gaze. She had piercing blue eyes and knew that they were one of her better features. She let him notice them.

"Girls too, for that matter" he finally said, unconsciously wetting his lips with his tongue, as if a little embarrassed to admit it. She knew enough to know what that meant. "Girls always interested me a damn-sight more than any book ever could."

"Reading can be a most pleasurable pastime" her words were innocent, but made him think of reading the sort of books that young ladies most definitely should not read. Turning away from his intense gaze, she continued "If you take the time, and find a good subject, or an author who interests you."

"Is that so?" he asked straight away, playfully.

"Tell me Miss Thornberry, if you had to select an author to recommend, to an unscholarly gentleman such as myself, little versed in the art of letters, whom would you call to my attention?"

"If I had to select just the one" she replied whimsically "I should say Mr. Henry Fielding. His novels possess a certain energy, and an easy humour that I believe you would find to be compatible with your own…" she looked him up and down, his casual gait, his long well-formed legs. She wet the edge of her lip, in a movement that he found more sensuous than Catherine could ever know, "… distinct personality".

"Very well" he said. "I shall endeavour to track down a volume of his, if what you say is an accurate reflection of my character." He stroked the cleft in his chin as he spoke.

"I am sorry if I am speaking out of turn my Lord" she said, newly serious, "but I presume that you did not ride out all the way to Harteston, and interrupt the academic formation of my charges, merely to discuss with me the pleasures of English literature."

"No indeed, I fear you have worked me out, Miss Thornberry, I had other business with you."

"Then what pray, brings you here this afternoon? I must remind you that I have a lesson to be getting on with. We have already provided quite enough of a spectacle for the children. I shall not be able to stop them talking about this for weeks."

"Of course Miss Catherine, forgive me my lack of consideration. I was merely wondering whether, given the great inconvenience that Thaddeus and I inflicted upon you yesterday, and the pleasure, which I presume to be mutual, which I found in your company, if you would consider something of a business proposal from me? I would like to offer you the post of governess to my young niece, who is my ward?"

Catherine was stunned. This was a most unexpected turn! An offer of work, at the Earl's estate? It was strange, and she was immediately confused. What did he mean by this?

"As governess?" her confusion was evident in her voice, and he seemed to see the need to explain, for he went on.

"Yes, as I said, to my young niece, who became my ward a few years ago. Her old Nanny unfortunately passed away not long ago, and she needs company, schooling and discipline. She is quite an agreeable girl, if a little stubborn at times – she is just fourteen - I believe her age is approximately that of many of your young charges, back there in the schoolhouse. Considering your qualifications in the field of education, your experience with commanding attention and respect from children, and the rapport we both share... I had hoped that you would agree – I believe that it would be of benefit to both of us, as well as to Theodora."

He eyed her appreciatively, but also almost pleadingly. She blushed and looked away.

Was that his motive? Coax her up to his house with work and then have his way with her, of an afternoon, after lessons were over?

And would that even be so bad a fate, she dared to think? The thought intensified her blushes, and she chided herself sharply for showing her feelings on her face.

"… I really do need someone to start almost immediately and I thought you might be willing to take up the post. I've advertised, but I am yet to find anybody else remotely suitable. I could easily match whatever the parish is paying you for schooling its' children, indeed I'd be willing to increase your salary significantly, if that were what it would take to secure your services. What do you say?"

"Oh, my Lord, this is most unexpected!" she exclaimed. Her head was spinning, questions consumed her.

What should she do? Abandon her employment for what might be a true respectable role, or might only be the cover for a strange and illegitimate affair? (Or perhaps it was an affair that would only ever take place in her imagination?)

Or should she turn down what was possibly the chance of a lifetime?

"I am of course, profoundly flattered that you consider me to be qualified to undertake so significant and personal a task as the instruction of your own niece. Only, I must consider my responsibility to the parish, to the children."

"Yes of course, we wouldn't want them to go uneducated, but I am sure that there are plenty of well-qualified young ladies in the county, who would be more than willing to take up such a vacancy, if it were to become available".

That was true enough, she thought. Why only the other day a young woman from Lavenham had come to the schoolhouse, enquiring about the possibility of employment there.

A replacement could certainly be found for her, her duties were not binding.

"There is also the question of my daily journey to your estate. It is some distance from my cottage, and as you are well aware, I do not own a horse or carriage of my own".

"The solution seems to me to be simple enough. I have, at the risk of sounding churlish, plenty of surplus room in my house. You could happily lodge there, if you wouldn't consider the prospect too improper or disruptive. Indeed, I would prefer you close at hand, to deal with whatever dramas Theodora may have, at odd times of night or day. Over the last two years it has become abundantly obvious to me that young ladies can be prone to some drama, which gentlemen are not well equipped to deal with! If your mother were to be in need of company at times, I could quite easily have my Steward, Featherstone, arrange to run you down in my carriage, if the walk were found to be too taxing for a young lady, or the weather were inclement."

He reeled it all off rapidly, as if he had already given this plenty of thought.

Catherine was astounded by the man.

"My Lord, you seem to have considered every possible eventuality! You make it very difficult for me to refuse your generous offer."

"I am a man who knows what he wants" he said, looking her straight in the eye, and raising his eyebrow in a way that made her feel he could look straight into her, and divine her improper thoughts. It was another overpowering moment, echoing the previous day, and she was once more under his spell.

"I know also how to go about getting it."

He turned and headed over to the tree where his horse was waiting.

"I would like you to come to Havisham Hall, to see the staff, to meet Theodora, and to allow us to discuss the salary and conditions, before you make a final commitment to the role – which I most heartily hope that you will accept. I shall have Featherstone send the carriage around to collect later this evening, if that would not be disagreeable to you?"

Catherine could barely contain a gasp. It was all happening so suddenly, he was inviting her to his estate already! Yet it was sensible – she wanted to see what situation she would be placing herself in, before she made such a commitment.

"Yes sir, if you feel that is necessary, I would be able to make such an appointment."

"Excellent. If you feel that we will come to an agreement, then please, plan to begin tomorrow. You will be returned to Hawthorn Cottage tonight after our discussion, to prepare for tomorrow. I'll see you at five o'clock then. Farewell."

With that, he swung once more into his saddle and with a small wave in her direction, set Thaddeus to a rapid pace out of the village. She wondered, idly, if he ever went anywhere at a more sedate pace.

Catherine was a little saddened not to have shared another kiss with him (impossible as it would have been, in the middle of the village street), but she was amazed at this gesture which seemed to be one of kindness and affection, as well as practicality.

Could it be possible? Was he laying the ground for an affair between the two of them? Or was this simply a position, with nothing more to it?

She could not possibly know, but, later that evening, she would surely come closer to finding out. Resolving to go along with the situation, to do her best for his niece, but also her best to further a relationship with him, she smiled. She would use all of her womanly wiles (unpractised as they were) to get what it was that she now knew she desperately wanted, more than she'd wanted any single thing before – that being Charles Rockingham, the Earl of Stanningfield himself.

She turned, resetting her expression to the serious one appropriate for a teacher, commanding the blush to fade from her pale, fair face, and went back into the schoolhouse to finish her lesson.

"You should hear some of the things they say about him in the parish" said her mother in a haughty, condemnatory tone, stirring her stew pot idly.

This was not the first time that Catherine had heard all of this, and she suspected it would not be the last.

"Mrs. Brown says that she once heard from a serving girl, who worked up there on the estate for a couple of years, that he's had mistresses all over the world - France, Holland, Spain, the West Indies, even in India. He's travelled widely so they say, and left a trail of jilted lovers and unwanted children everywhere he's gone!"

"Mother you can't honestly expect me to believe all of that! People will say anything down in the Inn, and in the tea shop, especially if it's about their betters."

"Betters? Better, him? I wouldn't be so sure. He might be of high breeding Cathy my girl, but mark my words – from what I've heard, he's a wrong 'un in other ways – or at least he has been – the things they say he's done! You just be careful now. They aren't Christian some of the things you hear. Why, they say he's got a child he fathered with one of his fallen women, up in that house, living with him! It isn't right at all that sort of thing, most improper. But then, that's typical of the nobility – their wealth lets them live by different rules."

"Mother I'm not interested in this sort of idle chatter. If you are so disapproving of my prospective employer, then why on earth were you encouraging me in this endeavour only yesterday evening?"

"Oh, not disapproving my child, not at all. These are only words of caution which I feel obliged to impart to you, as your dear mother. It would not be very responsible of me, would it, if I were not to share what I have heard from those that have a little knowledge of these things?"

"No mother, I suppose it would not be. But pray, do not torment me so!" Catherine was nervous. She could not be anything but nervous, the clock on the mantelpiece was ticking away and every stroke of its hand brought her fate closer. It was after four o'clock, and the imminent arrival of the Earl's carriage loomed large in her mind. She could feel a flutter of nervous anticipation, building at the bottom of her stomach, and her mother's gossip was only making it worse.

"He may be your prospective employer," her mother continued "- but I dare say he's prospectively a lot more besides. Keep a close watch on him child, and on yourself. I can see that you're taken with him! No good will come of an affair out of wedlock. You must do it for the family – convince him to marry you, not just use you."

She gestured once more to the coat of arms above the fireplace. There was so much pride and pressure invested in those symbols of her past. She looked at them and she pictured the knights of the de Quincey family, resplendent in their armour and with the same proud symbols painted on their shields and banner.

There was so much family honour to be lost and won, so many great names to try to be worthy of.

"Now eat your stew and we'll hear no more of it. You must first secure this employment that has been offered, and then take things from there."

Her mother handed her a bowl of stew. There was a little bacon in this batch, the village butcher must have put his prices down. That probably meant that it was on the turn. This poverty was all she had ever known, living on cheap stews and lighting their home with tallow wicks rather than the proud, but expensive, wax candles they knew they deserved. She could barely imagine what wealth she might see in the Earl's home.

It frustrated her, that she could not give her mother more, that she seemed trapped in this simple and bare life. She longed for something greater. Perhaps that chance would come.

"Oh mother" she said, with a melancholy tone. "I hope you do not feel that I am abandoning you".

"Not at all child, not at all!" Mother Thornberry replied immediately. "You're all I have in the world, it is true, but I always knew this day would come. You're a pretty young miss and I've done all that I can to bring you up correctly. It's only right that you should go off in pursuit of a husband."

"Thank you, mother. Thank you for understanding, you have indeed, been a wonderful parent."

"No need to thank me child, it was the least I could do. I only regret that I couldn't provide you with the sort of home and fortune that our family history warrants. But no matter, 'blame that on the ancestors', as my own mother would have said. There's no call for you to worry about me. I have friends in the village; I have my reading and my needlework to occupy my days. The truth is that, ever since you were old enough to take that job at the schoolhouse, my time has, for the most part, been my own. As I said, I knew this day would come eventually. Hoped that it would, in any case."

"I hope that it will possible for me to secure a marriage proposal from him. After all, his intentions remain something of a mystery. But..... I must say that, if I am to marry, and marry for our family improvement, I am glad that he is a man that I find attractive.  Although, I do feel rather terrible, plotting like this, to capture his attentions – it seems so cold a way to go about it."

"That is true enough, though he wouldn't be the first wealthy gentleman to fall for a pretty young governess."

Her mother smiled reassuringly.

"Don't worry you head about it being cold and calculating - marriages arranged in such a way are the standard thing amongst the *ton* – if it isn't you, he'll likely be forced to marry some chit he doesn't care for at all. Play your cards right my Cathy, and I shall be seeing somewhat less of you in the coming years. Do your family proud".

Catherine looked down into the stew, and tried to take a mouthful of the steaming stew. Try as she might, however, she could not seem to force the food down. She was too nervous, too distracted. Anticipation was building in her stomach. She looked around at the small cottage she had known all her life. The thatch on the roof might be uneven, there might not be all that much room for two women, the bricks around the fireplace might have gone black over the years, but this was home - her home, which she had cherished, her refuge from the world.

It had always been her intention, someday, to move on from it, and yet now, looking at it and considering all that it meant to her, she was sad.

To be doing so, to take employment in an unfamiliar house, with a man she barely knew, yet whom she suspected she was falling in love with, made it doubly difficult.

There was a knock at the door. Catherine promptly abandoned her bowl of stew and went to open the door. It stuck a little, in its wooden frame, painted ultramarine blue, as worn as the rest of the cottage. Standing in front of her was a tall man with a thin, grave face and grey hair, dressed in livery.

He had lace at his cuffs, and a black velvet doublet, emblazoned with the coat of arms of the Stanningfield family. This, she thought to herself, must be Featherstone.

"This is Hawthorn Cottage, in the village of Harteston?" he said, peering inside to see Catherine's mother by the fireplace. He looked underwhelmed at the little cottage, but then, Catherine supposed, he was used to a stately home.

"Yes, indeed it is." she replied promptly.

"Then you, I presume, are Miss Catherine Thornberry?"

"I am."

"Very well. I am to escort you at once to Havisham Hall. My master informs me that he made an appointment with you earlier this afternoon."

"He did, yes."

With an acknowledging nod, Featherstone stepped to one side and gestured courteously for her to step through the door. She walked to the carriage with a sense of unreality, and was surprised again as, when she reached for the door, Featherstone spoke again.

"Please" he said in a serious tone of voice "- allow me."

Catherine was quite taken aback. She was unused to being served in this way. She had always had to run her own errands and carry her own luggage. This was quite a new sensation, the feeling of being waited on. The simple act of opening a door had suddenly become something of significance.  She waited, bemused, as he let down the steps, opened the door, and ushered her in.

"Oh. Thank you very much, Mr…?"

"Featherstone" he said firmly, confirming that she was correct as to his identity.  He paused, the door in his efficient, professional grasp. "I am the Steward of Havisham Hall, and I have served his Lordship for many years. I am not generally a coachman, these later years, but that's where I started, and I do enjoy the occasional excuse to drive." His smile was infectious, and she found herself relaxing a little.  She looked around the interior and was immediately struck by the plumpness of it, the finery.

"This is a magnificent coach. I have never before been in such a beautiful conveyance! I am not the wealthiest girl in the county, as I am sure you could have surmised". His face lit up at her praise of the carriage, and he nodded cheerfully as he closed the door.

"Let us be on our way."

With that, he stepped away, and she felt the carriage rock as he climbed up and took the reins. Catherine lay back against the seat, and stared around her in amazement – here she had been wondering what wealth she would see in the Earl's house, and already the interior of the carriage outshone any house she had ever been inside!

There were silk cushions, plumped up and accommodating, and the softest upholstery she had ever had the pleasure to sit on. The interior was decorated tastefully but richly, with gold renderings of the family crest on the two facing walls of the carriage. Catherine could not help but gasp at the sheer luxury of it, and wondered how much it all must cost.

She placed her feet on a perfectly positioned foot rest, and looked out of the window to wave goodbye, not for the last time, but with a certain finality, to Hawthorn Cottage and the poor but contented life she might well be leaving for good, come tomorrow morning, if all went well with her interview with the Earl, and her meeting with his niece.

Her mother, convinced that Catherine would, indeed, leave her forever, come the morning, stood at the window wiping tears from the corners of her eyes, as the carriage pulled away.

Johnson sighed, his frustration with Charles' fidgeting evident in the sound, although he gave no other indication of anything out of the normal.  Finally achieving a last tug of the cravat into place, he stepped back and eyed his master speculatively.

At home, Charles Rockingham was wont to be considerably less formal than most of the ton, and, even when preparing to interview a prospective governess, this seemed a little excessive a fuss about his appearance, compare to his usual behaviour. The Earl considered his appearance in the large mirror, which graced the wall of his dressing room, and nodded in satisfaction.

He looked every bit the cool, in control Earl.  A pity, he thought to himself, that he did not feel anything like that.

He was annoyed with himself – a man of thirty two, with a history of very effectively seducing a range of delectable women, should not feel nervous about conducting an interview of a very ordinary village woman, however physically attractive he might find her.  Yet, ridiculous as it was, he found himself exactly that – nervous, unable to stand still, and worrying.

He was just worrying about this because the need for a governess was so desperate, that was it, surely that was all it was. What if she decided not to take the position? What if Theodora took one look and decided to hate her?

He refused to consider that as an outcome.  This must work.  The mere thought of any of those terrible women, who had applied for the role by post, in response to his advertising, was enough to make him shudder.

He was, he assured himself. Only concerned for Theodora – the fact that he wanted Miss Thornberry, that the image of her, soaked in river water, all her curves exposed to his gaze, haunted his thoughts, had nothing to do with the nervousness.  Nothing at all.

Charles strode down the hallway to Theodora's room and tapped firmly on the door, entering when the maid pulled the door open.  At 14 Theodora was beginning to see herself as rather grown up, and to demand that she be treated that way – when of course, she remembered.... She was still child enough to be easily distracted by kittens, and toys at times.  She was what some might call wilful, a characteristic which Charles chose to see more as an indicator of her strong character - character that reminded him all too much of himself at the same age.

Smiling at him, in a way that was almost able to be interpreted as impertinent, but not quite, she dipped an elegant curtsey to him.

"Good afternoon, sir." Her voice was clear, and reminded him of her mother's – a voice made for singing, for bringing those hearing it to awe of its beauty. He shook the moment of sadness away – that was the past.

"Good afternoon Theodora, I am glad to see that you are ready, and suitably presented.  Please come downstairs and wait in the blue parlour.  I will speak to Miss Thornberry in the drawing room first, and then, if I feel that she will suit, I will call for you to come and meet her."

Seeing a frown start to take shape on Theodora's face, he continued speaking, hoping to prevent its settling into place.

"I pray you, do not make any assumptions about her until you meet her – being judgemental about a person that you have not met is very impolite, and most unladylike. I think that you will be pleasantly surprised."

That last comment was enough to make Theodora pause – surely any woman working as a governess would be stern and harsh, with no sense of humour and nothing to like about her? Still, she had come to know that, even though the Earl could be impetuous, even occasionally prone to temper, he was, at heart, a very honest man.  She had good reason to know that he hated subterfuge, and would be open and fair if he possibly could.

Nodding her acquiescence, Theodora let the frown dissipate, and followed him out of the door, and down the elegant, sweeping stairs.

With Theodora settled in the blue parlour, accompanied by her maid, and supplied with tea and scones to keep her occupied, Charles took himself to the drawing room to wait. Waiting proved trying. He could not settle, and his nervous energy drove him to pace, rather like a horse stabled too long, that needed to gallop out its tensions.

He alternately stared out the windows across the terrace to the gardens, and paced across the room, listening for any sound of the carriage returning. With difficulty, he resisted the urge to run his hand through his hair, or to tug at his cravat – ruining Johnson's artistry would not help him make a good, and convincing impression on Miss Thornberry.

And yes, he realised, he wanted her good opinion. That a peer of the realm should care for the opinion of a schoolmistress was not at all normal, but he did. He assured himself, yet again, that it was just because he needed to solve the governess problem. It was, however, getting harder to believe his own assurances.

He eyed the brandy decanter, where it sat on the sideboard, and then turned away – maybe later – for now, he needed to be clearheaded. Another five circuits of the room, and he feared that he was wearing a path in the carpet (which was Aubusson, and a family treasure), when, finally, he heard the crunch of gravel beneath the carriage wheels, as it drew up at the front of the house.

He strode out, calling the key staff to attend, and went to the doors.

Catherine watched the familiar countryside from inside the carriage, trying with all her might not to break or dirty anything. That would have been a most inauspicious start to her new employment, assuming that this interview resulted in her being employed, which was, perhaps, presumptuous of her. She was determined to make a good impression, and to not give off the sense that she was unused to this sort of high life, and to wealth. She supposed that was silly as he knew of her circumstances, yet she felt the need to not appear common and poor.

She might have been born and raised in a humble cottage without much wealth behind her, but she was from a great family going way back, and this sort of thing ought not to overwhelm her too much.

Nevertheless, the stew pot by the fireside and the often grubby-faced children in the crumbling village schoolhouse all suddenly seemed a very long way away. The little stew that she had managed to eat sat in a leaden lump in her stomach, and nervousness made her feel mildly ill.  But along with that, a growing excitement infected her, a fluttering in her stomach, pushing the lump of stew aside, was the result of just the thought of seeing him again.

Her mother might want her to capture the Earl's affections for the family honour, but she found that she was just as interested in capturing his affections for herself.  Never before had a man made her feel like this, and the warmth that flooded her body at the memory of his arms around her on the horse, of his lips against hers in that kiss, was a disturbingly pleasant sensation.

She looked in greater detail at her immediate surroundings. This was the first real opportunity she had had to get a look at the Earl of Stanningfield's crest, and she was most impressed by it. A great shield in the shape of a kite was at the centre of it, with an oak tree, tall and proud in the middle, three little gold balls she knew to call 'besants' assembled over it. Above these was a strip, and in that field five three-pointed stars. Around the edges of the shield was an intricate design formed by thorns and laurel leaves, curving symmetrically around the edges.

These were held in place by two mythical beasts, griffins she thought, with the wings and heads of eagles but the bodies of lions. Magnificent creatures, proud and mighty, much like Charles Rockingham himself. At the bottom in a curling scroll read the family motto: *Fortitudine et Honorem*.

She knew enough Latin, from her study of what books she could get, to know what that meant: 'strength and honour'.

A simple motto for an ancient family. Looking at the great coat-of-arms she dared herself to think that a de Quincey panther might complement the design nicely. Maybe at some point in the near future, she thought to herself.

Outside, the landscape rolled by at a pleasing pace. She was not used to travelling at this speed, having walked everywhere for the bulk of her twenty-four years, but she could still make out familiar sights.

The late afternoon light shone on fields of golden wheat, ripening in the May sun. In a few months' time, all of the fields around would be consumed by all the busy activity of the harvest - with gangs of boys running behind the haywains, sweating out their day's labour.

There were trees as well, many oaks and elms, tall, green and mighty. They broke up the monotony of all the rolling fields and gentle hills, looming over the crops and the haystacks. The trees were resplendent in their summery finery, so many shades of green; emerald, shamrock, Kelly, viridian and Lincoln. England, she thought, was not such a bad country on a fine day such as today.

What a balmy and beautiful early summer evening to be going up to Havisham Hall to meet her new life.

She heard the wheels of the carriage crunching on gravel, and presumed that they must have reached their destination. They came to a halt, and Featherstone opened the carriage door, lowered the steps and helped her down.

She was indeed correct, they had arrived at the most splendid house that she had ever had the privilege of seeing. Two ornately carved balustrades converged on a single, elegant rise of steps leading upwards, towards the front door.

Assembled around it was at least part of the household staff, what appeared to be the Butler, the Housekeeper, and a number of footmen, standing to an obedient attention waiting for her.

The idea of it shocked her – surely she did not merit such a welcome.

The house was at least five stories high, and she tried to count the number of windows running across each floor, each pair seemingly a single room. She quickly lost count, and started to feel rather giddy at the vastness of the place.

The entire front façade was beautifully plastered in a creamy white and yellow and above the main entranceway a stern plaque, held aloft by two marble-carved cherubs, proclaimed once again the family motto, *Fortitudine et Honorem*.

The grounds were all as wonderfully well-kept as the house itself, manicured lawns in two rich shades of green.

The trees tastefully dispersed across the meticulously kept grounds appeared to extend for many acres around.

She could see an enormous fountain in the near distance by the entrance to a yew-tree maze, and over on the other side in the distance a fine little pagoda by a duck pond. Such splendour!

What wealth this man and his family must possess! What a wonderful home!

Standing in front of all of it, offering a hand and a charming smile, as confident as ever in his stance and posture, was the lord of the manor, Charles Rockingham, third Earl of Stanningfield, stepping out from between his servants to welcome her, Miss Catherine Thornberry!

"So good of you to come" he said finally, stooping to kiss her hand. "I hope that my humble abode is to your satisfaction".

"Sir, it is the most wonderful house I have ever had the privilege of being invited to!" For a moment Catherine abandoned all composure. She was taken aback, awestruck by Havisham Hall and all the majesty it seemed to promise. Any pretence of sophistication, that such things seemed normal to her, was stripped away.

"It is most kind of you to say so" - the Earl was as cool and composed as ever. "I've recently had the façade re-plastered; the old place was starting to look a little shabby. I'm having the grounds remodelled as well; they are currently set down to my grandfather's tastes, which I regret to confess I do not myself share."

"I cannot even begin to imagine how one could go about improving such a house!" Catherine gasped. "To me, it already seems more perfect than I had ever imagined any home could be!"

"You flatter me. However, when you have passed the great bulk of your life in a place such as I have here, I suppose it starts to seem a little dull to you."

He turned her to the side, and motioned his staff forward. "Miss Thornberry, this is Wilton, my Butler, and Mrs Cartwright, my Housekeeper."

She acknowledged the bow and curtsey that they gave her, feeling rather overwhelmed by it all, and turned back towards the Earl.

"Now let us not tarry, come, we have business to conduct." Without a moment's hesitation he placed his gloved hand on the small of her back and urged her up the steps, into the interior of Havisham Hall.

On the inside the house was, of course, just as splendid. It was exactly as Catherine had always imagined a stately home such as this to be, only more so. To actually be here, and seeing it in person, taking in all of its antique delights, she was quite overwhelmed. A marble staircase led up to the top floors, with rich blue carpet draped over its central axis, inviting one upwards. The floor was remarkable, an austere black and white, polished to a sheen she had not even imagined to be possible.

The decoration was remarkably tasteful, the Earl had evidently dispensed with the centuries of aristocratic clutter, which she had always presumed would decorate a house like this, in favour of simplicity and grace.

There was a great clock standing at the centre of the landing above the staircase, gilt-edged and superbly rendered, solemnly ticking away. Two enormous mirrors sat either side of the entranceway, and Catherine turned, to see her entire body perfectly reflected back, for the very first time in her life.

She was amazed, and then instantly felt conscious of the simplicity of her own dress.

Despite wearing the very best that she owned, a dark green frock that she had always considered to be elegant, next to all of this finery, and to the Earl's superbly tailored clothing, she felt a little shabby and ashamed. She turned away from the mirror and saw, by the side of the stairs, a massive portrait of the Earl, Charles Rockingham, striking a powerful pose with his hand on his hip and a hunting dog at his side, grinning in that casual, mischievous way of his.

"There I am of course" he said proudly. "We used to have a portrait of my ancestor, the first Earl of Stanningfield, in this position, but I must confess I couldn't bear to look at the old boy every day. Do you think the artist has captured my likeness?"

"Oh, very much so, my Lord. Why it is as if you yourself were sitting in the picture frame, regaling us with your smile."

"I am pleased to hear you say so. Regrettably I had to dispose of the services of the first artist I employed. He was technically gifted, but he wanted me to pose in the nude, like one of those Roman or Greek fellows. Most unorthodox, all I required was a straightforward portrait, fit for the present age, such as this one here." Catherine did everything she could not to giggle nervously at the thought of the Earl posing naked.

She pictured it vividly, the mighty thighs, the strapping chest, the bare and impressive manhood (well, what she thought such a thing would look like – she did not exactly have anything to go by! Occasional glimpses of the village boys swimming in the stream when they though no-one was looking did not provide much of a reference).

It required all of her powers of concentration not to blush red all over with excited embarrassment. The flutter at the base of her stomach, and the tightening of her breasts as she imagined it were most distracting.

"Let us go into the drawing room" the Earl declared. "We can discuss the position, and the necessary arrangements in comfort there." He led her into the next room, and once again it was all Catherine could do to stop herself from gasping in awe. The drawing room was immense, and so airy and sophisticated in its design. The high-ceiling and great windows on one side gave one the impression, almost, of being outdoors, whilst yet remaining in the warmth and comfort of the house. Everything was fresh, light and open, and she could feel herself smiling at the wonder of it.

A wooden parquet floor stretched across the entire room, once again polished to shimmer like water. To one side was a long elegantly upholstered couch, an equally elegant small table set before it, and a pretty silver dish atop a lace covering upon it. In the centre of the room was a magnificent Aubusson carpet, well placed to be lit by the spectacular crystal chandelier that hung above.

At the other side of the room were several chairs and couches, plusher and more inviting than any she had ever sat on, assembled around smaller tables, and set to allow the warmth of the fireplace to reach them in winter.  The entire room was designed so that the chairs and couches afforded a view through the huge windows, to the gardens beyond.

The Earl ushered her to a chair, close to the windows on that side, and then sank onto the chair beside her, once she was settled.

"Can I offer you something to drink? It may be a little late for tea, but I have plenty to offer you. Some Madeira, or a lighter wine? I am told that Featherstone has recently acquired a superb Champagne that I could have brought up from the cellar – I believe it is the latest rage for the ladies of the *ton* - if you would like a glass of wine?"

"Oh, I do not think it would be proper of me to indulge in strong beverages at such an important meeting. Tea will suffice for me."

"Are you quite sure? You are more than welcome to make yourself comfortable; if we come to an agreement, and you feel that you can care for Theodora, then you are to be living here permanently as my niece's new governess, after all."

"I appreciate your generosity my Lord, but I fear it would be best for me to stick to tea."

"Very well," he reached out and pulled the rope which hung to the side of the window, to summon one of the servants. A middle-aged woman with a thick-set brow appeared in a maid's uniform at the entrance to the drawing room.

"Yes, my Lord?" she was working hard to conceal her Suffolk accent.

"Polly, would you be so kind as to bring some tea for our guest?"

"Of course sir, at once." She disappeared promptly to fetch the tea. The Earl rose to his feet and went over immediately to the drinks cabinet to the side of the room.

As he spoke, he poured himself a glass of a brown liquid, which Catherine took to be brandy, from a crystal decanter.

"You will forgive me if I indulge in a little brandy, Miss Thornberry?"

"Of course."

At that moment, Polly returned with the tea, and placed it on the table beside her, eyes bright with curiosity. The Earl waited until Polly had left the room before he continued.

"Good. Now I believe that I laid out the essentials of the position, which I am offering you, in our rather… extraordinary meeting at the schoolhouse in Harteston."

"Yes sir, indeed you did."

"It is pleasing to see that you were paying attention then. In brief, you would be required to attend, six days a week, to educating my young niece, Theodora. As I have previously informed you, she is a most pleasant girl who is simply in need of the hand of a capable governess. I infer from your professional employment that you would be more than qualified to undertake such a task. I will, of course, offer you a salary more than adequate – significantly more than the parish has been able to pay you. I will also offer to supply your mother with a more than adequate quantity of food, delivered each week, from Havisham Hall's supplies. I would not wish you to be concerned for her, without you there to care for her."

He turned, glass in hand, and walked back across the room, to stand directly in front of her.

"All that I really require from you Miss Thornberry…" now he was looking directly at her, standing so close to her.

His eyes were the same colour as the brandy in his glass.

She felt her pulse quicken at the proximity, a stirring beneath her petticoats, a flutter in her stomach, "… is a firm commitment, once you have met Theodora. The position would require you to leave your current post as schoolmistress, and to come and live permanently at Havisham Hall."

A jolt of pleasure ran through her. So he was serious! She could move into this wonderful house and begin a new life! But was he serious about her? Would yesterday's kiss ever be repeated?

"Are you in agreement Miss Thornberry?  Is this position one that you can see yourself taking?"

Catherine paused, her heart beating fast, and thought – she could not really refuse – her mother's care assured, and so much more money for herself – enough to truly improve both their lives.  And, truth to tell, she did not want to refuse, she wanted to be near this man, more than was proper, more than she should, but she wanted it nonetheless.

"Yes, my Lord, I believe that I could be happy in such a position."

"Most Excellent!"

He spun away a moment, and deposited his glass on the table. Again, he tugged on the bell pull, as Catherine carefully poured herself tea, into the beautiful, delicate china cup that she had been given, and sipped to ease her nerves.

Polly reappeared, and was asked to bring Miss Theodora to the room.

Moments later, the door opened to admit a young girl, a girl on the verge of womanhood.

She was tall, and showing signs of great beauty to come.  Her figure was still childishly slim, but the hints of curves were beginning to show.  Her hair was dark, but not as dark as the Earl's, full of gold and reddish highlights as the light touched it, where it was drawn back in a simple knot.

"Come in, Theodora.  Miss Thornberry, may I present Miss Theodora Rockingham, my niece.  Theodora, this is Miss Catherine Thornberry.  It is my intention that Miss Thornberry become your governess.  I have asked you to come here so that you might meet each other, before we finalise that arrangement.  I realise that most guardians would simply employ someone, without consulting you in any way, but I choose to be unconventional – I would prefer that you actually get on with your governess."

Theodora, dipped into a suitably polite curtsey, then stood and raised her eyes to Catherine's face.  They were startling eyes, of an intense green, with flecks of blue, unlike anything that Catherine had ever seen.  The effect was breath-taking, in the pale, beautiful face. Catherine smiled, captivated. This was no milksop aristocratic miss – there was intelligence, curiosity and character in that face.

"Good afternoon Miss Theodora, I am most pleased to meet you." Catherine's voice was as warm as her smile.  Perhaps, she thought, this role could be more pleasant than she had ever imagined – for surely this was a girl with a thirst for life, who would learn, and want to learn, although, perhaps, not always the things that young ladies were expected to learn!

Theodora's eyes widened at Catherine's friendly tone, and her words came without apparent thought.

"You are not at all what I expected, Miss Thornberry!"

The Earl tapped his foot, looking at Theodora with some mild annoyance.

"Oh, I am sorry Miss Thornberry. I do sometimes speak before I think! I was just so surprised."

Theodora blushed a little, and her eyes flicked to the Earl for a moment. Catherine's eyes followed, and discovered a fleeting expression of amusement cross his face, before it went back to calm and impassive.

"I…. well, I rather expected a governess to be older, and somewhat more….. stern.." She sounded so confused by the fact that Catherine was not like that, that Catherine found herself laughing – a clear joyful sound that startled both Theodora and Charles, then brought a smile to their faces.

"Thank you Theodora, thank you! I have no wish to be old and stern. Thank you for being honest and telling me your thoughts – although, perhaps, for polite society, you may need to curb that tendency a little – the *ton* are not often forgiving."

Charles looked on, making no comment on this interaction, but Catherine was sure that she saw him relax, saw the tension drop out of his shoulders – perhaps he really had been worried what she and Theodora would think of each other. This was not, in her opinion, the behaviour of a hardened rake.

"So, Miss Theodora, do you think that you could stand to have me as your governess? That we could go along together well?

Theodora stood thinking, hesitating, then suddenly flung her arms around Catherine, in the sort of hug that one would expect from a small lost child.

Startled, Catherine froze a moment, then gently eased her arms around Theodora. In a small, slightly shaky voice Theodora spoke into Catherine's shoulder.

"Oh yes, please Miss Catherine, I have been so lonely since Gran died. I so want to have someone to talk to, to help me. I promise to even really try to learn – yes, even the things I hate learning – please do say yes Miss Catherine."

Smiling at Charles, over the top of Theodora's tousled head, Catherine spoke.

"Yes Theodora, yes my Lord, I will take the position. I think that Theodora and I will rub along famously together. Let us conclude the formal arrangements, so that I may return here to take up the role as soon as possible.

Theodora relaxed against her at the words, and, as Catherine gently stroked her hair, lifted her head, those amazing eyes positively glowing.

"Thank you, Miss Catherine, thank you."

She stood back, a little embarrassed now at her actions, but smiling still.

"Thank you Theodora." The Earl's voice was warm, his expression relieved. "Now please go and finish you tea, whilst miss Thornberry and I sort out the arrangements."

Theodora curtseyed again, then positively bounced out of the room. It was the happiest that Charles had seen her look since Mrs Walsh's death.

Charles came to Catherine, and took her hands.

She felt a little frisson run through her at his touch, and looked into his face with wonder. When he spoke, his voice was deep, and she felt some great emotion in him, just below the surface.

"I did not expect that, but I am more than happy that it happened that way. This lifts a great weight from my mind, for I genuinely care a great deal about Theodora. Most unfashionable for a guardian, I know, but there it is. Come, let us be seated and complete our agreement." He turned, and led her to the couch, still holding her hand.

Catherine was intensely aware of him, of the heat of his hand on hers, of the scent of him, a heady mixture of brandy and something herbal, like sage – he must be wearing a cologne of some sort – all underlaid by the tantalising musk of the male body. She shivered a little, remembering that kiss again, wanting, if she was honest with herself, for him to kiss her again. She sat on the couch, and he stepped to the sideboard, picking up a sheet of paper that lay there, then came to sit beside her.

"I am, as I said, very happy that you have chosen to accept the position. I had hoped that you would do so, and that Theodora would be at least accepting. So this has worked out considerably better than I had hoped. I am sure that you will be happy here. I will do everything in my power to make it so." He watched her as he spoke, those brandy coloured eyes sparkling.

"I have taken the liberty of drafting a letter informing the parish that you have accepted alternative employment. All that it requires is your signature…" he leaned in closer to her, smiling in that way that made her feel quite breathless, and placed the letter in her hands.

She could feel his breath falling on her, see the lines where he had shaved his shapely jaw – she felt an irrational desire to run her finger along that line. "… and I will interpret that as a commitment, to me, and to the position as Theodora's governess. Here is an employment agreement between us, which I have already signed, in the hopeful expectation that you would be accepting the role."

He turned away, and produced the second paper from his pocket, and placed it in her hands.

Catherine quickly scanned the letter to the parish:

*Dear Sirs,*

*I regret to inform you that I leave the position of schoolmistress at Harteston Parish School vacant, with immediate effect. I have been offered alternative employment elsewhere, as a governess, and have decided to take up this new position. I have every confidence that you will find a suitable replacement in a very short time. Please convey my condolences to the children; I am sorry that I could not see their schooling to its conclusion.*

*Yours faithfully,*

*Catherine Thornberry*

She looked up. The letter was blunter than she might have made it, but it communicated the point.

Catherine looked out of the window at the splendid grounds, around the magnificent drawing room, and into the handsome face of the Earl.

Without another moment's hesitation, she took up the pen that was sitting on the small table, and inscribed her signature onto the bottom of the letter.

Turning to the other papers, the agreement for her employment, she gasped, raising shocked eyes to his, when she read the promised amount of her wages. It was much more than she had ever expected – more than anything else, it mad the vast gap between their stations obvious to her.

To him, this amount was unimportant – easily paid, as just a minor expense. To her, it was a life transforming amount.

It was also much more than she believed governesses were usually paid. Doubts assailed her – was he simply generous? Or did this payment presage an expectation of what he might want from her, beyond the tasks of a governess?

Shaking the doubts aside, she signed – it was too late for doubt, and she had discovered today, with Theodora's arms around her, that she wanted to be here, no matter what. And, if her mother's wishes came true, and she should manage to engage the Earl's affections, deeply enough for marriage, then she would not be at all unhappy about that either.

She handed him the papers. He smiled, and offered her further tea, which she declined, suddenly in a hurry to get back to Hawthorn Cottage, to pack up the last of her small collection of belongings, to prepare for tomorrow.

The Earl stood, and bowed to her, graceful and elegant, then took her hand and assisted her to rise. He pulled her towards him, a little more than necessary, and steadied her with a hand on her waist.

She stilled, so close to him, her eyes caught by his, his rich masculine scent filling her nostrils, her heart beating hard.

She dragged her eyes away from his, only to have them fix on his lips – those full, firm lips that she had felt on hers, but a few days ago. Her breathing became ragged and her eyes fluttered half closed.  She wanted him to kiss her again. Now.

He was so close, his breath brushed her lips, as she unconsciously licked her tongue across them. Somehow, the distance between them had disappeared, she felt the hardness of his chest against the softness of hers, and the heat of his body warming hers.  His lips came down on hers softly, his tongue tracing the contours of her mouth, until she moaned a little sound of pleasure.  As her lips parted, so his tongue slipped between them, exploring and caressing the warm cavern of her mouth.

He made a small sound, almost a sound of desperation, and crushed her hard against him, the kiss becoming deeper, demanding. The world melted away, there was nothing but him, his body against hers.  Then suddenly, he pulled away.

"I apologise Miss Thornberry, I should not have…  It is inappropriate for me to impose myself on you.  You should go – you need to get back to your mother, and arrange your things. I will have the carriage brought around."

His look was regretful, but full of desire, and she thought about it all the way home.

The memory of the kiss haunted Charles throughout the evening, and kept him awake at night. If he had wanted her before, he wanted her doubly so now. Yet he should not. She was an innocent, she was now his employee, damn it, and Theodora needed her – more than he had realised.

His mind might rationalise it, but his body disagreed – he lay in bed, unable to stop thinking about her, his cock achingly hard, even after he had given himself some relief earlier. This may be the best thing for Theodora, but if he continued this way, it might make him quite mad. He was not used to not being able to have a woman that he wanted.

To add to it all, he reminded himself, he was betrothed.

The fact that, for the last three days, that fact had completely escaped his mind, was a rather damning reflection on how he felt about Lady Blanchette. He did not wish to dishonour Catherine, yet he wanted her.  Again, he realised, with a sense of shame, it reflected poorly on him that he had so easily taken Blanchette's virtue, yet he did not want to dishonour Catherine.

He chose to see that as an indication that he was growing more responsible, less of a rake.  For to see it as anything else was unthinkable, was something fraught with so much complication that it could not be considered.  None of which made any difference to the fact that he wanted Catherine more than he had ever wanted any woman since Monique. Mentally, he shied away from the possible implications of that thought, and brought himself back to thinking of the most boring things that he could, in the hope of finding sleep.

Eventually, exhaustion took him, and he slept, all too short a time before Johnson came to wake him, and prepare him for the day. Once he was assured that Mrs Cartwright had prepared a suitable room for Catherine, not too far from Theodora's, in the servants' section of the same floor of the house, and that everything was in readiness for her arrival, he asked Featherstone to arrange the carriage to collect her.

Featherstone again volunteered to drive, and Charles smiled, willing to let him do something below his standing in the household, simply because it pleased his loyal retainer to do so.

*

Catherine stood near the fire, watching her mother, who sat, determinedly keeping herself occupied with sewing, staving off her tears by force of will.  Mother had been happy to hear that Theodora was a child who needed love and care, who wanted to cooperate – for she could not imagine anything worse than trying to teach a child who had no interest in every doing anything that you wanted.

But still, the thought that she would only see Catherine occasionally was hard to deal with right now. Catherine felt the same – they had cried in each other's arms the previous night – both sad and happy tears.  For now there was a chance that Catherine might engage the Earl's affections, and, even if that did not happen, between the money that he would pay Catherine, and the food stuffs that he had promised would be delivered to the Cottage, this would be the first year since Catherine was born that Mother could be certain they would not starve, even if she did no paid sewing for anyone else.

It was an odd thought to have even that much security, after so many years of just scraping through.

Catherine's small collection of possessions were gathered near the door, waiting for the carriage to come and collect her. It was, when all brought together, a pitifully small amount of things. Compared to what was in the huge house that she was going to, this might as well be nothing – but it was all she had.  Her few dresses and other clothing, her sewing basket, and her small collection of precious books.

She turned as she heard steps on the path, and opened the door before Featherstone reached it.

"Good morning Miss Thornberry." Featherstone smiled, and looked around. Spotting her luggage, he turned back to her, an expression of surprise on his face.

"Is this all, Miss?"

Embarrassed, she looked down, twisting her hands in her skirt, then took a deep breath and answered.

"Yes Featherstone, this is all. We have never been wealthy enough for more."

His expression shifted to sadness, and his voice was kind when he spoke.

"You've done very well with what you have, and I know that the parish children are the better for your teaching. As will Miss Theodora be. We are all so glad that she took to you – she can be a handful, but she has a good heart. She's been too sad since old Mrs Walsh went."

She nodded, brought to the edge of tears again by the unexpected kindness. He took up her meagre possessions, and she turned to hug her mother yet again, promising to come and visit very soon, then turned and walked to the carriage, before the tears took hold again.

Her mother stood in the doorway, watching, until the carriage was out of sight. She walked back in, closing the door softly and stood a moment, looking at the de Quincey family tree. Then, in a whisper barely above silent, she spoke, before turning back to her sewing.

"Oh mama, grandmamma, and my dear grand aunt, maybe there is hope yet, maybe Catherine can restore what we lost, what I so foolishly threw away."

# Chapter Ten

"But Miss Thornberry" squealed Theodora "I don't understand, why should I have to learn another silly language like French? I can talk in English perfectly nicely, my Gran said so herself".

Catherine sighed. It had been a week now.  A week in which she had barely seen the Earl, after he had greeted her on her arrival, and provided her with a maid and a footman to assist her with getting settled in.

It almost felt as if he was avoiding her, and she worried that he regretted that kiss in the drawing room so much that he could not bear to see her.  It was a depressing thought.

She had been given two small rooms in the servants' section of this floor, quite close should Theodora need her, but enough to give her some privacy.

Even though the rooms were small for this house, they were still bigger than the whole of hawthorn Cottage.  With just her tiny collection of possessions in them, they felt oddly empty.  They had no personality yet, and she had nothing more to put there, to make them feel homely.  Ah well, that could come with time. For now, she needed to deal with Theodora's frustrated stubbornness.

On days like this, it seemed that her new post might not be quite as easy as she had hoped. Theodora was, as the Earl had said, and as she had seen when she met her, a pleasant enough girl, but she was stubborn, and obstinate at times, and had no desire to learn anything that did not interest her.

"There are ample reasons, my dear" she replied wearily. "All the pretty young ladies in society know a little French, so that they may converse with gentlemen. You won't ever find yourself a suitable husband if you can't express yourself in the French tongue."

"I don't believe you!" the child fairly shouted back. "Why on earth should that be the case! We're English after all, therefore we speak English. Why should we waste our time learning all these other ways of speaking?"

Catherine looked around the nursery. Her surroundings did not offer much inspiration for responding to the girl's questions, but they were pleasant enough. Theodora was passing her girlhood in far greater comfort and splendour than she herself could ever have imagined.

Although, thinking about it, she realised that she had heard that Theodora had only come here, to the Earl's wardship, about three years ago.

Apparently, before that, she had lived somewhere distant, in lesser circumstances.

Idly, she wondered where. Catherine wished that, when she had been a child, she had had such wonderful toys. Theodora's toys were most splendid: beautiful china dolls in real silk dresses, a superbly carved rocking horse, and the most ornate doll's house with every imaginable detail and accessory.

The room was perfectly laid out for a young girl, with a light shade of pink on the walls and big bright windows offering views of the countryside all around.

Still, what had been appropriate for a girl of ten or eleven, was daily becoming less appropriate for a girl of fourteen, growing fast towards womanhood.

Despite, or perhaps because of, all this, Theodora was no scholar. She looked for any opportunity to get out of her studies.

She was bright, and quite capable, but most study did not interest her – she would rather run in the gardens, play with puppies in the stables or sneak into the kitchens and get her fingers into whatever cook was making. It made life an interesting challenge for Catherine.

"Imagine for a moment…" Catherine replied at last "…that in the near future you are given the opportunity to go on a trip, the Grand Tour, to France, perhaps with an Aunt or other older relative. On your travels you will surely encounter some interesting French persons of distinction and quality; perhaps some handsome young gentlemen you wish to converse with."

Theodora stared at her, the stubborn expression as yet unchanged.

"Now, tell me Mistress Theodora, how frustrating would it be to find that you could not speak to them, or understand a single word that they said? Would that not be terribly annoying? Would you not wish that you had listened to Miss Thornberry and practised your French, back in your nursery, were such a situation to arise?"

"No. I think not."

"Pray tell, why?"

"Because I cannot imagine any French person has anything of interest to say to me. I am English, and I will have English friends, who are perfectly capable of speaking to me in English. That is all that there is to say."

"But there are also many interesting books that you will not be capable of reading if you do not learn French, books that your beloved English friends may have read, and which they may wish to discuss, and which you will be unable to comment upon."

"If that is to be the case then so be it. I doubt that there are any interesting books in French anyway, and anyone who would want to read them would be nothing but a dullard." Catherine was on the point of furnishing a response to this when suddenly her thoughts were interrupted by a voice from the door:

"Theodora, stop aggravating your new governess so, it isn't polite."

It was the Earl, dressed far more casually than was proper, in a flattering shirt, which was unlaced enough to reveal a triangle of skin at his throat, and with only a waistcoat over it, leaning against the door frame and smiling at both of them.

Catherine was briefly worried that her heart was going to leap out of its place in her chest; it picked up its rate of beating so suddenly. She suppressed a gasp of delight and turned to face him.

"My Lord! I thought you'd gone out?"

"I thought I'd give old Thaddeus a rest today. Been riding him pretty hard of late, I don't want to risk injuring the horse."

"That is most kind of you."

"Indeed, I can be generous, on occasion. I hope that Theodora hasn't been giving you too much trouble?"

"No indeed, she has been most obedient - although we were just in the midst of a dispute about the various merits of studying the French language."

"*Quand j'etais petit, j'ai appris beaucoup de la langue Francaise, et elle m'a servit tres bien*. There. What did I just say to you Theodora?"

The girl looked sheepishly down at her feet, embarrassed by her ignorance.

"I don't know" she mumbled in response, blushing.

"There. Now if you don't want to grow up feeling like that all the time you'd best get your nose in some books pretty sharpish. Have we a French-English dictionary in the nursery?"

"Indeed we do" said Catherine. "I was just about to set Theodora some exercises from it."

"Then we have all of the pedagogical resources we require. In that case, you won't feel any guilt if you leave Theodora in the nursery for the present time and come and take a walk with me around the grounds. We wouldn't want you to waste away in here all your days, would we?"

With that Catherine felt her heart lurch upwards once more, and a fluttering in her belly which she could not contain.

So that was why he was here! What a charming interjection, she was quite overcome! Yet, why now, after she had barely seen him for days? He did not seem in any way sensible, but a part of her most definitely did not care for sense. She felt flushed, nervous and excited, and quivery in ways that she had never felt before.

"Yes sir" she said, quite calmly. "I think that would be quite agreeable, provided you do not think your niece's schooling assumes a higher priority?"

"Indeed not, she needs to learn some self-discipline. Get down to your studies Theodora, or your place in high society might be forfeit. And that would be a great pity, given what your family went through, to ensure you the opportunity that you have."

Theodora nodded seriously in response. It was obvious to Catherine that there was something more complex behind the words, some shared knowledge between the Earl and Theodora, something that Theodora cared enough about, to change her behaviour for. At least for now.

The Earl held out his arm firmly to Catherine, and she took it without a second's pause.

"Now you've no excuse. You simply must come and take a walk with me in the grounds. It's disgraceful that you have been here over a week, and I have not yet shown you the beautiful gardens – I have been remiss." And with that they were off.

92

Up close the grounds were even lovelier than she had imagined they could be. Catherine had never seen grass so well-kept, or flower beds so carefully planted and maintained. They walked arm in arm through a charming little rose garden. On either side of them, banks of red, white and gold flowers grew high and haughty, and let off a rich scent.

"I suppose much of this must be quite new to you" he said, pausing for a moment to sniff the head of an especially tall flower. It was vast and bright red, and the smell was evidently pleasing to him.

"Theodora loves this garden, but she will only sit here by herself, and she won't tell me why."  He sounded frustrated by this, but did not say anything further about it.

"It certainly is new to me," she confessed readily. "We have a little garden back at our cottage in Harteston where mother has always liked to cultivate herbs for cooking, and a few pretty flowers, but nothing of this sort."

"That sounds charming, in its own way. I am unused to small houses or modest gardens. I suppose I take all of this…" he waved around him to indicate the grounds of Havisham Hall "… for granted.  Ever since I was small I have been surrounded by splendour, and by a large and dedicated staff. Do you know that it takes twenty men, employed full-time, all year round, to keep all of this horticulture in order? I suppose it is pleasant enough, but a great deal of effort and expense goes into maintaining all of this pleasantness."

"Pleasant? The word does not do it justice. It is positively beautiful, the whole thing."

"You are generous in your description. I have seen greater gardens in my time; the grounds of the Palace of Versailles for instance, or at Leeds Castle, down in Kent. But my own little parcel of England is pretty enough in its own right, of course. Have you travelled at all, Miss Thornberry?"

"I'm afraid not."

"No, I suppose your instructional duties at the school would not have permitted it. It is good to see a little of the world if one has the chance. I have been fortunate enough to voyage far and wide in my time, and it is true what they say, it does broaden the mind. But then I suppose you have your reading for that?"

"Yes, I do. Reading can open up new experiences and possibilities as well."

"I imagine that it can, though I have rarely taken great pleasure in it myself. I did, however, look into this Fielding fellow whom you recommended to me. I have ordered a copy of his *Tom Jones* from a publisher in London, and I am looking forward to commencing reading it."

Catherine was quite taken aback! To think that she, a plain and simple girl as she was, had already had some effect on the mind and habits of this great and noble gentleman! How was it even possible? She thought now of other changes that she might effect in his character, if, as it seemed, she had some strange power of influence over him.

Perhaps she could turn him away from his reputed rough and roguish ways towards the affairs of the mind, the heart, and the soul. It would be both a satisfying and a remarkable effort.

They had come to rest on a simple but sturdy bench in the shade of a great oak tree. It was a rather impressive tree, possibly the largest that Catherine had ever seen. It towered above them and its bark was tight, hard and sinewy. She brushed her back against it and could feel the roughness of it, tough and turgid, but pleasing nonetheless. It was one of many new sensations that he seemed to be experiencing now, all at once.

"Tell me…" said the Earl in his languid manner. "… this innkeeper's boy, who you have mentioned to me as your sweetheart, how advanced is the affair between the two of you?"

"I must confess sir, most of that was a fabrication. I am familiar with the boy in question, and have been since I was a girl. He is, as you say, a most attractive young man, but it would be dishonest of me to claim that there was anything of significance between us."

"I see," he said with a chuckle. "So you lied to me because you knew it would provoke my interest?"

"Oh no sir, not a lie…"

"There is no need to protest, Catherine," he said, calling her by her first name for the very first time. He was leaning very close to her, looking her straight in the eye.

Catherine felt her heart pounding away inside her breast, so close to his that she wondered whether he could hear it or not. Immediately her mind went back to that last kiss in the drawing room, to the feel of his body against hers.

Desire trickled through her, making her feel weak and shaky.

Her hands were damp and she shivered slightly in anticipation, and the hope that he would kiss her again.  She wanted to feel that way again, to taste and feel him, no matter how wanton that might make her.

"I know young ladies and their fey and fickle ways. I can forgive you. In fact, I rather admire you for it" and with that, he broke his charming grin and leaned forward, like an inevitable force, until his lips met hers.

The kiss started gently, but she could feel the full vigour of his passion in it. She melted against him, wanting this, even whilst she knew that she should not.

At first that knowledge, a strange and nagging instinct, telling her (in her mother's voice…) to resist, to pull away and say that this was not what she wanted, disturbed her, but she quickly pushed the thoughts away, sure now that this was, in fact, what she desired, intensely so, and she had known it all along.

She felt his tongue, muscular and well-practised, push her lips apart, as she sighed at the pleasure of the sensation, felt it penetrating her mouth, lapping skilfully and sensually at hers, encouraging her to explore his mouth and tongue with hers.

He cradled the back of her head and pulled her towards him, so that her bosom was pressed against his breastbone and she could sense their two hearts beating in unison. His breathing was as uneven as hers, and the thought that she could raise such a reaction in a man like this excited her.

His hands were assertive, she was quite taken along by them, and as his hands held the back of her head, they tangled in her hair pulling and tugging her to him harder. Rather than feel pain or dread at this however, it caused a thrill to run through her entire body, and she could feel the quaking anticipation right in the centre of her, hot, wet and shaking as it had been on that ride only a short week before. Today those feelings were stronger, the warmth and quivering sensitivity spreading through her whole body from the points where his hands touched her.

A thought surfaced momentarily, through the haze of sensation, that this was so soon after they had met, she should not be feeling like this, behaving like this, quite willingly being seduced by him, in the grounds of his estate!

Yet it felt right. She started to think about the wonders of the heart, the mysteries of what makes one person more desirable than another, but she was too distracted by the Earl's burst of passion, and the sensations of his hands on her body, to really focus on anything else.

Their teeth touched as their tongues swirled together, and his lips melded to hers with bruising passion. She found his forcefulness strangely arousing, the intensity of his need for her astonishing. He pulled back a little for a moment, as if he was going to stop, and she instinctively slid her arms around him, pulling him back towards her. With a groan he returned to kissing her, whatever hesitation he had felt gone, in the face of her response.

One hand slid over her neck, then her shoulder, tracing the soft shape of her, drifting down to caress her breast, to brush her hardened nipple through the thin fabric of her dress. Catherine gasped at the sensation, at the burst of pleasure that ran through her, as his fingers teased at her flesh.

Moments later, he took her hand and pressed it firmly against his manhood which she could feel now, hard and throbbing, upright like the oak tree that concealed their tryst from any prying eyes.

She was shocked, for she had never touched a man so intimately as this, but she was also excited and aroused – this seemed the most natural thing in the world at this moment, and all thought of consequences had fled her mind.

Before conscious thought could intervene, he lowered her to the ground beside the bench.

He was firmly on top of her, almost pinning her down with his mighty arms like a leopard trapping its prey. Catherine arched her body into his, finding herself even further aroused by his forcefulness – the sensations confused her, but were so wonderful that she wanted more. She grasped him to her, running her hands over him, her fingernails scratching lightly over his skin, where his open shirt gave her access to touch. He kissed her lips, and kissed and nibbled at her neck, and down to the soft rounded tops of her breasts. There was almost something of wild animals to them, biting and scratching at each other on the green summer grass.

His fingers slid under the neckline of her bodice, encountering her hardened nipples, lightly pinching and brushing them, making her arch and squirm in his arms, panting and moaning. She had never thought that her breasts could feel this way!

At the same time, she felt his hand making its way forcefully under her petticoats, towards her inviolate womanhood - she did not resist, in fact she willed him further on, guiding his hand with another arch of her body against him. His touch on her legs trailed higher, and her breath hitched as the amazing sensations flowed through her.  She deepened the kiss in response.

Without a moment's warning he was there, touching her most intimate place, rubbing and drawing tiny tactile circles with his fingers, building her moist anticipation up into frantic, feverish gasps.

A passing thought – her mother was right – she had had no idea at all about what this could do to her!

He kept on kissing her but she could no longer kiss back, she was panting uncontrollably, her breath forced out of her, enraptured by his motions. He nibbled, licked and sucked at her neck and she felt him slide a finger inside her, working it gently as she gasped at the astonishing sensation.

He moaned against her neck, but was obviously trying hard to hold back, to ensure her pleasure.  Another finger joined the first, and his thumb moved outside her, over that one spot that caused waves of intense sensation to flow through her.

"Catherine" he groaned her name.  She gasped, undone by the need in his voice, and arched up hard against his hand, as pleasure slammed through her, beyond anything that she could have expected.

Moments later, as his clever fingers continued their work, she felt the sensations building again, and found herself crying out - "Charles, please, oh please, I need….." she had no idea what it was that she needed, she realised, except that he could give it to her.

She felt him move, lift her skirts higher, and ease his weight back off her a moment – she felt oddly bereft without his weight against her, but, before she had time to protest, he was back, his fingers sliding out of her, and suddenly replaced by the feel of his manhood at her entrance.

She froze for one second, but his hand returned, slid between them, working away at her most sensitive spot, and she arched against him, pushing her hips up, seeking the completion that she needed. It was too much for him to stand – any hope of going slowly was gone, and he thrust himself into her, meeting her need with his.

Her eyes flew open, and her body contracted around him, as the sharp pain of his entry touched her.  He leaned down and kissed her, beginning to move very gently inside her, and the pain slipped away, replaced by new sensations that excited and tantalised, promising ever greater pleasures. She felt him moving inside her and knew that the long vigilance of protecting her virginity was over.

She did not care. This was all too brilliant, too intoxicating to bother with any of that. The Earl, her Charles, moved above her, in her, thrusting harder as he took his pleasure and it was all she could do not to scream in delight. She felt the impending approach of that ecstasy again as he held himself closer and tighter to her than she had ever been held before.

They shared each other's bodies and flowed into one another gladly, their cries from the pleasure of it all filling each other's ears. Then, with a sudden intense groan Charles thrust hard into her, and stilled. He was spent, He let his weight fall onto her with a sigh, and she trailed her fingers over his back as he lay there, enjoying just being able to touch him, feeling his body still in hers.

After a moment, he rolled over to the side, sliding out of her, easing his weight off her, and tucked his manhood back into his breeches. Catherine lay there for a moment, wide open, skirt still pulled aside, feeling warm and whole, but already yearning for him to touch her again. She stared into the sky and felt that it was entirely within her reach.

"I can only hope that experience was as pleasant for you as for me? I am sorry if I was somewhat.... Forceful in my actions, but... you have aroused my passions so much...." Charles spoke, still breathing unevenly.

"Oh yes, my Lord, that was…. most agreeable" her voice was dazed. She felt immediately that she should have found better words to express the enormity of what she felt, of the whole new world that had just now opened up before her.

*

Charles looked at Catherine, still lying on the grass before him, in a state of relaxed abandon, and his heart constricted painfully in his chest. Guilt overwhelmed him, and a sense of despair. He was silent, yet inside his thoughts he was ranging at himself. *'What have I done? I am now more than a fool, I am a worse rake then ever I was before! For all my grand resolutions to not diminish Catherine's honour, to not treat her as I did Lady Blanchette, here I am, guilty of doing exactly that.'*

*'At least,'* he thought, with a slight ironic smile, *'I did, this time, have the consideration to bring the lady to pleasure, before reaching my own.'* That, he had to allow, might also have been because the lady in question was so responsive, so passionate in return, that it had been easy to pleasure her.

He still wanted this woman, wanted to know her better, to have the chance to know her body, over and over, not just in a hurried tryst in the gardens like this.  The despair settled over him – no matter what he wanted, no matter what self-recrimination he indulged in, he had no choice but to marry Blanchette, for he had given his word.

Duty was a terrible cross to bear.  He had no idea how he would ever make reparation to Catherine for what he had just done, in the foolish throes of passion, but the least that he could do was to tell her the truth, now, before his courage failed him.

He looked at her again.  She was watching him, her passion hazed eyes half lidded, her expression dreamy, her intense blue eyes darkened.  He was about to hurt her desperately, he knew it, yet there was no other choice.  Taking a deep breath, he choked back his feelings for her, and spoke.

*

"Good. I am glad that, for this moment, I could make you happy. Because now I am afraid I have a most regrettable confession to make." She sat up suddenly. Much of her giddy pleasure subsided at his newly serious tone. She was confused and puzzled – he had gone from passionate and powerful, to hesitant and serious, almost unhappy, looking so fast.  She could not imagine what he might be about to say. He was frowning for the first time in their acquaintance, and looking not at her, but off into the distance, back towards the house. Sitting up, carefully rearranging her clothes and smoothing her skirts, she studied his serious face.

"Pray tell sir. I am sure that I am quite capable of receiving your confession, whatever it may be." She did everything she could to sound confident and firm, but she could feel a new dread coming over her.

"There is no easy way to tell you this.  My actions have been reprehensible, no matter how strong my passionate care for you may be. I regret to inform you Catherine, in light of what we have just shared, that I am engaged to be married."

"What?! To whom?"

Her voice rose uncontrollably as she spoke, her first reaction one of horror, and of denial that he might be speaking the truth.

Who was this man? Were all the rumours about him true? Should she have trusted more to her mother's vague warnings? She realised, in a wave of shame, that she had not thought beyond the moment at all, that she had wantonly allowed her passion for this man to overcome all of her good sense. It would seem that her mother had been, lamentably, correct.

"To Lady Blanchette Cavendish, daughter of the Earl of Derbyshire."

Catherine was plunged into a state of shock. This was all too much!

He had used her, abused her, had his sordid way with her and now he was off, to marry a fellow member of the nobility and leave her to take care of his little niece, as if nothing had happened between them! It was all just too awful.

She had a sudden urge to be sick. Every last touch of dreamy pleasure left her body in a rush, as if she had, again, been plunged into the icy cold water of the stream.

"I am deeply sorry Catherine. I am profoundly fond of you, and I hope that we can remain friends. I had never intended, never expected, what is between us to come to this, so fast. But around you … I can't seem to help myself – I wanted you so very badly, and I believed you to feel the same."

"Friends? Sir, I am appalled! To speak of friendship at such a time, really! Your conduct is truly low, beyond all realms of caddishness! When were you planning to tell me this, pray?"

"I'd hoped to inform you as soon as I could, but…"

"As soon as you could?" she interrupted him, too aghast and angry to respect his higher status as her employer and as an aristocrat. "But only after you'd had your way with me, is that so? Take what you want from me and then leave me here in disgrace so as you can marry someone better?"

"It isn't like that Catherine, believe me! I had no say in the matter, if it were up to me I would not be marrying her at all. As I say, I am extremely fond of you, but I'm afraid my family is set upon a suitable match to a Lady from a noble house. I fought this match for years, but, it has been formally agreed – I am duty bound to marry her." Catherine felt as if he had punched her in the gut. It was all too horrible.

"I understand. A penniless schoolmistress from the disgraced de Quincey family isn't good enough for the esteemed Earl of Stanningfield. I understand, my Lord. But you will likewise understand if I have developed a strong and sudden urge never to speak to you again."

With that, tears gushing down her face, still hot and red from their moment of passion, she hitched up her skirts and ran back into the house to cry out all her shame and regret, leaving him no opportunity to say anything further.

*

Charles watched her go, his face a picture of anguish. If he was honest with himself, he had to admit that his feelings for this woman had grown, at a rate which shocked him.  He wished, with everything in him, that he had never agreed to marry Lady Blanchette.  But he had.

His life seemed to suggest to him that he only ever hurt any woman that he actually cared for.

It was a depressing realisation.  He would find a way to continue around Catherine, without his feelings for her intruding – for Theodora's sake, if nothing else.

He could only hope that, with time, she might forgive him.  The thought brought him no comfort, and the prospect of the long years ahead, in a marriage to a woman that he did not particularly care for, seemed darker and emptier than ever.

For several days Catherine did little but tutor Theodora and cry. She would wake in the morning, prepare herself a simple breakfast of brown bread and milk, in the pantry, and set about convincing her employer's niece that reading and study were worthwhile pursuits.

Try as she might, she could never quite seem to connect with the girl on the subject of learning, although she found her very pleasant to deal with as soon as they moved their activity or conversation away from the schoolroom.

She was rather disappointed that, when it came to languages and literature, Theodora remained stubborn and headstrong.

Catherine had wanted so desperately to learn, as a girl, and books had been impossible to afford in so many cases, that she struggled to imagine being surrounded by them, and not wanting to learn.

"I simply cannot see the purpose of this book." Theodora declared, when they set about trying to read *Robinson Crusoe*, a novel that Catherine had naively thought would be exciting and modern enough to hold Theodora's attention. "Nothing that is described in it actually took place did it?"

"Well, no, I suppose it is unquestionably a work of fiction." Catherine replied, weary after having repeated a similar routine for days. In some ways, this one girl was more work than the entirety of Harteston Parish School. "But it is based on real events and experiences, and it can tell us a lot of truth about what it means to be human, even if the characters and events are not real."

"I don't understand what you mean". Theodora implored her. "If it isn't real, what truth can there possibly be within it?" The effort was tiring and demoralised her yet more. It seemed that the Earl was gone, she knew not where, and she certainly was not going to ask.

She told herself that she was glad of it, that it was for the best, that she would simply get on with her life.  But her heart and mind were not so co-operative – she found herself listening for his steps in the hall, and desperately hoping to see him.

At the end of each hopeless day, Catherine would head once more to the pantry, there to collect a simple meal which she would generally eat on her own.

Cook left out bread, cheese, some cold meats and perhaps some soup or pie for her, and she would simply help herself.

The servants considered themselves distinct from her, despite the fact that they were all live-in employees of the Earl, and stuck to their own already formed circles and cliques.

On one occasion, Catherine had tried to engage Mrs. Cartwright, the housekeeper, or Polly, the doughty woman who had served her tea on her first day at Havisham Hall, in conversation, but the prickly old servants were remarkably dismissive of her efforts.

"Nice to see you Mrs. Cartwright" she had said, warmly.

"And you likewise, Miss" she had said in a haughty tone, before simply carrying on her allotted rounds and ignoring Catherine entirely.

Often she did not even look her in the eye, and Catherine soon gave up on even exchanging pleasantries with her.

She did manage to make one friend, however. There was a young maid called Anna, who she would often see down in the pantry, loitering without any apparent purpose.

After some time, Catherine decided that it was best to ask her what she was doing down there, after all of the other servants had departed.

"Oh, nothing Miss." Anna spoke somewhat defensively. "Just, er, looking out for mice, that's all. Don't want them running all over the place getting at the grain or the flour now, do we?"

"A worthy endeavour I suppose" Catherine replied, suspiciously.

"But it seems a strange time to be going about it. Do you not have any traps, or some poison you could lay down to save yourself the effort of stalking them at all hours?"

"Ah, yes, I see you've got me there Miss. Yes, you're right; doesn't make a whole lot of sense really, me doing that, does it?"

The maid stood in the pantry door, grinning apologetically, and Catherine could not help but feel a small sense of warmth and affection towards this girl. At least she was willing to talk to her! She could not have been much younger than her, and had a kind face, pretty in its own way, with pronounced dimples on the cheeks and freckles.

Her thick dark red hair was held back by her maid's headpiece, and she wore the uniform of a serving girl lightly, as if it did not quite suit her to be in so lowly a position within the hierarchy of the house. Catherine felt a kind of kinship with her, instinctively, she knew that here was another woman who had lived her life with very little, yet had some pride and confidence, and had made the best of what she had.

"What I was actually doing – it's Miss Thornberry, isn't it?" Catherine nodded "... was hanging about here hoping to speak to you. See, we all know how the Earl has treated you. Now don't you ask me how or why, we just know, that's all, been working here more than long enough to know what's what, that's all I'll say."

Catherine was startled – she had not thought that the servants might be aware of her foolishness, or her disgrace. She flushed with embarrassment and shame, at the thought that they all knew. Anna went on, the words coming in a rush:

"I'd just like to say that I think it's a disgrace, what he's done. You've been really very brave carrying on the way you have in the education of young Theodora, in the light of all that's happened, and I, for one, am just about brim-full of respect for you. Brim-full. I'm sorry if any of the other staff have been a bit unfriendly with you as well, they don't mean anything by it, it's just their way with strangers, see. Most of them share my high opinion of you, at least those that haven't been here for so long that they'll just support his lordship and never question him no matter what. Well anyway, I've talked plenty now, but I just wanted to say, you do have at least one friend here at Havisham Hall."

Anna beamed a big grin at her, slightly embarrassed to have said so much all in one go, but sincere in her expression of friendship. Catherine was full of gratitude for this kindness.

"Thank you Anna. That's very nice to hear."

"In any case, I'll let you finish your supper, but just so you know, should there be anything you require, anything at all, just ask, and I shall do my best to assist you in whatever way I can."

"You are too kind. Thank you again."

After finishing her soup, Catherine retired, as she did every day, to her quarters. The quiet isolation gave her space to think, to not have to keep on pretending that everything was normal. Unlike the grandeur of the main part of the house with its elegant drawing rooms and sumptuous decoration, her two rooms, which she had been shown to by the housekeeper on that first night, were in the servants' quarters, and were therefore very plain and simple.

Admittedly, they were in the better part of the servants quarters, on the same higher floor of the building as Theodora's suite of rooms, with a lovely view out over the gardens from the small window, but still, they were plain. Somehow she had not yet found a way to add anything to make them feel more homely.

She had a small bed, serviceable enough but not anyone's idea of especially comfortable, and, in her tiny sitting room, a bare, unvarnished desk, the wood of which had chipped away over the years and which gave her splinters if she ever tried to write on it.

There was a modest, single shelf attached to the left wall adjacent to her bed, where she had put the few books that she had, and a little cabinet in the desk, as well as one small closet where she could store her clothes. The walls were whitewashed and cracked, with much of the paintwork, which had probably been applied decades ago, at least, flaking away.

There was a slight smell of lingering damp throughout the room, which she had noticed had started to get into her hair and clothes, an indignity she had not expected to suffer on moving to a grand and stately home.

Perhaps the rooms had been empty for a long while before she came to them.

She was grateful for the small window on the back wall, with its pleasant view of the grounds at the back of the house, but it let in so little light by late in the day, that she was often forced to light up the precious supply of candles that she was afforded, to have light enough to read by.

The boards of the bare wooden floor would creak as she picked her way back into her room of an evening, to read and re-read the novels she had with her, or compose letters in which she falsely reassured her mother that she was happy and that all was well.

She was just sitting down to write such a letter, pen inches above the ink-well, when an unexpected knock at the door made her jump, it being so unlikely that anyone would seek her out here. Startled for a moment, she placed the pen back down and went to the door. She was utterly shocked, upon opening the door, to see her employer, the Earl, standing in front of her, wearing his crimson smoking jacket and looking far more nervous, indeed almost sheepish, than usual. Despite her decision that she never wanted to see, or speak to him again, she found her traitorous heart beating faster, and a sensation suspiciously like happiness rising inside her.  She repressed it firmly.

"I hope I am not disturbing you" he said immediately, in a subdued tone.

Despite everything that had happened between them, or perhaps because of it, she still felt a flutter in her stomach, and a growing warmth in her intimate places, at the sight of him — her body remembered the pleasure, even if her mind was focussed on the hurtfulness of his actions.

"My Lord! This is most unexpected. No, I suppose you are not disturbing me."

She tried as hard as she could not to be rude or churlish towards him.

He was still paying her a wage after all, and a more generous one than it needed to be, at that. And, in the end, no matter how frustrating the girl was, she did like Theodora, and did not want to leave, and doom her to a cranky and unforgiving governess in the traditional mould.

"What, pray, brings you to my humble quarters at this hour?" Her voice was hard, all of her repressed hurt hidden just under the surface of her words.

"Please Catherine…" he said, moving into her room without her permission. The house was his property, but she baulked slightly at this sudden invasion of her little corner of privacy.

"I wish you wouldn't speak to me in that tone – it is terrible to hear such coldness in your voice. I wanted to come and see you, to express my profoundest regret at how I behaved, and at having betrayed you as I have."

"Some, sir, would say that your apology is long overdue."

"Yes, I can see that you would perceive it like that. I've had to go away, this past few days, to finalise arrangements for this accursed wedding. Had I been here, I would have redoubled my efforts to demonstrate my regret to you, at every opportunity. Can you forgive me?"

She looked him straight in his dark, compelling eyes. He looked sincere in his intentions - indeed Catherine almost thought that he looked genuinely distressed. It had been decent of him to come to her like this.

Although, his mention of the wedding made her feelings of hurt all the sharper again.

"I can sir, but with a heavy heart. You have stripped me of my innocence, and my honour, and deceived me quite deliberately. I trust that our relationship will heal, but it will take time - time that I am only willing to grant you for Theodora's sake."

"Oh Catherine!" he said, plucking her hand from her side and holding it against his breast for a moment. He pressed a kiss to the sensitive flesh of her palm quickly, and let out a great sigh of relief.

"My heart swells with affection for you, I cannot thank you enough. Believe me when I tell you, my very soul has been swallowed by guilt these past few days. I wish I did not have to marry Lady Blanchette, with all my heart, but alas, a gentleman of my station must consider his duty to his house and successors. And I have given my word on it, some time ago — it would bring her great dishonour should I cry off at this late stage. I had never expected to meet someone else, someone who affected me as you do."

Her skin tingled where his lips had pressed, and a warmth spread through her, her nipples tightening in response. No matter what she thought, her body had very distinct opinions about his closeness.

"Thank you for your candour, sir, and I am pleased that you regret your actions. Now however, I should like some peace and quiet in which to write my letters, and then the space required for a good night's sleep."

He looked pained at her cold response. A tiny, guilty part of her was glad that she could still wound the heart of a man like the Earl.

Perhaps their relationship was not quite as broken as she had initially thought – if he could seem to be so wounded by her words, could it be that he told the truth, when he spoke of his affection for her ? That thought raised a tiny flutter in her heart, a little piece of hope.  A hope that she fiercely repressed, by reminding herself that he was to wed another, that, no matter her feelings or his, there was nothing here for her.

"Of course!" he said humbly. "How tactless of me, I shall leave you in peace. Only, whatever may have happened between us, and whatever uncertainties the future holds for both our fates, know that you will always occupy a pre-eminent position in my heart."

He paused to plant a solemn kiss on the top her head, smiled weakly, and left at once. Maybe, just maybe, despite his past indiscretions and his lusty habits of life, Charles Rockingham wasn't such a terrible man after all.

Charles sat in his study, the scatter of papers, all relating to his upcoming wedding, cluttering his desk.  The organisation, and cost, involved in a wedding was truly horrifying.  He didn't care.  Thank God his mother had chosen to live in the Dower House when his father died.  He would have gone mad by now where she here in the house with him.

She was currently wedding obsessed, as the union between Charles and Lady Blanchette was the culmination of 20 years plotting on her part.  He would have found it amusing, were he not one of the major characters in this farce.

He could not get Catherine out of his thoughts.

The feeling of utter despair, which had overtaken him when she ran from him in the grounds, had stayed with him all through the last few days as he had visited tailors and dealt with all of the trivia associated with the wedding and managing the alarmingly large influx of guests that was expected.  It had only eased this evening, when he had finally managed the courage to go to Catherine and apologise, again.

This time, she had listened long enough for him to ask her forgiveness, and she had been gracious enough to grant it.

But the coldness in her voice had chilled him to the heart, and the uncertainty of her manner towards him made him castigate himself even more, for the utter fool that he was.  He knew that passion made him forceful, and could overcome him – why had he put either of them in a position where that could happen?

He knew the answer – because he was selfish, because he wanted her, and he had not considered the impact of his actions on her future.  He did not like the answer, but he accepted it.

His thoughts ran round and round, an endless circle going nowhere, and found no answer.  In eight days, he would marry. No matter that he did not love, or even care for, the woman he would marry, no matter that he had come to care for Catherine, had come, dare he even think the word, to love her.  There was no way out.

No solution which allowed everyone to be happy, and still be true to honour and duty. He could not even lose himself in drink, or any other pastime – there was too much to do.

He would have to simply push his feelings aside and immerse himself in the management of the house and the estates, and the preparation for the guests' arrival.

Yet still he sat, ignoring the papers, and stared at nothing, Catherine's face haunting his thoughts. There was only one idea that had come to him, which might, in some way, allow him to have what he wanted. It was a thought that he was ashamed of, yet it came back to him – for surely that would be better than nothing at all?

He pushed the idea aside. It was not right. But it nagged at him. Annoyed, he pushed himself away from the desk and took himself to his chambers. It was late, and there was much to do tomorrow. Perhaps if he rose early and took Thaddeus out for a gallop, he might face the situation with better grace.

*

And so it went, for the next four days. Charles dragged himself through the day, dealing with interminable preparations, meeting with his mother to deal with everything that she demanded, taking Thaddeus out each morning in an attempt to ride out his frustrations. Catherine haunted his thoughts, and, when he saw her in the house, he ached to draw her to him and hold her. He forced himself to turn away instead, with a polite greeting, and escaped to another part of the house.

On the evening of the fourth day, he sat again in the study, nursing a large brandy, and considered the morrow. In the morning he would ride.

In the afternoon, Lady Blanchette and her family would arrive, as would some other guests, and the major activities would begin.

Three days after that, he would be wed.  It was still a surreal thought, and it appealed less than it ever had before.

He ached for Catherine.  He wanted to touch her, kiss her, hold her, feel her body beneath his. The thought that he might never do so again was unbearable. Yet he must accept that reality. In a sudden fit of frustration, he downed the brandy in one gulp, and smashed the glass on the stones of the hearth.  Turning, he took himself to his bed.

The next day the house was full of unfamiliar people, and frantic energy, as the Cavendish family arrived from Derbyshire with Lady Blanchette. With only three days to go until the wedding, there was an enormous amount of preparation to be getting on with.

The kitchens became a hive of activity as the chefs prepared all manner of dishes; stuffed geese, pigeon pie, plum pudding and turtle soup, endless platters of fruits, meats, pickles and cheeses, and of course, the *piece de resistance*, an immense wedding cake.

The deepest cold cellar was full of prepared items, and more ingredients where delivered continuously.

Catherine could barely move for all of the extra staff taken on for the effort, and was forced to sip her soup and nibble her bread and cheese in a tiny alcove off the pantry, keeping out of their way, lest she be trampled underfoot.

Anna had the unenviable task of helping them to scrub dishes, although that was not part of her normal work, working her way through a seemingly endless cycle of huge copper pots and pans. Cheerful by nature though, she whistled a merry tune and got on with her task.

By contrast, Catherine felt even more morose and heartbroken. She had seen Charles, in the distance, a couple of time in the day, always surrounded by his new relations to be, looking as handsome as ever, and even more unattainable. She sternly reprimanded herself for caring, but still could not help but look for him everywhere she went.

She had been overwhelmingly shocked when she discovered just how soon his wedding was to happen, with her shock rapidly turning to bitter anger at him, all over again, followed by despair.

If it were not for the need to keep Theodora quietly occupied in the midst of the chaos, she might have simply run from the house and not come back.  But…. where would she go?  She could not return to her mother, and tell her the terrible truth – her mother would be so disappointed, and would harp at her about it forever after. Anna broke into her gloomy musings with a question.

"How much of this feast do you think will be left over for us?" she asked Catherine with a cheeky grin.

"I reckon about half. These posh types don't tend to eat all that much. They wouldn't be able to squeeze their way into their fancy frocks and coats if they did! I'm not complaining! I can't wait to sink my teeth into a piece of that cake!"

Despite the sadness in her heart, and her deep regret that this wedding, which shamed her by its very proximity, and by stealing from her the man that she had believed that she loved, she laughed along with Anna, and felt a little spark of excitement at the prospect of seeing all of the beautiful clothes and decorations associated with so grand a wedding.

Regardless of anything else, this whole episode in her life was giving her a chance to see inside the lives of the nobility, which she would never have otherwise been able to do.

Before her duties with Theodora began for the day, from her little window at the back of the house, Catherine watched the preparations.

The servants were setting up the gardens so that guests feeling too warm in the ballroom would be able to take the air outside, surrounded by beauty, and with refreshments close to hand. Tables and chairs would be laid out throughout the gardens, providing places for guests refresh themselves, should the banquet presented indoors prove inadequate to their needs.

One of the terraces outside the French windows from the house had been set up as a stand for an orchestra to regale the guests outdoors with music, in addition to the musicians engaged in the ballroom where those so inclined would enjoy themselves dancing.

She had to confess to herself that it was all very exhilarating, the prospect of all of these grand celebrations, and the presence of so many of England's wealthiest and most important people, here to celebrate love and marriage.

Well, she corrected herself, marriage anyway – there was not much of love associated with most wedding in the *ton*.

She only regretted that all of this decoration, and the enormous feast being prepared down below was not for her wedding to Charles, but for that of another, a Lady with a real title and more money than she could ever dream of, rather than a penniless governess with nothing but a pretty face, a certain cleverness, and an old link to an ancient family to recommend her.

She did not even see Lady Blanchette until the next day when the Earl formally presented his household to his bride to be. They were, after all, to be her servants as well as his, once the match was complete, and he thought it prudent to introduce them now.

They all lined up in the entrance foyer of Havisham Hall, in their finest livery, from the butler and the steward, right down to the junior groundskeeper and scullery maid, as Lady Blanchette, her father Lord Derbyshire, and the Earl passed along the line.

Lady Blanchette was undeniably pretty. She had a small, heart-shaped face that was dainty and well-proportioned, with pert lips and piercing blue eyes the shape of almonds. Her dark glossy hair was beautifully dressed.

She wore a sumptuous dress, in red and black, which accentuated her womanly figure, curved at the hips, and, though she was not a tall woman, she had a certain gravitas that Catherine presumed came from the inevitable effect of her breeding and of the authority that is automatically granted to those of the aristocracy.

Each of the servants bowed or curtsied to her, without her saying more than a few words to them.

Lord Derbyshire, who seemed to be rather old and wore his thin grey hair in an old-fashioned manner, appeared bored by the entire exercise, dawdling at the rear with his hands behind his back.  He appeared to be focusing more on the family paintings of past and present Earls of Stanningfield, than on the staff of Havisham Hall. However, when the party got to Catherine, who was standing near the end of the line, wearing her best green dress, Lady Blanchette thought to say a little more than usual:

"And you must be the governess?" she said immediately, in a voice as clear and crisp as a mountain spring.

"Yes, my lady." Catherine responded as demurely as she dared. "Catherine Thornberry is my name."

"And a charming name it is too!" Lady Blanchette said, somewhat too brightly. Catherine was unsure what to make of her manner. Did she know about what she and Charles had done under the oak tree? Surely not.

"Charles has told me all about you. He says you are the cleverest young lady in all of Suffolk, and one of the prettiest besides. I can see that he was not exaggerating in his praise."

"You are too generous, Lady Blanchette." Catherine said, curtseying awkwardly.

"I will be most honoured to have you as a member of our household. I am sure that, with your attentions focussed completely on Theodora, she will learn, and not be a nuisance to us at all."

Blanchette fixed Catherine with a steely gaze. Though her mouth formed a smile, Catherine sensed a certain coldness in her bearing, the smile did not reach her eyes.

The sentiment expressed by her words did not appeal – Theodora did not deserve to be shut away from the Earl, and from the other activities of the house.

Catherine saw a momentary expression of displeasure cross Charles' face, where he stood beside Lady Blanchette, then it was gone.

She mumbled in reply "Thank you my lady. I am deeply honoured" and the Earl's bride-to-be passed on down the line.

Catherine's eyes met Charles' as he passed, and she noticed him throw her a wry little smile. She had to bite the inside of her lip to prevent herself from smiling too broadly in response. Instead she chose a stern and disapproving expression, hoping that it would make him at least a little sad.

That night Catherine lay awake in bed, writing in her diary and pondering Lady Blanchette's words and actions.

She was unsure what to make of them, and had little experience of high society, or the whims of beautiful, powerful young noblewomen, to draw on.

The idea of recording her thoughts and feelings from this strange period of her life had come to her a few days before, and now she set about it, scribbling notes to herself in an empty journal, by candlelight.

She had settled to a sort of sleepy peacefulness, finally starting to accept that there was nothing that she could do – he would marry another, no matter how much her heart ached, when, with a suddenness that caused her to sit up and gasp, the Earl burst into her room, without any sort of a knock or any kind of prior warning.

She instinctively recoiled in fear, but when she realised who it was her heart leapt in foolish hope and she felt a crazy urge to smile and laugh.

"My Lord!" she said, her breathing suddenly hurried and uneven, "… why what on earth are you doing here?"

"Hush, my Catherine" he said, turning to close the door and drawing his finger to his lips to command her to be quiet.

At this show of authority she stilled and sank back deeper into her bed, shutting the diary and placing it on the floor as she did so. Suddenly realising that she wore only her night rail, she drew the covers up to her shoulders, feeling vulnerable and unsure.

Charles came further into the room, tip-toed over the creaky floorboards and perched himself on the edge of her bed with a rapid, smooth movement, as if he'd practised this before. In the dim light of her small candle, he looked as handsome as ever. She could make out the edges of his jawline and his high, well-crafted cheekbones.

As before, she felt an urge to reach out and touch his face, to trace his jaw.

"I just wanted to say Catherine" he began, gazing at her passionately " – that, though I may be obliged to marry Lady Blanchette in a mere two days' time, my thoughts have been constantly of you. I cannot stop my mind from returning to thoughts of you, again and again, and I do not believe that any woman has ever had such a profound effect upon me before. As strange as it may be to say it, at a time such as this, I think I love you, Catherine Thornberry."

Catherine sat up. She was, of course, surprised and deeply flattered, happy beyond words and despairing at the same time, filled with great sadness and anger. She could feel the same shaking in her bosom and quivering sensation in her body, and especially between her legs, that Charles Rockingham had always caused in her.

Now she knew that those feelings were wanton desire, it made no difference – she found that she craved his touch, even whilst she hated their situation.

She had hoped, had in some way, already sensed that this was what he felt. There was a connection between them, some force that seemed to be drawing them together. A force strong enough that it overcame her anger, overcame her resolution to be sensible, and made her want simply to be in his arms.

No matter how set in stone his dynastic marriage into the Cavendish family might be, she had come to realise that nothing could change the feelings that they shared. Which only made the situation all the more painful and impossible.

"I know" she said. "- and I care about you very deeply, nay, I love you, as well, Charles Rockingham. You may be a cad, but you are also the most wonderful man that I have ever had the privilege of knowing – but…."

Before she could finish her sentence he had grabbed her, and was kissing her passionately, frantically holding her body close to his. The angry words that she had been about to say were swallowed by his kiss and all thought of them slid from her mind, as the onslaught of sensation from her body took over.

The same warm and powerful sensations, which she had felt under the tree on the grounds, overcame her, and she surrendered herself to him. It was delicious, it was everything she dreamed of, she felt safe and desired in his arms, even when she knew that none of this could possibly be.

Still kissing her, he pulled the bedcovers away from her body, stilling her protest with another kiss, trailing kisses from her mouth, down her neck, across her collar bone and down the upper slope of her breasts, as his deft fingers undid the ties of her nightrail and pushed it aside to allow him access to her nipples.

Her fingers tangled in his hair, holding him to her, as she gasped and arched up to him when his warm mouth and clever tongue found the hard peak of her breast and proceeded to lick, suck and nibble on it, creating sensations in her body that she had never imagined possible.

Sensations more intense even than those she had felt when he had taken her in the grounds, sensations that she wanted to explore, to feel more and more of.

Continuing his loving treatment of her breasts, suckling one and then the other, one hand supporting his weight above her, his other hand reached down and slowly drew up the hem of her nightrail, trailing his touch up the silken softness of the skin of her inner thigh as he did so.

She was squirming, arching her body against him, feeling heat building within her, and moisture gathering between her legs, in that most intimate place.  Her breathing was ragged, and she found herself helplessly calling his name then making little mewling noises as her body was flooded with sensation.  He slid up to kiss her mouth again, and her breasts ached for him to return to them, until that sensation was overridden by the next, as his fingers slid inside her, and began to work at bringing her to a peak of pleasure.  He moaned aloud as he touched her moist folds, finding her so very wet and ready for him, and the sound and feeling of his moan against her lips aroused her even further.  She felt that she had no control whatsoever over her, oh, so wanton, body, and her hips rose to meet the thrusts of his fingers, as she felt the irresistible wave of pleasure grow within her.

It was amazing, it was wonderful, she wanted more, needed more, even though, at the same time, it was so strong a sensation as to be unbearable.  Helplessly, she found herself at the peak of pleasure, and falling, falling, over it, into an indescribable and wonderful place.

As she fell, she felt his fingers leave her, and instantly missed the warmth of the intimate connection. Moments later, as she reached for him, pleading wordlessly, he came back to her, and slid his deliciously hard cock inside her.

It was slower than the time on the grounds, and she revelled in the sensation of being filled, of no pain whatsoever, only a delicious sense of fullness, and of sensitive nerve endings being stroked by his every movement.

Charles kept his movements slow, and deliberate, the effort obviously costing him much concentration, but when Catherine reached up, sliding her hands under his loose hanging shirt, and gliding them over the sculpted muscle of his body, he lost all hope of control, and began to thrust into her, feverishly, hard and fast, bending his head to gently bite at her nipples or lick and suck them.

She clutched him to her, her body contracting around his, and found herself about to come again, about to fall into ecstasy.

She cried out as she came, and the sight, sound and feel of her tipped Charles over the edge too. They collapsed into each other's arms, to lie still, and sated, and both pretending desperately that tomorrow did not exist.

But tomorrow did exist.

After a short while, Charles gently disentangled himself from her, and sighing, put his clothes to rights. "Oh my Catherine, I love you, but I am still honour bound to leave you. I see no way out, and that leaves me feeling dark despair. I want you desperately, but I must marry another. Perhaps, …… would you consider…. Could I possibly ask it of you… would you be willing to be my mistress?"

Catherine looked at him, suddenly feeling cold and abandoned, all of the beautiful, warm afterglow of their lovemaking blown away by the icy wind of his question.

She was hurt, shocked and offended, and spent no time considering it, before snapping "No!" and turning away from him.  Charles reached out a hand to touch her, but she pushed him away. "Leave me alone!" she demanded, turning from him and pulling the covers over her head.

She felt the bed shift, heard him move, hesitate, then sighing, leave the room.  She waited until she heard the door click shut, and his steps recede down the corridor, before letting herself indulge in tears of wracking grief.

Leaving an equally miserable Charles, with no choice but to steal off back into the night, returning to the life that he was duty-bound to lead, elsewhere, away from her.

The day before the wedding, Catherine took a day's leave and went back to her mother's cottage in Harteston. It was not a difficult decision to make, the house had become so consumed with pre-wedding activity that she could barely sleep, let alone find a moment's peace or privacy during the day.

Theodora was to have a part in the wedding, as an attendant, and had been excited by all of the fuss, by the more adult styled new gown that had been made for her, and by the increasing scale of the preparations.

She had been more distracted than ever before, speaking constantly of the impending marriage rather than focussing on her learning.

This had, quite predictably, made Catherine's task an impossibility, and so she had taken the liberty of writing a note to her employer:

*My Lord Stanningfield,*

*I regret that it has become necessary for me to temporarily quit Havisham Hall for Harteston. My mother has taken ill, and I am required by her bedside at once. I offer my sincere apologies for any disruption to the affairs of your household, or to Mistress Theodora's education.*

*Yours faithfully,*

*Miss Catherine Thornberry*

It was a brief and blunt letter, but she expected him to understand. The fact that her mother was not really ill, caused her a twinge of guilt as she wrote, but she felt that she needed some unquestionable reason for her actions.

The very thought of him and of their intimacy drove her to distraction, and she was tormented many times a day by reminders of his betrothal to another. Equally distracting was the idea that he could even consider asking her to be his mistress – did that mean that he really did love her, and could not bear to lose her? Or did it mean that he really did not love her, and was merely looking for a relationship of physical convenience?

She was so very confused.

Sitting in the middle of the preparations for a wedding that was not for her, between the man she loved and a woman she could not warm to, was simply too much to bear. She resolved to spend the next few days back in the village, away from this strange form of torture until after the wedding was over.

Without lapsing into painful or unseemly levels of detail, Catherine told her mother about the situation in which she found herself.

She had expected Mother Thornberry to be angry with her, and to insist that she had made a mistake, but she was more compassionate than she had expected.

"Well, as they always say, the course of true love never did run smooth" she said, hugging her daughter close, with warmth and affection.

The stew pot was in its usual place over the fire, filled with a rich smelling stew that had obviously benefitted from the food sent by the Earl. Catherine's single bed was warm and freshly made, and outside, the Forget-me-nots were emitting their sweet scent. Everything seemed to be in its right and proper place.

"Oh mother" Catherine whimpered. "How can I bear it? I feel as if my heart could only ever beat for him, and yet he is to marry another. I fear that I will be forever sad and alone."

"Don't talk such rubbish child!" her mother replied at once, patting her cheek to make her point more forcefully.

"Even if this rather unfortunate situation does not play out as you desire, well, there are plenty of other handsome young gentleman out beyond the four walls of this cottage, who would be inclined to take a shine to a pretty and clever young Miss like yourself. If you can attract the affections of one man such as the Earl of Stanningfield, why then should you presume that you could not catch the eye of another?"

"But mother, I may never meet such a man as him again, in all my life! And I would want a man such as him, a man that I could love." she exclaimed, with a hint of desperation in her voice.

"It is not every day that one is saved from drowning in a stream ten minutes' walk from one's own house by a handsome young Earl! You speak as if every man in the kingdom was as good-looking and charming, or as if every other young buck with wild oats to sow had a great name, house and estate behind him! Occurrences such as these are rare, indeed, I feel I may have drawn out more than my allotted due of good fortune already. And now to see him spurn me and marry another, it is all too much for a fragile heart to bear."

"You forget one thing my dear" said her mother, with a twinkle in her eye. "He has expressed his love for you. His marriage to this Lady Blanchette is taking place against his will, despite her many virtues and excellent pedigree, the result of a contract made when they were mere children, as I understand it. If he was sincere in the expression of his heartfelt desires, then you should not abandon all hope just yet."

"I do not know mother. I cannot stand it. To think of him wed to another for the remainder of his days - for the remainder of my days, to come to think of it – it is enough to make one lose all desire to go on living."

"Don't talk such rot girl! Why if we all simply gave up on things every time we faced a little difficulty, then none of us would be here at all! Had I given up, then you and I most certainly would not be here today.  You must hold your head high, take some pride and carry on as you were. There is nothing else for it."

Mother patted her cheek once again, and went back to stirring the old pot.

# Chapter Sixteen

Charles had not slept – he had lain there and thought of Catherine, feeling lost and achingly sad. Here it was, the day of his wedding, and he still really had no interest in marrying Lady Blanchette. He desperately wished that he could marry Catherine. He wanted a woman that he loved, not a typical *ton* marriage. He wanted a woman who could care for Theodora, even though she was stubborn and strong minded, not a woman who saw her as an inconvenience.

He wanted, most importantly, a woman who loved him, with whom he could share passion, not a woman who simply submitted to him because she had to, as his wife. There was still no solution that would give him all of that.

When Catherine had rejected his suggestion that she become his mistress, he had been happy – for he did not really wish to put her in such as position, where she would be looked down on, and scorned.  Yet there was no other way in which he could retain his honour, do his duty and also have Catherine.

Perhaps duty was not so sensible a way of life after all, if it made people so terribly unhappy. Honour he could still see some value in – in fact, in this case, he felt that what he was about to do was distinctly dishonourable, even if it was his duty.

The thought galled him.  Even through his most rakish days, he had still held to honourable behaviour, as much as he could. *'Yes,'* said that insidious voice in his mind, *'the last time that you acted in a truly, regrettably dishonourable fashion was Monique – and you vowed not to be like that again….'*

Irritated, with himself and the world, he pushed the thoughts away, and forced himself to rise, ring for Johnson, and prepare for the day.

*

Against her instincts, and possibly her better judgement, Catherine decided to go along to see the wedding. If pressed on the matter, she would have struggled to immediately explain why. Perhaps it was a desire to firmly close that chapter of her life, and to demonstrate to the Earl and his new bride that she bore no bitterness towards them, in spite of what had happened.

Perhaps part of her genuinely wished Charles Rockingham well, and desired only to express her fondness for him through this gesture of contrition.

She did, most genuinely, regret the way that they had parted, when he came to her room that last time.

But perhaps there was a part of her, some dark instinct for power inherited from the de Quinceys, which suspected that everything was not entirely over between herself and the man that she'd presumed to love. That she still, very much, loved.

After their amazing lovemaking in her quarters, she had surmised that she still, despite the demands of his family, had some power over him, held him still in her sway, although his asking her to be his mistress had shaken that a little.

It was impossible to say for certain, but she knew, at least, that she did not feel utterly resigned and miserable as she took the walk along the country roads to St. Jude's Church at Harteston, but rather had a, probably foolish, sense of hope and possibility.

She knew that St. Jude, patron of the parish, was the saint of lost causes, and perhaps this gave her some strange sense of hope.

It was a very attractive church, which she knew well. Two great and ancient yew trees stood over the entrance to the churchyard, marked with a wooden gatehouse painted black. Passing under these, the splendid medieval tower of the church loomed over the visitor, a reminder of the power of the almighty.

Its sturdy Gothic stones had been laid down in the late Middle Ages, back when Suffolk's agriculture and the wool trade had made it the wealthiest county in England, with even its most modest parish churches built on a grand scale.

Age-old Gargoyles leered down at her, as they had at visitors to this church for hundreds of years, threatening and promising in equal measure. Atop it all was a weather vane in the shape of the Archangel Michael, warrior-messenger of the heavens. He was leading her, as he had led legions of the faithful in the past, into her very own battle. She smiled at her fanciful thoughts, and turned to the church entry.

She was almost late, and most of the guests had already filed into the pews for the service. Catherine was, by some margin, the most modestly dressed of them all, wearing the same plain grey dress that she had worn the day that Charles had accidentally tipped her into the Shimpling Stream.

It was not an accident that she wore this humble garment, which she knew held great sentimental value for her, and hopefully for today's groom. Sliding inconspicuously into the very back of the church, she easily avoided the gaze of all the various grandees in their finest frocks and elegant suits.

So many of the gentlemen wore the tall hats that she understood were just coming into fashion in London society, along with bulging complicated white cravats and collars. The ladies, many accompanied by servant attendants, wore corset bodies, covered by bodices of beautiful silks, which seemed tighter than it was possible for any bodice to be, pressing their figures hard into an elegant curved shape. Their over opulent and spreading skirts made pools of colour in the shaded church.

Though she admired the appearance of them, Catherine was privately glad that she was not smart or wealthy enough to be expected to wear such uncomfortable looking garments. Not smart or wealthy enough yet, anyway.

The organist droned out a few pious bars of music, and the assembled congregation all took their seats. Catherine perched on the end of the rearmost rank of pews beside a formidable older woman, who threw her, and her modest garments, a disbelieving glance before facing the altar.

With the guests all seated, she could suddenly see him, her lover, looking more marvellous now that he ever had before, in a superbly tailored black coat with an immense white flower in his button hole. His hair was more buoyant than she had seen it, worn high and thickly curling, as irrepressible as ever.

He stood next to the reedy-faced vicar, mumbling something to a gentleman she presumed must be his brother, based on some similarity in their appearance, who was holding a small box, which likely contained the wedding ring.

What glorious diamonds or other gems might be encrusted on that ring! She allowed herself to fantasize about it slipping, glistening and wonderful, onto her finger. Her eyes met those of the Earl for just a second and she blushingly turned away. He had seen her though, of that she could be certain.

The organ piped up again and Lady Blanchette entered. Catherine had to admit that the woman, who was to break her heart forever, looked glorious in her wedding dress. It was as pure white as freshly-fallen snow, with her glossy dark hair covered by a fine veil that gave the woman's face an air of innocence and piety that it did not, on its own, possess.

She held a fabulous bouquet of hothouse flowers of types that Catherine had never even seen before.

Her dress had such a long train flowing out behind her that it took six attendants, including her young charge Theodora (who looked even more excited than before, if that was possible!), with a ring of flowers around her head. Theodora, stubbornly herself, grinned as she recognised her governess and Catherine could not help but beam a smile and a subtle wave back.

The bridal party reached the altar and the organ came to a prompt halt. Catherine could see the Earl whispering something, most likely some compliment, into his betrothed's ear, before the Vicar started up.

"Dearly beloved, in the presence of God, Father, Son and Holy Spirit, we have come together to witness the marriage of Charles Rockingham, Earl of Stanningfield, and Lady Blanchette Cavendish, to pray for God's blessing on them…" Catherine was too preoccupied with her own thoughts to properly take in the priest's words.

He plodded on through the opening prayer and words of welcome, and the wedding guests dutifully listened. She could not see Charles's face from her position at the back of the church, and had no opportunity to surmise how enthusiastic he was feeling about all of this, now that the moment had actually arrived.

"If anyone present knows any reason why these two may not be joined together forever in Holy Matrimony, let him speak now, or else forever hold his peace." Her heart lurched forward slightly at this familiar, ominous moment.

Being careful not to move her head to bring attention to herself, she scanned the room with her eyes.

No-one stirred, no hands were raised. She would not be relieved so easily then. Unexpectedly, Charles had turned around slightly, causing a murmur to run through the church, and once more she felt his gaze fall upon her. Again, she looked down at the floor rather than meet his eyes directly. She heard the vicar start the vows:

"The vows you are about to take are to be made in the presence of God, who is judge of all and knows all of the secrets of our hearts, therefore, if either of you knows any reason why you may not lawfully marry, you must declare it now."

Silence hung heavy around the church. The vicar allowed for the customary pause, used to passing over these formalities with nothing happening. Catherine could just about make out Charles, shifting his weight uncomfortably, at the front of the church. Nevertheless, it seemed that he would keep his silence, until, suddenly, he cleared his throat and spoke:

"I know a reason."

The vicar took a step backwards in shock. This was most improper, most unexpected, in fact, completely unheard of at a wedding of the nobility! He seemed unsure even of what to say in response.

"You do, my Lord?" he said at last, nervously.

"Yes. If, as you say, God knows all of the secrets of our hearts, then I'm afraid he would be rather appalled at mine. I love another, and have lain with her outside the bounds of wedlock. Surely that would be cause for me not to enter this marriage in the eyes of God?"

"Charles!" The Earl's mother stood up in horror from the front row. "What is this madness?"

"Do your duty boy!" said another, possibly an uncle. "This is no time for pious confessions! We're here for a wedding!"

"You may very well be…" said Charles firmly, turning now to face the congregation. Lady Blanchette kept her silence, the veil disguised the expression on her face. "… I however, have no intention of going through with this. I am sorry Lady Blanchette, but I cannot marry you. I have already given my heart to another, and it would therefore be false of me to take these vows now."

There were cries of outrage throughout the church.

Charles' mother surged to her feet, shrieking. "Who, pray? Who are you talking about Charles? What the devil has overcome you?" his mother sank back, almost fainting.

The vicar tried to protest this unseemliness in his church, but he was drowned out by the newly raised commotion.

"Catherine Thornberry." Charles' voice thundered, reaching straight to her, at the back of the church, as he answered his mother's question.

Catherine stood up, and it was all she could do not to cry out in delight, though she felt rather faint and shaky with shock. Her heart beat so hard that she shook with it, and her breathing came short.  He had declared her shame to everyone here, and she did not care, for he had also declared his love for her.

Could this really be happening, and to her? Such drama!

Her heart overflowed with joy and she was filled with a desire to sing.

"She has quite overcome me, and I have loved her since the very first time I saw her" he was walking towards her, striding purposefully down the aisle of the church. She clapped her hands to her face in shock.

All eyes were upon her now, some scowling, some simply confused, but a few of the old-fashioned romantics present seemed to be smiling. The old woman sitting next to her gave her a quiet nod of appreciation.

"Those of you who have come here to witness a staid and predictable dynastic marriage may be disappointed" he declared to the assembled throng "- but I freely admit that I care not."

Now he was before her, dropping down onto his knee. He did not have a ring on his person, so he simply held out his hands as a gesture of devotion to her.

"Catherine Thornberry, would you be my bride?" she gasped audibly.

Everyone there, Lords and Ladies, members of wealthy and powerful families, grandees who had come to see an exchange of vows and property between grand old families, all craned their necks at her in expectation. There was a sense that the entire church full of people held its collective breath.

She could not have said anything other than:

"Yes. Yes of course, I'll marry you!"

With that, Charles Rockingham rose to his feet and, in one powerful sweep, gathered her up in his arms and kissed her with a passion the like of which many watching in that church had never even seen, let alone felt. Cradling her close in his strong embrace, he turned and carried her towards the altar, to stand before the vicar expectantly.

Lady Blanchette drew herself up stiffly, and with a repressed hiss of anger, turned and strode from the church, followed by her closest family.  Charles watched her go, with no regret, and turned to the vicar.  "Please do continue – we have a wedding to complete!"

A short while later, to the enthusiastic applause of the guests, Charles kissed Catherine again, as his wife, and swept her up to carry her towards the door, leaning in to whisper "Thaddeus awaits, my Countess." She giggled uncontrollably as he threw the church doors open.

They passed on out into the world, free and in love, with the sound of an entire church's rapturous applause ringing in their ears.

AR
Arietta Richmond
Regency Historical Romance

The Derbyshire Set - Book 2
Regency Historical Romance
The Captain's Compromised Heiress
Amazon Bestselling Author
Arietta Richmond

The Derbyshire Set ~ Book 2

Regency Historical Romance

# The Captains Compromised Heiress

## Arietta Richmond

# Dedication

For everyone who had the grace to be patient while this book, and the ones before and after it, were coming into existence, who provided cups of tea, and food, when the writing would not let me go, and endured countless times being asked for opinions. And for all the writers of Regency Historical Romance, whose books I read, who inspired me to write in this fascinating period.

ARIETTA RICHMOND

# Chapter One

The moment that Lady Blanchette saw Captain Westbury's uniform, she knew that this party had not been a mistake. For days now she had argued with her mother and sister, insisting that it was all too soon, too close to the nightmare that had been her aborted wedding to the Earl of Stanningfield, for her to be able to cope with society once again. They had recited the same old arguments; she needed to move ahead in her life, she couldn't go on moping and crying, over having been jilted at the altar, for ever more.

The incident may have stirred up a scandal in Derbyshire society and beyond, but she was still one of the most desirable young ladies in England, with a substantial portion as well, and would surely find a suitable match soon enough.

She had dismissed all of their reasoning and sulked, but, in that instant of her first sight of Captain Westbury, with her heart pitter-pattering like a cantering mare, all that could be put aside. Hope, romance, and desire all rose suddenly within her, fresh sensations once again.

'Captain Henry Westbury of the Coldstream Guards, heir to The Most Honourable Sir Thomas Westbury, Marquess of Bevington.'

The footman, in his sumptuous livery, made the announcement over the sound of the room's chatter, and it took an immense effort for all of the ladies present to maintain their calm demeanour and resist the urge to turn, as one, and stare at this new arrival.

His rank and title spoke for him - a soldier, so gallant and well-attired, and also with a claim to one of the great estates in England.

Such a man would be a desirable husband for any daughter of a noble family, and all present were immediately aware of that fact. Not only this however, but from the perspective of a young lady, with ideas about romance learned from novels and whispered gossip between sisters, this Captain Westbury was an exceptionally handsome gentleman.

His golden hair sat thick and lush upon his head, immaculately curled, matching the colour of his shining brass buttons. The military stock and collar, in the dark facings of his most esteemed regiment of guardsmen, seemed almost to frame his face like a painting, and perfectly emphasised the delicate curvature of his bone structure, slender and pleasing.

There was serenity in his blue eyes that nevertheless, when matched with his glorious mane and shimmering scarlet uniform seemed to give him an inner strength that radiated outwards.

He was tall and well-proportioned, with long-legs clad in skin-tight buff breeches and high leather boots, designed for the parade ground and polished to a glinting sheen.

His entire manner and bearing was confident, even heroic, and he strode out into the room with every female eye fixed discreetly, or not so discreetly, upon him.

Blanche suppressed an urge to laugh. Could it really have been only a few hours ago that she had been sitting in the library of this very house, her house, here on the edge of Amfield Moor, morosely carrying on a conversation with her sister Charlotte about her desire to run away and be done with men and society for good?

'Oh Blanche, you must not talk such rubbish!' Charlotte had declared back confidently.

'Why just because one eligible bachelor has spurned you does not mean that they all will! What happened in Suffolk was a freak, a bizarre little incident that historians will look at a hundred years from now and declare to be one of the strangest occurrences in the annals of the English gentry! You were just unlucky that's all'.

'But Charlotte…' Blanche had replied, trying with all her might not to burst into tears once again. '… What if it's me? What if there is something about me, which Stanningfield, Charles, found profoundly unattractive? What if it's all somehow my problem and men don't take to me?'

'My dear Blanche, I am not sure what that is even supposed to mean. Why, you're pretty, you're clever, you're from an exceptionally good family, if I do say so myself. Don't talk rubbish! If you are to declare that you have certain deficiencies of appearance or character that make you unattractive, what possible hope is there for me?'

They had shared a little laugh at this. It had always been known to both of them that Blanche was, as the eldest and the prettier of the pair, the one who would be first to find a husband.

She secretly suspected that Charlotte resented her for this fact, but her sister was kind and knowing enough not to let on. The truth was that Blanche's failed marriage put Charlotte in a very awkward position. It was unlikely that a betrothal would be sought, or agree if proposed for he, until her older sister was herself wed.

Indeed, in her worst moments, Charlotte did wonder if, as the youngest, there was a chance that her family might decide they would rather not be parted from her ever, if she did not have the chance to seek a husband soon. An unsaid tension was growing between the two sisters, despite Charlotte's willingness to try and stem her sisters' tears.

'Here is my personal guarantee' Charlotte had declared, smiling. 'If you don't have attractive and suitable gentlemen positively queueing up to ask you to dance with them at the ball tonight, why then I'll personally ride naked through the streets of Chesterfield. You have that as a guarantee, signed by my own hand and sealed with the Cavendish family crest!'

Blanche was rather shocked by that image, but had laughed nonetheless. They had shaken hands in a comical imitation of City gentlemen, and embraced.

The truth from Blanche's perspective was that she had never doubted Charlotte's prospects of finding a man. She could be very funny and was shamelessly flirtatious, and their mother had never suggested keeping either of them unwed.

Perhaps the younger of the Cavendish sisters knew that having a moping spinster ahead of her in the marriage queue was no good to anyone. Whatever her motives, Blanche was glad of the kindness. Now that Captain Westbury had made his appearance she was more than glad.

In fact, she was positively delighted that her mother had decided to host this house party, and ball (the fact that it allowed her mother to indulge in her penchant for bringing together unwed persons of distinction was a side benefit, from Blanche's point of view), and that so many had decided to come. None had yet raised the subject of her unfortunate jilting at the hands of Charles Rockingham, Earl of Stanningfield, many of whom present privately knew to be an eccentric and impulsive sort of a man in any case.

For a while she had sat at the back of the room gathering her courage and resolve, sipping at a glass of ratafia, while Charlotte batted her eyelashes and laughed at the men's jokes, but now she pressed forward, concealing half of her beautiful heart shaped face with a fan, and casting what she hoped were dark and mysterious looks with her piercing gaze. She could see immediately that Captain Westbury, who was still by the door exchanging pleasantries with his hosts, her mother and father, had noticed her.

She was not in the least surprised when he ignored several of the ladies nearer the entrance, blushing and fiddling with their hair, and made straight for her. The newfound sense of confidence, that this created, carried her into their conversation with a strong sense of her attractiveness, and of the ample possibilities this evening, and the rest of this week, afforded.

'Lady Blanchette, I assume?' he asked wryly, bending to kiss her hand in a single, practised motion. Her heart fluttered and she felt something new stirring in her, low in her body. It was a sensation she was quite unused to, a trembling and a warmth. She had felt desire before, had felt nervous, had felt many things, but never exactly this.

It startled her, but, if pressed, she would not have said that it was an unpleasant sensation. She looked at Captain Westbury's clean-cut jawline, and felt his firm hand around hers and the sensation came on all the stronger.

'You presume correctly, Captain Westbury' she replied, barely making eye contact. She could see that Charlotte, on the other side of the room, had noticed and was now watching, distracted, no longer all that interested in the red-haired fellow she had been flirting with.

'Tell me, what brings a soldier of the esteemed Coldstream Guards to our humble occasion at Amfield?'

'Why, the same things that attract anyone to an occasion such as this - the promise of society with one's peers, of hunting, and the prospect of meeting, and conversing with, attractive young ladies.'

'And I trust your hopes in that regard have not been disappointed?'

'Certainly not.' He had a direct and bluff manner of speaking that she suspected he had learned in the military.

'I had heard about his Lordship's fair young daughters and assumed that reports of their grace and beauty had been exaggerated.

But now that I am able to make a reconnaissance with my own eyes, I can see that they were quite understated in their praise'.

'You think so? And may I hope that it is not daughters in the plural that you are here to make an aesthetic appraisal of?'

For the first time she allowed herself to make full eye contact with him. Their eyes met, two pools of intense blue, each hinting at fascinating hidden depths.

He seemed momentarily taken off guard by her quip, and her heart picked up its pace once again, at precisely the same moment that the string quartet on the far side of the room increased their tempo.

Was it the music, she thought for a second, that was making her feel like this, or the company?

'I shall have to see.' He responded coolly. 'After all, it would be ill-mannered of me not to make the effort of acquainting myself with all of the young ladies present, would it not?'

'I suppose that depends on your perspective' she said, with a flutter of her fan.

'Nevertheless' he said, regaining some composure, 'I was considering asking you to dance with me at once, and I would consider it most disappointing if you were to refuse. May I dare to hope that there may be a space on your dance card – for this very dance?'

Blanche made show of consulting her dance card carefully, even though she knew exactly what was written on there – which was, due to her hiding in shadows earlier, precisely nothing. She looked up, and was immediately caught again by his deep blue eyes.

'Would you be so very disappointed Captain? I suppose in that case, I should feel duty-bound to accept.'

With an intriguing smile, that promised much but gave away almost nothing, she placed her hand daintily on his offered arm, and allowed him to take her off to the centre of the room to dance.

The Right Honourable James Blackwood was a lot more than just the heir of the Viscount Selby. Aside from his title, he had rather a reputation, some of which was hard-won, but some of which never seemed to stop chasing him. He was renowned as one of the best shots in the kingdom, having brought down a reputed two score and a dozen grouse on the Glorious Tenth three years ago. He was also a superb huntsman, a fine addition to any party, hard-riding and with a talent for scenting a fox.

All admirable traits. But, unfortunately, perhaps, in addition to these he was a gambler, a drinker, and a notorious rake. He hosted parties at his house in Nottinghamshire which were known to go on for days and days of rowdy cavorting – the sort of parties where the ladies present were certainly not of the nobility.

He was friends with strange and dangerous men; poets, painters, Italians and Turks, and had travelled far and wide.

Some said that he had killed a man in Greece for bringing him the wrong vintage of wine. Some had said he had seduced the Mistress of the King of Prussia, and been banished from that kingdom for ever. It was even said, in a few especially sensational whispers, that he had fathered the present dauphin of France in an especially daring and violent affair before the conclusion of the wars with Napoleon. Whether there was any truth to any of this was impossible to establish for certain, and Blackwood himself never deigned to comment.

What was undeniably true, and what formed the basis for much of this reputation, was that Blackwood was one of the most skilful seducers in England. There was a trail of conquests behind him, and many of them had let the world know about his skills. He was good-looking, but not exceptionally so.

There was an edge of darkness and danger to his appearance, from his jet black hair and cynical eyes, to the shadows that seemed to cling to his jawline and the easy way in which he raised his left eyebrow, as a comment, in itself, on the conversation.

His lip seemed to form a permanent slightly sardonic half smile that was, apparently, still beguiling to the ladies, and he rarely raised a true smile, even at the best efforts of ladies and gentlemen alike to stimulate his sense of humour. His voice had a resonant, rasping tone that came from his years of hard-living, and from the musky cigarillos, which he imported directly from the West Indies, and smoked with frequency.

Young ladies often flinched from him at first, but they soon found that what they first experienced as a sort of dread quickly turned into fascination, and then passionate attraction. Blackwood knew the effect that he had on people and he knew how to use it to get what he desired.

When James Blackwood heard that Lady Blanchette Cavendish had been abandoned at the altar by Stanningfield, a former companion of his, his interest was piqued. Lady Blanchette was an intensely pretty girl and he had made her acquaintance some years ago.

She was already betrothed then, but he had still done all that he could to ingratiate himself, inviting her fascination, coaxing her to laugh at his remarks even when they were not all that amusing, leaving confident that she would think of him more, and even allow his image to stray into the realm of her fantasies.

He considered her very attractive even by his own high standards, the equal at least of many of the ladies in the courts of Europe that he had visited in his time. It amused him, in a somewhat twisted way, to be able to draw the affections even of ladies promised to another, especially to someone like Stanningfield, with whom he was no longer on such good terms. So when the invitation to a week-long house party and ball at Amfield House had arrived, he had been pleased.

He had suspected at once that Blanchette would not only be present but in a fragile state, still mourning the loss of her promised husband, shaken by her embarrassment in front of society, and most likely receptive to the advances of an attractive and well-bred bachelor, whom she had already met.

He estimated that most of the other gentlemen there would be young, inexperienced, a little over-enthusiastic and unpolished in the art of seduction, looking to start a serious affair rather than a pleasurable liaison.

He would therefore stand out in the room, due to his reputation and his manners, and he knew for a fact that Amfield House was plenty big enough to accommodate the fruition of a seduction.

Anticipation had roused his manhood to turgidity, and he had set out for the ball, attended by his loyal valet, Buckham, and with late night pleasure on his mind.

'The Right Honourable James Blackwood, heir to the Viscount Selby.'

There was an almost audible gasp in response to the announcement of his arrival. He was wearing his best black dress coat, and his cravat tied in the manner most fashionable in London society. He glanced casually around the room, immediately taking command of his surroundings. Young ladies looked at him in awestruck fascination and gentlemen with instinctive unease. A number of the younger gentlemen present immediately made very unsubtle defensive shifts to shield their sweethearts from his sight, and potential attentions.

Blackwood almost laughed. He was well used to this. Soon enough they would be slapping him on the back and boasting to him about their hunting prowess, trying as hard as they could to ingratiate themselves with this notorious dandy before he ingratiated himself with the women they desired.

For now though, their reaction at hearing his name was one of mild panic.

The only people in the room who did not seem scandalised at his appearance were his hosts, the Earl and Countess Derbyshire, but then they were rather older than most of those present in the room (save the well-attired chaperones who sat around the fringe looking mildly bored), and did not move in circles where the principle conversation was salacious gossip.

They had always considered Blackwood to be rather charming, and greeted him now with a warmth and grace he rarely received elsewhere.

'Ah, James!' declared Lady Derbyshire, beaming. She was a large woman in every conceivable sense, taller and heftier than her husband, with a booming voice and open manners for a lady of her station.

'So excellent of you to come, I had feared an occasion such as this might prove a little drab for an experienced and well-socialised fellow such as yourself!'

'Not at all, My Lady.'

Blackwood smiled, kissing her hand politely as she offered it.

'There is little on this good earth I value more than a good house party and ball at Amfield House, with persons of quality. The hunting here is always excellent.  Regarding the room, I can see that you have excelled yourselves once more.'

'I see you have not lost your powers of flattery!' said Lord Derbyshire, shaking his hand firmly. 'I should hope that you do not employ them on the delicate sensibilities of the young ladies present, my dear Blackwood!'

'Indeed not, My Lord.' Blackwood replied promptly 'My wild oats are quite sown, your guests need not fear my bachelor's status. I fear that, as the heir to a humble estate, I am used to certain habits of ingratiation as a necessary function of my society...'

'You are as modest as you ever were!' said Lady Derbyshire, casting him a wry glance.

'Now you must excuse me' Blackwood said to his hosts, privately keen to move beyond these formalities. '- I shall now avail myself of your no doubt excellent punch, and make my salutations to your charming daughters.'

'Well we would not wish to deprive them of your excellent company, Blackwood', chortled Lord Derbyshire, blinded to the intentions of his guest. 'We shall attend to greeting the rest of our guests. I believe young Blanchette is already developing a fondness for a young officer of the guards, see over there?'

Blackwood followed the line of his finger to Blanchette, and their eyes met. She was indeed dancing with a young, blonde fellow in a soldier's uniform.

He sensed a mild shock in her as she noticed his presence, as if she were immediately distracted and unsure what to think.

'Best break 'em up before anything unseemly breaks out, eh?' said Lord Derbyshire, with a wink.

Blackwood smiled in acknowledgement of his host's saucy joke, and, as the music came to a conclusion, and the dancers left the floor, started his move across the room.

'You will forgive me my sudden interjection...' he said in his husky tone. The pair, who had been moving to the refreshments table, turned to face him. The officer, whom he observed, with a tiny note of regret, was a terribly handsome young fellow - and taller than he was – looked somewhat taken aback. Blanchette however, looked immediately delighted. A spectacular smile quickly spread across her face.

'Mr. Blackwood!' she exclaimed in delight. 'Why it's been such a long while since we have seen you! So good of you to have come!'

'You look absolutely divine' he said at once, wearing his easy confidence lightly. He reached for her, sliding his fingers over the sensitive skin of her palm in a caress that was effective even through gloves, and unseen by anyone else, as he bent kiss her hand. He looked up and saw that she was looking right at him, the pupils of her shimmering blue eyes dilated slightly. He could already sense that their attraction was mutual. 'It is quite worth the ride up from Nottinghamshire, just to see you again. It was so good of you to invite me.'

'Not at all! You were certainly atop my proposed guest list.'

'You are too kind. As you are well aware, occasions such as this have a tendency to bring out the absolute worst in me' they held each other's gaze as Blanche giggled lightly. His touch was already working.

'But then we wouldn't want a boring and tiresome ball now, would we? Or a tiresome week, for that matter – hunting only goes so far for amusement.'

'Why no, sir. Most emphatically not – I have been quite bored enough in my life.'

'I am sorry.' Captain Westbury cut in assertively. His interruption disrupted a moment of dark excitement, of quivering attraction growing in Blanchette's bosom. She turned, and for a moment it was he who had the lady's attention. He went to place his hand on her shoulder but she shifted instinctively to the right to avoid it.

Instead, he stepped forward to place his powerful military frame between Blanchette and this dark and, to him, somewhat ominous looking intruder.

'I do not believe we have been introduced, Mr...?' he said the 'mister' disdainfully, placing stress on Blackwood's lack of estate or title.

If only, Blackwood had often thought to himself on occasions such as this, my old uncle Selby would do the decent thing and be deceased, and let me inherit his Viscountcy!

'Blackwood.'

'Pleased to meet you sir, I am Captain Henry Westbury of the Coldstream Guards.' He spoke with the rat-a-tat tone and graceless clarity of the officer's mess.

'Charmed' said Blackwood ironically. 'It is pleasing to see that we have a trained warrior in our midst. Should Bonaparte escape from St. Helena and deign to invade Amfield Moor I am sure we shall be quite safe with you around.'

Westbury, rather shocked at the disrespect implied, made to stutter a reply but could not think of anything. 'Aha!' thought Blackwood. 'This bounder might have the looks and rank, but I've got all the wit!'

'Now excuse us, I fear we may be occupying a little too much room on the dance floor, we'd best retire to the fringes. I trust you shall enjoy the remainder of your evening, Captain Westbury.' Blackwood threw Westbury a cruel glance, and led Blanchette, who already seemed to be under his spell, away from her handsome Guardsman.

## Chapter Three

'So what can you tell me of the French ladies, Mr. Blackwood?'

'Well, they are certainly fair, and very fashionable. So many of them have a worldly sort of air about them, as if nothing you could do could possibly impress them. They are far more assertive than the English girls as well. In France, it is very often they who lead the gentlemen, and not the other way around.'

'Heavens!' said Blanchette, fascinated by Blackwood's experiences. 'I cannot even imagine such a situation!'

'Nor could I until I went there, but I am compelled to report that many of the things one hears about the ways of French ladies are true. They are not however, my specialist subject. Until the conclusion of the war of course, France and its manifold delights were quite closed off to us.'

'And with good reason!' Blanchette cut in. 'Bonaparte had designs on the whole of Europe!'

'I suppose that all depends on your point of view' said Blackwood, casting his troubled glance into the middle distance. 'Politics has always bored me terribly. I have often thought it would be best if all the governments of the world would simply abandon their little schemes for the dominance of one another and let those of us who appreciate life more live as we pleased. The Italians understand that, for example…'

'That is most unpatriotic of you, Mr. Blackwood!'

'Perhaps it is' he said casually. Blanchette was quite scandalised but she could not shut off her ears or eyes from the intriguing observations and opinions of this man. The very fact that he felt at liberty to make her feel scandalized caused a delicious shiver to run down her spine.  His was quite the most dangerous company she had ever kept, and that excited her more than it should. It was as if, in his company, none of the usual rigid formality and expectation of society seemed to apply, and one could simply say whatever one wanted. Or for that matter, do whatever one wanted…

'…but I have always found that the Italians appear to have their priorities set right. We English, and others of the northern nations on the continent, are so uptight, so proper, so concerned with our little plans and designs, with commerce and politics.'

'And it is right that we should be so!' chuckled Blanchette, aware that she was playing devil's advocate.

She had seen none of the world beyond England's shores and could only guess at what it was like from what she heard from men like Blackwood. It was entirely possible that his opinions were correct. 'Through our industry and our unparalleled constitution, we have come to rule half the world!'

'... and if that is what concerns you, Lady Blanchette, then that is all well and good. However, I am interested in more than money and colonies. I am interested in the heart and soul of man, and indeed...' he leaned closer to her and placed his strong hand on hers discreetly. There were no chaperones nearby to chastise him, and Blanche's mother and father were, again, distracted by new arrivals at the door.

A small part of Blanchette was fearful of this rogue, who had sailed the seven seas, but most of her was glad that no-one was looking on. Her heart thundered beneath her stays and her womanhood prickled with heat. She felt as if she had never been so excited – was this, she wondered, what they meant when they spoke of lust ? Did she desire this man, in a carnal way ? She had felt desire before, of that nature, though she would not admit it to anyone, but it had never felt like this.

'... the heart and soul of woman, as well.' Blackwood almost whispered in her ear. She held fast against his proximity, if only because if she leaned any closer to him in turn they would soon be atop one another. Not that, at this moment, she would mind being hard up against his strong body, but.... There were too many people around them, who might, at any moment, turn and see, such a thing was unthinkable, here.  Well perhaps not unthinkable... but certainly not acceptable!

'Pray tell Mr. Blackwood...' she said, feigning innocence. 'How do the fairest ladies of Derbyshire County compare to those of say, Italy, or France?' She leant forward, and wriggled away from his disturbing touch, if only temporarily.

Then she looked him straight in the eye, for a lingering moment that said more than any words ever could.

'How do we measure up?'

'Well-' he replied, with a whimsical little smile '- all company is mixed, of course, it is rare in heaven or earth to find a room filled exclusively with young ladies whose prettiness is beyond question. But I would have to say that the best amongst present company...' he looked at her again, steely and wry, a glint of something hungry in his dark eyes, as if in his mind he was already tearing off her bodice and hitching up her petticoats. She didn't allow him to hold her gaze, and instead cast a glance off to the left, where she assumed Captain Westbury would be skulking around feeling thwarted.

'... would be a match for any of the greatest beauties of the world.' Blanchette's stomach did a little tumble. She could feel the hairs on her arm prickling, standing to attention. Her hand strayed down to brace her against the back of a chair next to where they stood, her legs were suddenly shaky, and it seemed that a lightning bolt ran through her as his hand brushed her elbow. She was hot and felt strangely warm and damp between her legs, all for him, for this dark and handsome traveller, this seducer, this knave. Just from a short conversation, and a light brushing touch – what was happening to her?

She was a well-bred young lady, she should not be thinking like this, and she should certainly not be enjoying it!

Yet… she knew that she was capable of enjoying this, for she had explored that possibility before… she shut those thoughts down. She was not going to remember, to even consider, such things.

Yet the temptation was too great – she had spent so long expecting to marry Charles, yet she had never felt this level of excitement with him.  No, whispered an insidious little voice in her mind, you have only ever felt anything like this with the man beside you now, and, for a moment earlier, with Captain Westbury….

Blanche made a sudden decision – tonight, she would be brave, would act on her own desires, regardless of what a well-bred young lady "should do", and would leave dealing with any consequences for tomorrow.  With her past, surely nothing she chose to do would make her any worse off!

'Mr. Blackwood,' she said in her best impression of a plain and simple maiden 'I would be most honoured if you would accompany me to the library. We have a fine selection of volumes about various parts of the world, I would be interested in your opinion of their veracity…' she turned her head slightly to the right, watching his reaction from the corner of her eye. She could not help but notice his open gait, the strength of his posture, and the proximity of his body to hers.  His beautifully tailored tight fitting breeches displayed his body to perfection, and left her in little doubt that he desired her.

'… and we also have a globe, and certain other accoutrements that I would be willing to show you.'

'That sounds most interesting, my Lady' he purred back. 'Lead on'.

The library at Amfield House was indeed impressive. It was well respected among the great families of central England for its elegant design and superb collection of volumes. High cases of shelves ran all around the perimeter from floor to ceiling, and some of the books were only accessible by ascending a ladder.

There were several sets of tables and chairs, all varnished to a sheen and beautifully upholstered, scattered about the room, with small piles of books upon them. A few larger couches were placed to one side. A cabinet of exotic curiosities, acquired by the Cavendish family over the years, sat in one corner, including a shrunken head from the Americas and a great claw, from an unknown creature, which some obscure relative had picked up in the South Seas.

At the back of the room, by a high window, was an escritoire, and on it, a great globe made at some point in the last century to commemorate the discovery of Australia.

'You have a very fine library' said Mr. Blackwood on entering, casually closing and locking the door.  He walked across the room, regarding Blanchette from behind with a heated stare that she could not see. She was shapely, and had always appealed to him, and their conversation so far had brought him to a pitch of lust that he had not felt for some time.

He supposed that it was the possibility of debauching such a delectable innocent, with her cooperation. At least he assumed that she was innocent – he wondered if Stanningfield had had the balls to take advantage of his betrothed, before he jilted her at the altar.

'I would certainly be interested in making an appraisal of your collections...' Blanche had stopped near the globe and, as he stepped up behind her, firmly repressing his desire to immediately fondle her easily reachable buttocks, she turned, and before he could utter any more inane formal conversation, Blanche had grabbed him, and was kissing him, inexpertly, but with feverish enthusiasm.

She was not entirely sure what had come over her, and knew that this was a most improper way to behave, even within the bounds of the 'unwritten code of possible improper behaviour' for unmarried ladies. Whilst she had certainly carried out some extensive 'exploration' with Charles, she had always waited for him to initiate it, and had been somewhat disappointed by the whole thing.

After the weeks of depression and tears since her aborted wedding to Charles, the effect of being so obviously desired acted like an aphrodisiac flowing through her, through her lips and tongue, her newly found courage fuelled by desire of her own.

Blackwood, though surprised for a moment, quickly regained his composure and took charge of the kiss, applying all of his expertise to deepening it, and taking full advantage of her enthusiasm.

They collapsed onto the nearby, large, well stuffed leather couch together, bound at the mouth.

Slowly, without forcing the issue or making her feel uncomfortable, he began to run his firm, strong hands all over her delicate body, careful not to scare her – he wanted her, he was so hard that it hurt, but he would take his time about it – these things were to be savoured, at least the first time, with such a woman.  Silently and smoothly he began to undo the tiny buttons at the back of her gown, then to loosen the laces of her stays, gently easing the gown off her shoulders, and kissing his way down her neck and onto the delectable top slope of her breasts.

Easing the fabric down further, his kisses following its path, he reached to ease her beautiful breasts up and out of the corset, just enough to reach her nipples.  Blanche was lost in the sensations, her breathing was fast and shallow, and her body seemed not her own.  It was as if she was someone completely different, some daring woman who knew what she was doing, knew what she wanted, and was not afraid at all.

Blackwood's tongue reached one nipple as his clever fingers found the other, and, as he caressed her breasts with an amazing contrast of warm mouth and lightly pinching fingers, she felt another jolt, as if she had been suddenly struck by some force inside her, and found that there were muscles clenching inside her, in response – muscles that she had never, prior to this day, suspected to exist.

She clung to him tightly, and though still almost fully clothed they seemed to be pressing into each other's bodies through the layers of cloth and undergarments.

'You are a most spirited girl Lady Blanchette.' His voice was husky, his breathing heavy, as she indulged her newly aroused appetite for kissing and exploration with kisses to his cheek and neck.

'Do you treat all of your gentleman admirers in this unorthodox fashion?' she drifted another kiss across the stubble on his jawline, and looked up at him as he leaned in closer to her. In an instant he was kissing her again.  She returned the kiss enthusiastically, pressing her body against him, as he ran his hand down over her hip, feeling her delightful shape, through the all too many layers of the fabric of her skirts, until he reached the hem, and could slide his hand up again, drawing those skirts with it.

'Only those whom I deem worthy of my affections, Mr. Blackwood.'

Her reply came on little gasping breaths as his fingers slid up the silken skin of her inner thigh, and then across the fabric of her drawers towards her most intimate place.

She arched her body up against him, and he bent to lick and suck at her nipples again, one then the other, as his fingers worked gently and insistently under her skirts.  There was much, much too much fabric still between them – he most strongly wished that he could see her body laid bare, but that would have to wait for another time.

He was deservedly proud of his skills in the sensual arts, of his understanding of what women enjoyed most – after all, he had spent years perfecting that knowledge.

It was a simple matter to ensure that what he did was having a deeply exciting effect on her.

Blanche was arching her hips and moving herself against his hand, tossing her head from side to side, moaning quietly, as he built the intensity of sensation, working her nub of pleasure mercilessly with his fingers. She quivered out a sigh and looked at him with eyes glazed with need.

'And tell me…' he added, pressing his brow against hers, breathing the words against her lips, whilst his finger never stopped in their work '… was Charles Rockingham considered suitable for such attentions?'

For a second, even deep in desire as she was, she was quite taken aback at his cheek. To raise the subject of her recent betrothal in her very own house! It was all rather too much to take in, all too shocking. But, as his fingers continued their work, and her body responded, regardless of her thoughts, she realised the purpose of his remark. He was asking after the state of her virginity. Just as he had coaxed these untamed passions out of her, so too was he forcing an admission of another sort.

'We did, commune, in a nature such as this, on more than one occasion.' She said it without either guilt or shame, even though she knew that society would say that she would feel both. She knew that she need not expect judgement from a man like James Blackwood.

'Very well. I do not make a habit of robbing un-betrothed ladies of their innocence. You may call it one of the few genuine principles I hold. But it seems, as you have already been quite stripped of all innocence, that I may proceed free of guilt.'

He did not say the rest of his thought, which was to the effect that he felt sure that he was capable of teaching her far more 'uninnocent' things than Stanningfield would ever have done.

She could not stop herself from laughing, and then kissing him once again, almost frantically. What a rare intrusion of honour into the conduct of Mr. Blackwood! His concern for her future prospects of marriage was quite admirable, and she could not help but feel all the greater affection for him.

After all, her current state of 'lack of innocence' was all her own fault, but at least here and now she could enjoy the results.

She pushed aside any thought of how she might deal with an eventual explanation to a husband, should there ever be one.

That was a problem that already existed, and what she did here today would not change that. Blackwood's fingers had not stopped their work, and her need was intense now, and seemed more important than anything else.

Blackwood abandoned conversation, his lust having risen to a fever pitch upon realizing that he could take her now, with no impediment, and have the pleasure, as well, of showing up Stanningfield as a poor lover, in the process. He began kissing her again, working his way downwards, from her lips which he kissed passionately, putting all of his well-practised sensuality into it, back to her delicious breasts.

He pulled her bodice further aside in what seemed to be single, clean movement and lifted her breasts further from the corset, fully exposing her pink nipples to his rampant tongue again.

All the while he continued to work his fingers ever deeper into her underclothes, until they slid through the slit in her drawers to touch her wet folds directly.

She writhed momentarily with pleasure at this instant of contact. He licked and lapped little circles around her sensitive breasts, drawing gasps and sighs of pleasure, and a growing shaking all through, all down to her dripping wet womanhood.

Any thoughts of resistance, or of pulling out of this mad, sudden seduction, which rose in Blanche's mind, were immediately suppressed. She had no desire to be anywhere but here, doing this, with this man, right now. Her nipples hardened further and seemed almost to push outwards from her body, her breasts newly swollen by desire.

Though she had expected it, the sensation of his fingers direct on her most sensitive flesh was not in any way dimmed by that expectation, indeed it was all the more electrifying for the build-up that had gone before.

His fingers continued to rub away in the same dextrous manner that they had worked when touching her through her clothes, moving over all of her womanhood, in ways that Charles had never touched her, and stimulating her further with every caress.

Shockwaves ran through her, emanating out from the point of his touch, and she could feel the wet desire pouring out of her as he increased the tempo of his motions. They continued to kiss, nipping at each other's lips with their teeth. She almost hissed back at him like a cat, but instead she lay back further on the chair and let her desire overrule everything, allowing him to do as he wished, revelling in the sensations which rushed through her body.

Leaving off his attention to her breasts, Blackwood worked his way under her skirts. For a second she wondered what on earth he was doing, but before she knew it she could feel it well enough. His tongue, muscular and well-practised, was pressing against her nub of pleasure, at first lightly, in gentle, rhythmical laps, but then with greater speed and intensity.

He started languidly, licking at her entire region with slow, deep tongue motions, but then began to concentrate his efforts on the one, most sensitive part, the heavenly dimple that sat just above the rest of it. He enclosed it in his whole mouth and with his tongue still working, pistoning away, he sucked hard and drew gasps of pleasure from her. She was quite overcome by physical sensation, all thoughts seemed to drift into the ether, and she forgot even who and where she was. This pleasure was all that there was. A huge wave of pleasure crashed through her, and she lay back, dazed.

Before she realised that he had moved, her lover had re-emerged into the light, and then she was kissing him once again, passionate kisses, expressing her gratitude for the pleasure that he had just given her. He allowed her a brief pause to collect herself, holding her in a powerful embrace that send warm shivers all through her. Then he was back to attend to her, not with his tongue or finger this time, but with his breeches about his knees, exposing his well-travelled thighs and firm buttocks to the air, his large cock hard and forward-facing, ready to deliver pleasure for himself, as well as for her.

He had not been this hard, or enjoyed himself this much for some time – there was a lot to be said for debauching supposedly innocent daughters of the nobility, rather than world weary widows and prostitutes.

Softly, he slid himself in, and she could feel herself glistening with wet readiness for his thrust, anticipation of the pleasure to come forming like a pool around her loins.

He pressed forward and she pulled him in with a lingering sigh, mellow but promising of so much more, of moans and screams of pleasure ready to burst from her lips, should he choose to cause them.

Blackwood savoured the sensation – she was deliciously tight around him, and oh, so responsive.

Blanche floated in the sensations, unable to prevent herself from comparing this to her previous exploration of intimate relations with Charles. Unlike her only previous lover, Blackwood did not seek to pin her down or impose himself almost violently.  His approach was so much more refined and practised!

Where Charles had seemed desperate, and hurried, Blackwood seemed almost to anticipate her sensations, appreciate her needs, and allow her space in which to feel and experience all of this. She was wide open with delight.

In one smooth and controlled motion he began to move. His entire body swayed with a singular rhythm, a pulse flowing through him and into her, undulating, gyrating, stimulating her in exactly the right place and sending sensations crackling up her all the way to the top of her head.

Her nipples were sensitive, unbelievably hard and extended out, towards her lover, and her entire torso was consumed with the same feelings of warmth and light.

Never had she felt so brilliant, so utterly intoxicated with another human being, so attuned to her own body and to what it was capable of, what acute pleasures could be conjured from within and without. As if she was whole, quivering with delight, quaking here, in her parents' very own library, sensing that she could be anywhere on earth and not care, just as long as these pleasures were there as well.

He held himself closer to her, as close in fact, as it was physically possible for two people to be.

Their lips and tongues locked once again in the same sensual dance as before and she could feel every pulsation of his body, ever hammering blow of his heart, fused almost to hers through her breast and bodice.

He gasped 'my lady…' and all she could pant back was 'James… oh God, James…'

She wanted to say more, to articulate her appreciation, all the superlatives and positive words that seemed to assail her, but she could not, she was too overwhelmed to speak.

Words were inadequate for these feelings, some deeper and more powerful language had taken over. And then, with a sudden groan, almost of pain, and a swift motion that extracted him from her before dire consequences and bastard infants could be risked, it was over. Blackwood tumbled aside, wheezing his smoky breath into the carpet. Blanchette lay back on the couch and allowed herself to fade slowly back into the room.

'There' said Blackwood, smiling, as he stood and adjusted his clothes, restoring his usual immaculate appearance. '... that wasn't so bad, I trust? I hope that I have delivered an experience of better quality than those granted you previously?'

'No sir' she replied, hazily, rolling to her side on the couch. 'Not so very bad at all.' He planted a firm slap on her rump, and she felt suddenly a little shocked and disoriented.

'As I expected - all English girls are whores deep down!' he exclaimed, suddenly seeming to care not a bit for her or her wellbeing. Was all that care and attention that he had just shown her just to get his own pleasure, with no deeper feelings at all? She was, in that instant, filled with feelings of shame and regret. However great the pleasure that she had taken with him, his sudden apparent lack of care left her feeling somehow used, and a little dirty,

Was everything one heard about James Blackwood true then? Had she just made a terrible mistake in surrendering herself to him so fully? And what would he expect from her, over the week to come?

He pulled her to her feet, and, as he helped her restore her clothing to rights, looked at her dazed expression with amusement, and said 'Come on then Blanche', calling her by the private version of her first name, though he had no right to.

'Let's re-join the party.'

Back in the ballroom, Charlotte was having a more trying evening than she had hoped for. She had watched, impassive, as her sister had first been approached by the most handsome man present, Captain Westbury, and then been taken off, presumably to some terribly exciting mischief, by the most renowned seducer in the kingdom.

Despite the need for a well-bred young lady to keep up a composed and good-natured air on an occasion such as this, she could not help but breathe an audible sigh. It had ever been thus. All of the gentlemen's attentions were focussed on Blanche, the oldest, fairest, and most desirable of the two. Charlotte was left to trail in her older sister's wake.

It was not that she wished ill of Blanche, or that their relationship itself suffered unduly. They had been very close since they were small, and had always got on well.

Their nanny, Miss Partridge, had always remarked that whilst other infant ladies could be expected to tear each other's hair out the moment they were left unattended, you could leave the Cavendish sisters in the nursery alone together for hours on end, only to come back and find them putting the finishing touches to a redecorated doll's house, or reading quietly to one another. She had a lot of fondness for her sister which was perhaps rooted in their very different characters. While Charlotte was clever and funny, Blanche was the more thoughtful of the two, and had a quieter and more intense nature.

She could, of course, be outgoing, even assertive when she needed to be, but Charlotte suspected that it was in part her sisters' ability to listen and play the humble and shrinking young maiden that seemed to attract men to her more easily. It was a great regret of hers that the century did not seem quite ready for women who knew their own mind and expressed it freely. She, of course, did her best to get the most out of her time at the ball. She fluttered her fan and let her eyelashes tremble invitingly, keeping her smile to herself and waiting for men to draw it out of her. The form was easy enough to imitate, but the conversation did not seem to be going her way:

'And what pray, have you been reading sir, of late?' she had said to a boisterous son of a Marquess, a regular at her father's hunts.

'Reading?' he had barked back. His face was already ruddy from the punch, despite her mother's insistence that it be diluted. 'I could never stand books. Can't see any purpose to sticking your head in a book myself. Fills the brain with all sorts of peculiar notions, most unnatural. As my father always maintained, the only diversions fit for a young fellow are hunting, feasting and whoring, and not necessarily in that order!'

His friends, big, arrogant, hunting obsessed younger sons to a man, laughed along at this. One might even have slapped him on the back.

'But surely sir, one must tire of the same three amusements? Surely the feasting and the, as you might say, liaisons of the other sort, must make it harder to pursue a fox after a time?'

'I have never found that to be the case' he replied disinterestedly.

He had hoped that this pretty-faced lady would be easier conversational game than she had proved. She was mocking him, and he was just about clever enough to realise it. 'You are a strange girl, Miss Charlotte. Now if you'll excuse me...'

A little later, talking to another gentleman, fair-faced but a rather slow conversationalist, she knew immediately that she had gone too far in the telling of what she had hoped would be an amusing story:

'I'd heard that, on the first chase of the season, it is customary for the ladies of the estate to play amusing pranks on the gentlemen, for a little light amusement, you understand...' the man, sandy-haired and well-dressed, allowed his eye to drift into the middle distance.

Women were not generally expected, on occasions such as this, to tell lengthy anecdotes, certainly not in order to amuse the men.

'... so a number of years ago, when I was only fifteen, we took the entire custom to an unprecedented new level. The fellows were taking a quick dram before they mounted up, and they had all of them left their riding boots by the parlour door, not wanting to tramp all through the house in dirty leather, you see? Anyway, just as they were getting ready, we snuck in and put a good dollop of custard into each of their boots! At first we'd thought that they would notice at once and that it might deter them from heading out, but to our surprise, they went out all the same, custard-filled boots and all! Eventually the rigours of the ride forced some of it to come out of their boots and all up their breeches, even staining the flanks of the horses. A lot of them were very startled, his Lordship the Earl of Gloucester I believe was on the point of calling for his horse doctor to examine this strange yellow affliction. It was only when Mr. Danvers, renowned up and down the land for his tremendous appetites, deigned to taste the stuff that they ascertained that it was only custard! Oh, how we laughed!'

'Hmm' came the nonplussed reply.

'I can see why that might cause some amusement to a few silly girls, unused to the pleasures of the hunt. Nevertheless, I can personally see no humour whatsoever in disrupting those fellows' leisure like that. I strongly advise that you indulge in no further such japes again.'

The young man then managed to find some distant relatives on the other side of the room who he 'simply had to speak to'.

Charlotte was just beginning to despair of conversation, parties, and men altogether.

Try as she might, she could never seem to strike the right balance, or conform adequately to the expectations imposed on her by society's rigid rules and demands.

She was considering retiring early to her bed, but, at her mother's look of concern, she sighed, put on a cheerful face, and went looking for someone else to talk to.

# Chapter Six

Blanche and Mr. Blackwood were able to sneak back into the ballroom easily enough. Cautious of arousing suspicion, they promptly parted ways on re-entering the room, Blackwood to talk with a few fellows he was acquainted with, over by the punch bowl, Blanche to the other side of the room to find her sister. Who was deep in conversation with a bored looking matron (one of those invited to ensure that enough chaperones were present) - a conversation that it would be most impolite to interrupt. Blanche felt a wash of disappointment, and paused, wondering what to do now.

Such feelings were almost immediately dispelled when she heard a slight but deliberate throat-clearing behind her.

Turning, she was met by the still splendid sight of Captain Westbury, standing on his own and sipping at a glass of punch. Held offered a second glass to her, and she took it gratefully.

Despite his dazzling uniform, he had the air of a man who was a little deflated, and certainly did not appear to be enjoying himself.

'I was concerned that you had fled your own family's ball, Lady Blanchette.'

'Oh no, sir' she replied rapidly.

Had he sniffed her out, somehow? Could he tell that she had not five minutes before had her petticoats and bodice pulled aside? Could he smell James Blackwood on her breath and in her hair?

'I was merely taking in a little air, that is all.'

'I see, and in the company of Mr. Blackwood, I understand?'

'Yes, yes I was' she stammered nervously. The façade had been erected but it did not seem to be standing up very well.

'Well after all, it would not be proper for a young lady to be going off on her own, even at her own party, and he is a most respected gentleman.' Thoughts of their encounter raced through Blanche's mind, and it was all she could do not to bite her lip. What elemental forces of lust had come over her just before?

She kept up staring into Captain Westbury's startling blue eyes, which gave her the feeling that he could see right through her prevarication, hoping to throw him off her trail somehow.

'He is. Though I must confess, I have heard rather mixed reports as to the reputation of Mr. James Blackwood. Even in the army one hears of these sorts of things, you understand.'

'Yes, but I believe his character to be quite reformed. People tend to settle down and mellow out as they get older, don't they, even bachelors of his…' she paused to think. Words were not coming easily under this sort of concerted pressure '…type.'

'Perhaps' Westbury replied sagely, casting a glance over in the direction of Blackwood. His dark hair and jacket could be made out instantly, as if he had a special aura pulling fascination, suspicion, and the bodices of young ladies all at once towards him.

'One does hear of such things, also.'

He paused, and they turned to watch the couples dancing, noting one particularly energetic young lady, dancing with an obviously besotted gentleman.

'That young lady certainly appears to be enjoying herself.' He spoke almost wistfully, as if he envied the girl her happiness.

'Indeed she does, Captain Westbury', Blanche replied. 'It is a predilection of young ladies after all, to desire the attention of handsome gentlemen at balls.'

He looked at her, strong, stern, but with a little hint of humour and understanding curling the edge of his lip. *'The Captain is an attractive fellow'* she allowed herself to think, even in her post-Blackwood haze.

'Is it now?' he said drily. 'Once more, I must admit that even in the army we are aware of such matters. It would be ill-mannered, would it not, were I not now to renew my offer of a dance?'

'Some might consider it so. Alternatively, some might consider it a show of undue favour, should I grant you two dances at one ball.' Blanche's tone was flirtatious. 'Personally, I always aim to keep an open mind on questions of social custom and propriety.'

'Well then' he said, extending his arm to her 'I shall infer from that what I will, and offer you my hand.' With a subtle smile and a tiny fluttering deep inside her, where earlier she had been penetrated by another, she accepted his hand and stepped onto the floor with him, to join the waltz.

'Tell me a little of the army, Captain' Blanche said, as they swayed around the floor.

'Did you see any action, in the recent conflict?'

'I certainly did. I was in Portugal, as a young Lieutenant, and then at Waterloo.' Blanche trembled at the very sound of the latter word. Waterloo! That great and terrible battle that had taken place less than two years ago! She had heard so much about it, remembered the news flying through the provincial towns and villages, celebrated with bonfires and the pealing of bells. Her parents had hosted a banquet to toast Wellington's victory, and she had there seen grown men on the point of tears, so moved were they by patriotic feelings of gratitude.

And now she was here, dancing in the arms of a man who had been there, who had braved French musket shots and bayonets and come out of it intact.

What a remarkable occurrence this was. She looked up at his strong chin and chiselled jaw and could not help look at him with a new admiration, awe even. For a few moments, James Blackwood was quite forgotten.

'I have heard that Waterloo was quite a battle, Captain' she said, suppressing her interest and excitement. 'It must have been a most traumatic experience.'

'I suppose it was a little' he replied sternly. 'The strange truth though, is that one does get used to these things. After terrible things have happened around you sufficient times, you become numb to them. You merely brace yourself and do what needs to be done.'

They swayed firmly to the right. His arms now felt stronger, the torso she could feel beneath his beautiful uniform coat all the more muscle-bound and magnificent. She was not just dancing with any old soldier here, some boy from the officer's mess dressed up for battle, this was a real-life war hero, impassive and unflappable, stepping along with her, in her parents' very own ballroom.

A tingling ran up to her bosom from her most sensitive area, and she knew at once that she desired him.

'But enough talk of the campaign trail, it is not an easy subject for even an experienced soldier to consider. Indeed it is one that we would all prefer never to need to think about again. I am more interested in you, my Lady.' She turned her head upwards sharply to meet his gaze, and could not help but feel flattered at his interest.

She could happily have gone on all night asking him about his gallantry and derring-do on the battlefields on Europe, but then she supposed, it was probably rather different discussing such matters when one had actually been there, and seen the horror of it all up close.

'Pray tell, what does a young lady of breeding discuss with a fellow like James Blackwood?'

'All manner of things sir' she said at once, a little defensively. 'There are many topics of conversation to pursue. His travels for example, or our respective opinions on various significant subjects.'

'Yes, I suppose that should all be plain enough. I have heard that he is a well-travelled gentleman, certainly.'

'Indeed he is...' she glanced around the room, and saw Blackwood, looking slyly in their direction. She was too far away to really make it out, but she could have sworn that she saw him raise his eyebrow at her, in an ironic acknowledgement of her new dance partner.

'...not in the same manner as you, Captain Westbury, but he has journeyed across most of Europe nonetheless, and seen the interiors of great courts and palaces.'

'- and the interiors of many great ladies as well, no doubt...'

'Sir! I find that allusion to be most improper. That is slanderous and scandalous talk!'

'- and those of many not so great ladies as well, one suspects.' Westbury was not put off by her outrage.

He seemed determined to weed out her secrets, to force a confession. The rational part of her simply put it down to envy, but she could not help but feel that he was vocalising her own conscience, and the anxieties she herself had felt, before and after her encounter with Blackwood.

There seemed to be a sudden need to confide in this bluff and honourable soldier, even if his speech was more direct than she was used to.

No, no, no – that would not do at all, she most certainly could not confide her thoughts to him.

But what could she say? Perhaps just a little sharing of confidences would satisfy him?

'It would be dishonest of me to claim that he does not exert a certain effect upon a young lady, upon my very own self in fact...'

'What an intriguing reaction!' Westbury whispered to her, conspiratorially.

'I must say, Lady Blanchette, you have aroused my interest. It is not just for your beauty, wealth and title, you understand, you are a most fascinating girl by most other measures as well. It seems that you do not think about the world the same way as other young ladies of my acquaintance.'

His words evoked a strange feeling of hope in her.  Perhaps.... perhaps this man could see her for more than her pretty face? She pressed herself closer to him, almost for comfort.

But where was he going with this? She desperately needed to turn his interest in her 'conversation' with Blackwood aside.

'You see, Captain Westbury, I have a confession to make...'

He looked at her, politely waiting for her to go on, although she could see that he would like to push her for more information, he did not.

'Mr Blackwood has been a friend of the family for some years - my parents are quite fond of him. I..... I ...' she hesitated, unsure of how to go on – she was telling the truth, but also, not all of it. 'A few years ago, as an impressionable young lady, I found him quite fascinating, and I fear that.... fascination.... has continued to exist, even through my betrothal to Charles.' She stuttered a little as she said it, and looked away, blushing, embarrassed.

He could not know that her blush was for her embarrassment at mentioning her aborted marriage, rather than her juvenile tendre for Blackwood.

'Understandable, I suppose, for a green girl.  But surely you see him differently now?  Forgive my bluntness, but I am concerned for your reputation.'

Blanche met his eyes, letting just a little of her confusion show.

How did she see Blackwood now?  Had it not been for his uncaring attitude in those few minutes before they returned to the ballroom, she would have said that he was everything that she had imagined, and more.

But now?

'I.... am considering my opinion.  Our conversation this evening was... most interesting.  And not quite what I expected.'

Captain Westbury looked ready to press her for more information, and she looked around, desperate to find a way out of this conversation, before she admitted everything to this man.  No matter how attractive she found him, his blunt and forceful probing of her private life was not something that she could cope with any longer.

"Now, if you will excuse me, I see that I must rescue my sister, or she will be trapped talking to the chaperones all evening!'

Blanche turned, and sped across the room to where Charlotte was still hopelessly caught in a conversation with Lady Eddleston – who was 90, loved to gossip, and insisted on telling, and retelling, stories from 40 years ago, as if they had happened yesterday.  She could only admire Charlotte's endurance, and dedication to upholding the family honour, by being nice to everyone, all the time!

Captain Westbury watched her go, a slight smile touching his face.  There was something going on there, and he meant to find out more.  Blackwood was a cad, if even half the things said of him were true, and Westbury could not bear the thought of Lady Blanchette with Blackwood.  His imagination was quite capable of conjuring up a very wide range of improper things that Blackwood would, almost certainly, like to do with Blanchette, and a rush of fury ran through him at the idea of it.

He forced his fingers to uncurl, before he snapped the stem of the glass in his hand, and silently vowed to watch both of them very closely as this week progressed.  He would discover Blanchette's secrets, and protect her from Blackwood if necessary.

Blanche's evening had been a whirlwind of emotions. She and Charlotte had both excused themselves and sought their beds early. Charlotte was feeling somewhat depressed and out of sorts after yet another pointless event spent trying, and failing, to have an intelligent conversation with a range of young gentlemen, and Blanche was feeling very conflicted by the events of the ball.

She had experienced many pleasures, and yet she knew, and had been reminded, by Captain Westbury's questions, that she had not made the right choice this time. Even if she had not admitted her behaviour to him, she felt that he had suspected it, and most certainly judged her for it. She had not made the right choice previously, with Charles, either, she now realised, but at least they had been betrothed at the time.

Yet the pleasure had been so intense – surely something so good should not be a terrible sin?  At the same time, she realised, somehow it felt as if something was missing, some depth to the whole experience that should have been there, and had not been.

This time, it was perhaps, as if something had been stolen from her, she felt almost used, and as if her liaison was illegitimate and should never have been allowed to happen. It did not matter the selfish pleasure that she had taken from it at the time, it had still been a foolish choice. A huge part of her wished that it had not happened, but there was no changing what had already taken place. She had had intimate relations out of wedlock with James Blackwood, and nothing she could ever say or do would change that immutable fact.

Her attraction to Mr. Blackwood was more deeply rooted than this evening. It had been growing, swelling inside her since she was little more than a girl, putting down roots and nourishing itself on fantasies that she had created from what she read in novels and spoke of in whispered conversation with her sister. When she was too young to be the object of a seduction she had considered him the most handsome and charming man in all the world, delighting her and her parents with his stories of exotic places and his unusual opinions, for which he refused to apologise or feel ashamed.

He was strong and dashing and lived as he pleased, he did not seem to care what others thought of him and he knew what aroused young women, and one could not help but admire all of that in part. Yet at the same time, she had long known, deep down that he was not completely a good man.

He was not nice, or honest, or honourable, and he cared more about his own pleasures and maintaining the dark reputation, that made it so easy for him to exercise fascination in others, (especially nubile young girls) than he did for the wellbeing of his many conquests. That much was painfully obvious now.  Yet part of her still wanted him.

What was she to do?  Could she be strong, for the rest of this week, if he tried to take advantage of her again?  Or would she let her own wanton, lustful nature override her sense again?

She had come to realise tonight, after much consideration, that he had intentionally encouraged her fantasies, her fascination with him, for all those years, simply so that he could, when he chose, take advantage of her.  As he had now done.

She was sensible enough, after her failed 'not quite marriage' and after observing the marriages of some of her friends, to know that she would be deluding herself if she tried to believe that she could change him.

Marriage would not reform his character any more than the love of a good woman. He had been this way too long to respond to the advice of others or to compromise for the sake of some girl's opinion. Knowing this did not stop her from still finding Blackwood compellingly attractive.

It would also have been delusion not to acknowledge her attraction to Captain Westbury, although this was now a very complicated phenomenon, working its way through the various alleyways of her mind.

He was probably one of the most handsome men that she had ever met, even more so than her former husband-to-be, who had run off with a governess and left her in disgrace, deeply embarrassed in front of society, and depressed enough to be easy prey to a man like Blackwood.

She had been fascinated by his unassuming nature and his quietly told tales of military heroism. A girlish instinct in her wanted little more than to submit herself to this strong and proud man. But despite that, their conversations had not been all that easy.

He had seemed wary of her and jealous of Blackwood, and had pressed her, as if expecting that she would confess her indiscretions – yet still she felt that she could trust him.

Perhaps he had spent too much time in the company of fellow soldiers and lacked in grace and panache. He seemed to have a sense of humour, and some understanding of ladies, but he was an enigma. She had too many questions over his character and his conduct to unequivocally admit an attraction to herself, though she knew it was there on one level.  But that level was very much physical – and she vowed never to let her lustful wanton nature overtake her good sense again!

Her mind was all awhirl, and it seemed that sleep would be a long time coming.

# Chapter Eight

The following morning, Blanche stayed abed late, having only fallen into a fitful sleep as dawn was fast approaching. Upon waking, she felt little enthusiasm for the day – how was she to face either Mr Blackwood or Captain Westbury with a calm face, and adequate social grace?

Once the sun was high outside her windows, and she had heard, drifting up from below, the sounds of the gentlemen setting off to hunt, she dragged herself from her bed, drew back the curtains on what appeared to be a quite disgustingly cheerful sunny day, and rang for Jane to assist her with dressing. She would, she decided, simply not think about how she would greet the two gentlemen, for now. Perhaps breakfast would improve her opinion of the day.

Charlotte looked up from her barely touched plate as her sister entered the breakfast room.

'Why Blanche, you look positively exhausted still – did you not sleep well?'

Blanche selected a small portion of eggs from the wide range of dishes laid out on the sideboard, and sighed as she sat down across from Charlotte.  They were alone in the room, and Blanche was relieved that she need not be concerned with social niceties for now.

'I could not sleep.  My mind is quite awhirl with the possibilities of the rest of the week.  I want so much to take this opportunity to get over the horror of being jilted, and to enjoy myself again, but I am so confused.  Both Mr Blackwood and Captain Westbury have shown me some attention, and I simply cannot decide who to like, what I think, what to do!'

Charlotte laughed, and clapped her hands together in some glee.

'See Blanche, I was right to tell you that being a part of this party was a good idea!  You complain of a situation that most young ladies we know would love to experience – how jealous they will all be! Why don't you just spend time talking with each of them, enjoy their company, and see what transpires?  I cannot imagine that either of them would be so taxing as company that you could not enjoy doing so.'

Blanche sighed, but admitted that, perhaps, Charlotte had the right of it. They finished their breakfast in amicable silence, then sought out the other ladies in the drawing room.

A morning of cheerful gossip and embroidery went a long way to restoring Blanche's equilibrium, although she was careful to make no comment when the ladies remarked on how handsome Captain Westbury was.

The gossip then turned to James Blackwood, with one of their neighbours raising his scandalous reputation, whispering of tales heard about his many mistresses. Blanche would, at that point, have liked the floor to open up and swallow her, but was saved from having to make comment by her mother, who quashed the discussion immediately.

"Rubbish" declared lady Derbyshire, "James is a delightful young man, so well-travelled and entertaining, I am sure that is all just foolish fabrication from person's who are jealous of his wealth and experience. I will hear none of it! Let us talk of other things entirely."

Blanche found that, today, she felt little kinship with these twittering sparrows of women. Had she once really enjoyed this silly spying into other's lives? Had she really been so shallow and uncaring, only looking for the thrill of hearing titillating information. Shockingly, she rather thought that she had been exactly like them. Was that, oh terrible thought, was that why Charles had cast her off?

Her gloom of earlier returned, and, pleading a sudden megrim, she hurried from the room. Perhaps if she spent the afternoon in her room, reading, she would feel more like herself. She need not come down for dinner – she could get Jane to bring her a tray.

With that plan in mind, she entered the library, heading straight to the shelves where her favourite books were kept.  The sound of the door closing behind her brought her to a sudden stop.

She spun around, to find James Blackwood in front of her, looking at her in a way that was certainly not how a gentleman should look at a lady. Her heart beat faster, and a dark excitement thrummed through her, accompanied by not a little fear.

Unconsciously, she took a step back, to find herself hard up against the bookshelves.

'Good morning Mr Blackwood.' Despite her best efforts, her voice shook a little as she spoke. 'I had thought you out hunting with the other gentlemen?'

"So formal Blanche?" The question was accompanied by a sardonic half smile, and a raise of that very expressive eyebrow of his.  He stepped closer, his body almost touching hers, trapping her against the hard shelves behind her. "As it happens, my horse had the inconsideration to throw a shoe, forcing me to return early.  But perhaps that is not such a misfortune after all.'

He reached up, and slid his fingers sensually down her cheek, to brush them slowly across her lips. No matter what she thought of his attitude, his proximity was intoxicating, and her body remembered his touch all too well, hear breathing was uneven, and part of her craved more, so much more.

He grinned, certain of himself, all cocksure arrogance.

'It would be a pity to waste this unexpected opportunity', as he spoke, his hands slid caressingly from her shoulders, down over her waist and hips, to cup her buttocks and pull her against him. It was immediately obvious that he was aroused, his manhood hard and ready, pressed against her through the layers of their clothes.

Blanche shivered, aroused despite herself, and horrified that she was.  Her hands came up to push against him, and he chuckled, interpreting her reactions as an enthusiasm for his attentions. She was shaking, but no longer from arousal.

'So excited to see me, my 'pure' little lady, with the heart of a whore? Delightful, you have no idea how much that pleases me. So much so, that I believe an immediate repeat of our pleasurable encounter is called for.  The gentlemen will not be back for some hours, the ladies are occupied, and the door is locked – I believe that makes the circumstances ideal.'

Blanche pushed against him again, harder, squirming in an attempt to free herself from his hold, but, it seemed, only inflaming his passions further.

'Mr Blackwood! I decline your suggestion.  I do not, at this point, wish to repeat our encounter.'  She tried for firm, but heard her voice shake as she spoke. He simply laughed, and bent to take her lips in a bruising kiss, lacking all finesse or gentleness, plundering her mouth with his tongue, as his hands hauled her even harder against him.

Taking one hand from her buttock, he started to pull up her skirts, obviously intent on slaking his lust with no concern for her words.

Blanche took advantage of that moment, when he had less grip on her, to twist violently sideways and out of his hold. Not fast enough.  He grabbed her arm and twisted her round to hold her against him again, her back pressed against his strong body, and his arm pinning her there, wrapped fully around her waist and trapping her arms against her sides.

Blanche was panting with fear, and an odd and horrifying excitement. When she had thought him mysterious and dangerous, she had not imagined quite this.

Blackwood's other hand came up to her bodice, stroking her breasts through the fabric, then sliding his fingers under the edge of her bodice to pinch at her nipple. She bucked against him, trying to get away, but he laughed again, a cruel laugh, full of his own dark pleasure in what he was doing.

"My dear Blanche, I do so enjoy it when a woman struggles against me.  You are such a spirited delight. But you do realise that I will have what I want, don't you?  You made your choice when you let Charles take your virginity in the first place. Because now that I know that, and have proven it for myself so delightfully, I can, of course, choose at any time to let the world of society know of your disgrace – subtly of course, but well enough to ruin your reputation forever. And then no-one would ever marry you, would they?  And, as I have no desire to marry, once I am bored with you, I may even allow you to marry, and not say a word.  But first, I will have what I want - so you will do whatever I say, when it comes to facilitating my pleasure. It is so lovely to know that you can be used, and that, regardless of what you say, I can make you feel pleasure – if I want to be so generous.'

He laughed again, and Blanche realised, with a sinking heart, that there was no escape, that she would do what he wanted. Not because she cared for her own reputation so much, but because such a disgrace would destroy her parents, and taint Charlotte's hopes for marriage as well.

'Enough delightful conversation. It is time for you to provide me a completely different kind of delight, my little whore.'

With another hard pinch to her nipple Blackwood shoved her forward, forcing her to bend over the high padded back of the armchair beside them. She did not fight him, a sense of despair settling in her as he pulled her skirts and petticoats up over her back and slid his fingers through the slit in her drawers.

'Let me make sure that you are ready.' He knelt behind her, one hand on her back to keep her still, and she felt his tongue on her most intimate flesh, brushing her with moistness, and triggering reactions in her body that she could not prevent, using all of his well-practiced skill to prepare her for his cock.

Her mind rebelled but her body did not – she felt numb and her body accepted his thrusts as he sated his lust, pounding into her, with little care for her enjoyment. It was, she realised, all about power – this man enjoyed the power that he had over her – his arousal had nothing to do with affection for her, only with controlling her.

As he pulled from her at the end, capturing his emissions into a handkerchief he held ready, she was grateful at least that he bothered to prevent illegitimate children. Shakily, she pushed herself upright, and set her clothes to rights.

'You may expect me to require your 'co-operation' some further times during this delightful house party, my dear Blanche.  I fully intend to enjoy myself while I have the opportunity so easily to hand. Don't look so shocked, my little whore – after all, if you remember, you seduced me.....'

Restored to his usual urbane elegance, he turned from her, so sure of his control as to not feel the need to say or do more, and left the room.  Blanche collected the book that she had come for and, megrim now quite thoroughly real, retired to her room.

# Chapter Nine

For the rest of that day, and all of the following, Blanche kept to her room, sending Jane for trays of food and drink when she felt able to contemplate eating, refusing to see anyone, and locking the door against any intrusion. She felt a deep sense of revulsion for herself, for all of the choices that she had made, that had brought her to this point.

Yet she had no choices left.  She would not hurt Charlotte any more than she already had.  If accepting Blackwood's now loathsome attentions was the price of her family's reputation, she would do so.  What horrified her most was that, at least in part, Blackwood's rough handling had excited her, that he was able to make her body react, at least to some extent, regardless of what she wanted.

Surely that was beyond wanton and lustful, and right on the edge, if not over the edge, of perverted.

She cried, she wrote in her journal, she slept and she watched out the window, being careful to stay hidden by the curtains, as the gentlemen rode out to hunt, the ladies took picnics on the lawns, and life went on around her, as if nothing had changed.

James Blackwood laughed and joked with the other men, rode off to hunt, and generally spent the time looking relaxed and rather pleased with himself.  She decided that she hated him even more for that.

Captain Westbury looked magnificent.  Quiet and authoritative, competent in everything that he did, it was obvious as she watched that the other men respected him, and his honourable behaviour was unquestioned. She knew that she could never have a man like him.  Not now, not after what she had done.  She was as ruined as a girl could get, and no decent man would ever marry her.  That did not stop her heart beating harder each time she saw him through the window, or stop her from imagining what things might have been like, if she had met Captain Westbury before Charles, before any of these sordid things had happened.

She remembered dancing with him at the ball, and wished that she had never let James Blackwood lure her from his arms.

The one question, that her mind skittered away from every time, was how she was going to deal with tomorrow.  She could not stay in this room for the rest of the week – her excuse of illness had already worn thin.  But once she left this room, she could not know where or when Blackwood might trap her, and demand that she service his lusts.

She could lock her room at night, but even that might not stop him – perhaps he could pick locks?

Late on the second day after she had taken to her room, Blanche emerged, having no trouble looking convincingly pale and shaky after her 'illness'.  She was, quite simply, terrified, but could hide no longer.  If she were to live with the consequences of her actions, it was time to start doing so.

She ventured downstairs to find all of the guests gathered in the drawing room, sipping pre dinner sherry and loudly discussing the day's hunting, and the plans for tomorrow. Blanche paused in the doorway, gathering her nerves and taking in the scene. Her sister looked determinedly cheerful as always, and was listening to hunting anecdotes told by old Lord Miltonhew, her parents were surrounded by their friends and engaged in happy conversation.

Captain Westbury drew her eye, resplendent in uniform and more handsome than ever, apparently discussing the war with some Lords whose sons had also served in France and Spain. Mr Blackwood was the dark to Westbury's light – he stood with a smaller group of men to one side, talking of travel and exotic adventures, making sure that he was the centre of attention. How typical.  How could she ever have found him appealing?  He was handsome, in his dark and dangerous way, but self-centred and vain in everything that he did.

She felt the last of her young girl's fantasies crumbling away to dust, leaving a much uglier truth revealed before her. She had paused too long.  Blackwood saw her.  He smiled at her across the room – it was not an attractive smile.  He gazed at her in a way that made her feel stripped of her clothes, and ashamed all over again, of everything that she had done.

Taking a deep breath, she moved into the room, choosing to go to her sister, and support her in being polite to the boring elderly guests. Boring old gentlemen were a much safer option than any other in the room.

Her movement brought Captain Westbury's eyes to her, and the sensation was so different from that of Blackwood's gaze, that she faltered a little as she walked. It was warm, and clear, and appeared to convey a genuine concern for her person. At her stumble, he excused himself from his conversation, and advanced to greet her, taking her arm to stabilise her as she recovered.

She leant into him, unable to stop herself, treasuring the momentary sense of security that his touch had brought. Then she pulled herself up.  That sense of security was utterly false. She had no security now, there was no help available.  She had made her choices, and there was no escaping them.

Captain Westbury looked at her, feeling her pull away, and asked, very quietly "is all well with you now, Lady Blanchette? You seem a little unsteady".  His voice washed over her, deep timbred and warm, and she was grateful for his concern.  But could admit nothing.

'I am much recovered, thank you Captain Westbury. Though still a little tired I fear.  I believe that I will retire early this evening.'

He acknowledged her words with a little bow, stepping back and releasing her arm.

"If I may be of any assistance, you have only to call."

She felt somehow colder for the loss of his touch. Resuming her path to Charlotte, she did not look back or, indeed, anywhere in the room, except at Charlotte.

Westbury watched her go, a slight frown marring his expression, before he returned to his companions.  As he turned, he caught Blackwood watching her, with an expression on his face that seemed out of place.  It carried echoes of lust, of anger and of something that might be jealousy.  He did not like that look.  He did not like Blackwood, for that matter, but civility must be maintained.

He was, however, more certain than before that Lady Blanchette was hiding something, something that had to do with Blackwood.  He was determined to uncover it, and he had the most disturbing feeling that the time was short to do so.

Dinner passed in a blur for Blanche, she ate little, and was continually aware of the eyes of both Blackwood and Westbury on her. She wanted to run from the room and the effort of staying there and behaving normally was exhausting. When the gentlemen retired to the study for port, she joined the ladies in the drawing room for tea, but struggled to make any conversation at all.  After an hour, she felt completely unable to continue, and excused herself.

'I fear that I am very poor company this evening Mother, I believe that I will retire, and hope to be in better spirits tomorrow.'

"Oh my poor child, of course you must go and rest, you must do everything necessary to get yourself well again".

She left the room perhaps faster than was elegant, or appropriate, but she was beyond caring. Taking a deep, relieved breath, she headed upstairs to her room.

The door to the study had been left open a little, as had the windows, to allow some air to flow through, and dispel the aromatic smoke from the cheroots that a few of the gentlemen enjoyed.

James Blackwood had positioned himself in the only chair with a clear view out the door, and down the hallway towards the drawing room door.

After having no access to Lady Blanchette for the last two days, his lust had risen. He did not like being denied. He was, for a fact, not at all used to being denied. It was more common for women to seek his bed than avoid it. Denial was not a sensation that he intended to become familiar with.

When she had arrived in the drawing room before dinner he had been pleased. He was sure to be able to engineer an opportunity to get her alone, and his cock had hardened at the thought. Then Westbury had had the presumption to go to her, and touch her.

His reaction had been strong – he wanted complete control of what was his, did not want any other man touching her. He had caught himself, pasted his mask of civility back into place, and not laid Westbury out on the spot. Although he had wanted to.

It only reinforced his need to have her, to have his pleasure, and to show her once again that she was his, until he decided otherwise.

He had hoped that an opportunity might present itself, and his patience was rewarded when he saw her, an hour or so later, slip out of the drawing room by herself, and head towards the stairs.  He excused himself from the conversation and slipped out the door to follow her.

Blanche reached the top of the stairs and turned down the corridor towards her room, she was not concerned when she heard light footsteps, assuming that it was one of the servants on an errand of some sort. She therefore emitted a rather loud squeak of alarm, when a hand grabbed her arm, a squeak that was rapidly cut off by a hand over her mouth.

She was pulled against a hard body, and knew at once that it was Blackwood – there was a distinct smell to him, of cheroots, and brandy, and something a little musty and not quite pleasant underneath it all.  'Shhh' he whispered, as he uncovered her mouth 'you wouldn't want anyone to see us, now would you?'

She shook her head, feeling her body shaking in his grasp, and knowing that her reaction pleased him, and fed his sense of power.  He pulled her along the hallway, and through the door of a small storage room, closing the door behind them.  Turning, he leant back against the door, effectively locking it with his weight, and looked at her, smiling in that unpleasant way of his.

"We don't have much time, my little whore, the gentle men will be expecting me back at any minute, so I think that I will forgo the niceties this time, and simply take my pleasure of you in the most expedient way possible.'

She watched him, unsure what was coming next, what he meant by those words. He carefully unbuttoned his falls, letting his long hard cock spring free. She shivered again, at the thought of what he might do with her now.

'Kneel' he commanded harshly.

Still puzzled, she did as demanded, finding her face almost hard up against his jutting appendage, in the small space of the storage room. He reached down with one hand, sliding it in the edge of her bodice to find her nipple, and took her hair in his other hand, pulling her head towards him.

'Take it in your mouth, little whore, suck and lick me, now!'

The command shocked her – this was not something that she had done before, or ever imagined doing, and, whilst she could imagine, based on the pleasure that his mouth had given her, that a man would want this, the idea of doing it to him repelled her. She cast about desperately for an idea, for a way out, but none existed, she was trapped.

'Now' he pulled her head harder against him, thrusting himself against her lips. She gasped at the sensation, and he took full advantage of that to push his cock further into her mouth. 'Suck' he commanded, sliding in and out of her mouth, as he had in and out of her body before. Despairing, she obeyed, wanting this done, as fast as possible, wanting to escape him, and his uncaring lust.

He groaned in pleasure as she complied with his orders, and within a few thrusts had spilled his seed in her mouth. She gagged, and turning, spit it forth onto the stacked linens at her side.

She wiped her mouth, and turned to see him, already restored to his sartorial best, watching her with amusement.

'That will do for now, my little whore, but rest assured, I will find a time to be much more leisurely about things, soon.'

He cautiously opened the door a crack, and finding the corridor empty, slipped out and away.  She stood, hating him, hating herself, hating the taste of him in her mouth. Her sense of shame and hopelessness redoubled, she crept out, and down the corridor to her room, where she kept her composure just long enough to ring for Jane to help her prepare for bed, and to bring her a cup of chocolate.

Once Jane was gone, and her door locked, she sat shivering in her bed, sipping the chocolate and letting it wash his taste from her mouth.  She was horrified anew – he had given up all pretence of wanting to give her pleasure, and was simply using her for his own.  He was the most shallow and selfish man she had ever met, and she quietly wept for her blindness in not seeing that before.

# Chapter Ten

Having cried herself to exhaustion, Blanche had slept surprisingly well, dreaming of Captain Westbury and light filled happy days.

The happiness lasted but a few minutes after waking, shattered when her memory supplied all of the unpleasant details of the previous evening.

It was obvious that she could not hide, that he would find her regardless and use her as he wished.  She was not prone to letting things beat her, although Charles jilting her at the altar had come close.

She would certainly not let this beat her now.

If she could just manage to get through the next few days, the house party would end, he would have to leave, and it would be much harder for him to get to her after that. She would do this, would survive this, for Charlotte's sake, of for nothing else.

She rose, rang for Jane, and dressed for the day. The breakfast room was empty, and she was grateful for the chance to simply sit in peace, not needing to converse with anyone, or make an effort to seem happy and interested in the day's activities.

She managed to eat. Although her appetite was small, she knew that keeping up her strength was essential. A flicker of movement caught her eye, and she flinched as someone came through the door, dreading the possibility that it was Blackwood. Relief followed fast, as Captain Westbury greeted her cheerfully.

'Good morrow Lady Blanchette, I trust that you slept well, and are feeling more yourself today?'

Blanche tried to sound sincere as she replied.

"Of a certainty, Captain, a peaceful sleep is always restorative. But is something amiss - are you not hunting this morning?" As she spoke fear flickered in her eyes – if the gentlemen had not gone hunting….. then Blackwood might accost her at any moment.

'Nothing is amiss, do not concern yourself – I had some business to attend to, and chose to deal with that early today. Whilst I do enjoy a good hunt, I am not so obsessed as to not be able to forgo the pleasure when needs must. Now that is dealt with, I can enjoy this repast and take the rest of the day at my leisure.'

She subsided, pushing the last of her food around her plate rather listlessly, but Westbury was not fooled, he had seen the flicker of fear in her eyes, seen her flinch and then recover when he entered the room.

Surely she was not afraid of him?  No, he could not countenance that possibility, it must be that she had feared to see someone else enter the room.  More secrets.  He did not like secrets – he was used to blunt honesty in the field, and found the veiled truths and cunning lies of society remarkably unpleasant.

So, what, or who, was it, that she feared?

Blanche watched him, careful sidelong glances taking the measure of his mood.  He was so well made a man, and even frowning as he did now, his face was not threatening.  She could not imagine him harming her.

She pushed away the thoughts that compared him to Blackwood, that reminded her of the terrible mistake that she had made, the mistake for which there was no remedy.

Such an honourable man would never consider her worthy of his attention if he knew of her ruin, of her wanton nature and foolish behaviour.

She could never have a man like him – such a man would turn from her in disgust.  But still, his presence in the room made her feel safer, and her heart beat faster with a hopeless yearning for his touch.

'Lady Blanchette?'

She had been woolgathering – he had spoken before, and now repeated his enquiry, looking at her in concern.

"Captain," she blushed as she spoke, embarrassed at her lapse "forgive me, my attention had wandered."

'Lady Blanchette, would you do me the honour of showing me the magnificent gardens of your home?  It seems that we have this fine morning to ourselves, and it would be a shame to waste the spring sunshine.'

Captain Westbury was more and more intrigued by this woman every time he saw her.  More and more concerned as well.  Ever since the moment when Blackwood had so rudely drawn her away from him at the ball, she had seemed distant, worried, afraid of shadows almost.  He wanted to know why.  He felt an unexpected urge to gather her to him, and soothe the look of tiredness and fear from her eyes.

"Why, I would be glad to, Captain."

She rose from the table and placed her hand on his extended arm, smiling as she did so.  It was the first unclouded expression he had seen on her face since the moment of their first meeting.

The secluded shade of the winding gravelled walkways through the beautifully laid out gardens produced an immediate sense of relief.  Walking through the house, and across the terrace, Blanche had feared to see Blackwood emerge from the direction of the stables and turn his terrible gaze on her.  She knew it was foolish to feel so, as he was far from here, hunting with the others, and would not give over that pleasure lightly.  But still, the tension did not leave her until they passed out of easy sight of other's eyes.

At first they simply walked, not speaking, appreciating the warmth of the dappled sunlight in the artfully placed small clearings among the leafy trees, and the delicious scents of the beds of carefully tended flowers. Captain Westbury watched her, watched the glint of the sunlight on her hair, where tendrils of it escaped from her pins, slid out from under her bonnet and drifted to curl over her shoulder. He wanted to touch it, to see if it felt as soft as it looked. He felt more heated by the warmth of her gloved hand, where it rested on his arm, than by the spring sunshine.  He felt.... well he did not quite know what he felt, except that it felt surprisingly like one of those warm and impossible dreams that soldiers have, only to wake to the depressing reality of war. But this was not, he assured himself, a dream.

They came to a clearing with a rustic bench, cleverly placed to provide a view out across the gardens to the lake, yet not be overlooked easily.  Without words, in perfect accord, they stopped, and sat, close against each other. Blanche did not want to speak, did not want him to speak, did not want to break the magic of the moment, this moment in which she felt safe, and as if anything was possible. She pushed her bonnet back, and let the sun touch her skin.

His arm slid around her, and her head tilted to rest on his shoulder, as if it was the most natural thing in the world that they should be at such intimate ease with each other. She allowed herself, for just this moment in time, to absorb every little thing about him, the smell of his cologne, the slight roughness of his coat against her cheek, the hard strength of his muscular chest beneath it, the strong beat of his heart, beating as hard as hers and the safe, protecting feel of his arm around her.

The moment seemed to stretch out, and she did not move as he raised his hand and gently caressed her face, tilting her chin up as he bent to softly kiss her lips.  There was nothing of demand in that kiss, more a savouring of sweetness, a delicate exploration of her mouth, and all the sensations bound up in soft lips and warm tongue.

She melted into it, savouring him in return, and thought with wonder how different this kiss was from any that she had ever experienced before.

But with that thought, reality came crashing back, as the truth of those kisses that she had felt before reminded her how impossible this was, how hopeless.  For she could not have this, she, ruined woman that she was, could not have a man like this, could not risk him finding out the truth.

Nor could she bear to lead him on, to allow him to believe that they might have something together, only to watch his gentleness and care turn to revulsion once he knew.  As surely he would know, the first time that he took her to his bed.

With a little cry, she pushed herself away from him, despair in her eyes. 'We cannot…. I should not have…….' Shaking her head she stood, and stepped back.  He reached out a hand to her, but, at the look on her face, let it drop, his eyes full of confusion, and some hurt.

'Lady Blanchette, I am so sorry, I never meant…. ' At his words, she gave one small sob, turned and fled back towards the house, the sound of her name on his lips following her into the trees.

He stood, watching her go, internally berating himself.

He had meant simply to enjoy her company, to talk with her a little, outside the rather stifling confines of the house, and well away from that bounder, Blackwood.  But it had been too much, had seemed so right, that, when she leant into him like that, so trusting, he could not help himself.  And so he had betrayed that very trust, obviously pushing her too far, too fast.

He was coming to understand that he cared about this girl a great deal, rather more than he had cared about any of the women in his past.  And now he had made her run from him.  He was an unmitigated fool!

A soldier did not run from his mistakes.  He squared his shoulders, took a deep breath, and wound his way back through the trees, considering his strategy. He still wanted to know her secrets, to know why she had seemed so afraid this morning, to regain her trust, and repair the damage that he had just done. And, whispered the little voice in his mind, to kiss her again, and have her stay.

The afternoon had passed in a blur for Blanche, and she was glad of the need for planning and organising, which gave her something to do, and kept her mother too distracted to look at Blanche too closely. Her mother had decided that tomorrow they should have another ball, before most of the guests departed on the following day.  Apparently she had received news that some important guests, who had been unable to attend until now, would arrive just for a day or two, tomorrow.

For Lady Derbyshire, that was an excellent excuse for another celebration.  The Cook and the Housekeeper were close to hysterics at the news, and the staff were in uproar with the rushed preparations.

Captain Westbury, upon reaching the house, had been almost knocked from his feet by two footmen, who were struggling to relocate a rather alarmingly large marble flower urn to the ballroom, at Lady Derbyshire's order.

They were most apologetic, extremely grateful that it was the polite and unflappable Captain that they had collided with, rather than one of the more acerbic guests, and cheerfully informed Westbury of the new plans afoot.

Faced with an afternoon of feminine bustle and chaos belowstairs, he rapidly amended his plans, and took himself to the stables. A good long ride would flush the cobwebs from his thinking, and give him time to think through the situation, and find some sort of strategy that might work. He would, he had decided, do everything that he could to convince Lady Blanchette to accept his suit.

Some hours later, much refreshed, and polished to perfection in his best evening dress, Captain Westbury felt up to the challenge that he was sure the next few hours would present. He would, no matter what, manage to speak with Lady Blanchette, to get her, somehow, to confide her secrets. He would also be watching Blackwood closely – he did not, in any way, trust the man.

Stepping into the drawing room, where the company was gathered for a pre-dinner drink, his eye went immediately to Lady Blanchette. She looked remarkable, more beautiful than ever, her lustrous hair swept up and artfully tangled through with ribbon, her gown a deep sapphire blue that made her beautiful eyes seem even more intense. She quite took his breath away.

He realised, with a start, that he had been staring, rather rudely, and turned his gaze away, only to find Blackwood glaring at him, with a look that could quite possibly melt a bullet in flight. A look that did not bode well for the evening's polite conversation.

"Ah Captain," Lord Derbyshire waved him over "you missed a capital hunt this morning ! We started in the north coppice and……"

Westbury tried his best to appear to listen, as Lady Blanchette's father regaled him with the entire sequence of events of the day.  His attention, however, was elsewhere.  Lady Blanchette had been speaking to one of the elderly Ladies, and turning, moved towards Lady Charlotte.  Blackwood smoothly removed himself from the rather raucous conversation of the younger set, and, equally smoothly, diverted Lady Blanchette from her path, taking her elbow to draw her over to the terrace doors.

She hid it well, but Westbury still saw the reaction in her body when Blackwood touched her, and the rather desperate glance that she threw over her shoulder, as he drew her aside.  No-one else noticed anything amiss.  It just seemed that two well acquainted young people were conversing politely, in full view of the room.

It was certainly not, to Westbury's keen eye, polite.  Blackwood kept a firm grip on her arm, carefully standing so that his body almost completely blocked the view of it.  Lady Blanchette's shoulders sagged, and she appeared most unhappy with whatever he was saying.

But, for some reason he could not fathom, she did not pull away from the bounder, did not demand that he unhand her, did nothing but listen. Doubt crept in to Westbury's mind. Could he be wrong? Could it be that she liked, even wanted, the attentions of the cad? Why else would she accept such improper handling? More than ever, he needed to talk to her, to know the truth, no matter how much the truth might hurt.

Moments later Blackwood released her and, with barely a nod, sauntered off back to the conversation he had left earlier. He looked smugly pleased with himself – an expression that Captain Westbury found he would like to wipe from Blackwood's face… with a fist.

Blanche looked somewhat shaken as she reached Charlotte, who gave her a considering look, but said nothing, beyond commenting on how well the colour of her dress suited her. They conversed for a while discussing all of the arrangements for tomorrow night's surprise ball, and speculating as to who the new important guests might be, as their mother had coyly refused to tell them.

Blanche carefully manoeuvred them, with the excuse of obtaining a drink, to quite the opposite side of the room from Blackwood, so that all of the guests, and a few potted palms too, were between them and the group where he stood. She felt better when he could not easily watch her. Her arm still felt soiled somehow, where he had held her, and her mind more so, by what he had said. All the while smiling, as if discussing the weather, he had informed her that he would come to her chamber tonight, and that he expected her to be ready and waiting to serve his needs.

He had looked across the room at Charlotte, and, quirking an eyebrow at her, had said 'your poor dear sister would be so terribly shocked if she knew what a little whore you are. And it would ruin her reputation forever, should anyone else find out.' There was nothing subtle about his meaning.

'Oh Blanche, you do still look so tired. You must make sure to rest properly tonight, so that you can enjoy the ball tomorrow!'

Charlotte held Blanche's hands between hers, looking so genuinely concerned for her sister that it tore at Blanche's heart.

She was saved from replying when Charlotte was summoned to her mother's side, going with good grace, but a little huff of frustration. Blanche looked up, desperate to seek safety in conversation, with someone, anyone, anyone but Blackwood. Looked up - straight into the brilliant blue eyes of Captain Westbury, who had magically appeared in front of her. Had she summoned him, like a knight to protect her, just with her thoughts? She pushed the whimsy aside, and smiled at him.

Right now, no matter how her heart hurt, no matter how strongly she had resolved, this afternoon, that she would not speak to him, not encourage him, she could not push him away now.

She wanted, rather, to cling to him, her relief at having someone to speak to profound. There was, she realised, something odd in his expression, as if he were angry with her. Well, that was not unreasonable, given that she had kissed him this afternoon, then pushed him away and run from him. Oh, she felt such a fool.

His normally sunny eyes were wintry, and he spoke in a somewhat harsh tone.

'After our conversation at the ball, I would not have expected you to allow yourself to be drawn aside by Mr Blackwood again. Could it be that, despite what you said, you enjoy his attentions?'

Blanche gasped, shocked that he could interpret what he had seen in that way, and he paused, seeing the seemingly genuine shock in her eyes. His anger pushed him on though - he had to know the truth.

'Perhaps that little confidence that you shared with me is not the whole of it? Perhaps he has taken advantage of your infatuation rather more than I had thought, or..... is this your choice, has he engaged your affections truly? Is that really what you want in a man? Most of the gentlemen present would consider you to be a most desirable match, perhaps even offer a proposition of marriage should you encourage them in the slightest, even given your previous disgrace. Nevertheless, if it were to be discovered that you had cavorted, shall we say, with a bounder like Blackwood, outside the realms of holy matrimony, why then that would present something of a problem, would it not? Of course, I am simply expressing comment on what might happen, should such a thing be suspected – I am sure that such a well-bred young lady as yourself would never allow herself to be placed in such a position.'

'I suppose it would Captain, should such a thing happen' she replied, her breath a little ragged.

Oh this was awful! The one man she most desperately wished to have care for her, was obviously already judging her, even without knowing the full truth of her depravity. Oh what a terrible mistake she had made, jeopardizing her future prospects, her potential relationships with decent, handsome men, like this Captain, for the sake of a few moments of lust.

And now she was trapped by her own foolishness, ruined beyond repair.

 '- and if such a discovery were to be made after a marriage had been arranged, why then that would be the doom of any hopes of securing a proposal in the future and of your position in society as well as that of your family.'

'Yes sir, yes it would!' the tension was unbearable. It was clinging tight to her like a bodice that didn't fit. She was burdened and had to lighten the load. The last few days of dark secret despair, with no one to speak of it to, weighed on her.  If the Captain already thought the worst, already despised her for her behaviour, then nothing she did could change that.  He was an honourable man, even if he knew, she was sure that he would not reveal his knowledge to the world.

She would cope, if he turned away from her in horror, just so long as her family were not ruined by her folly.  She must confess, must trust someone, and unburden herself!

For some reason she felt that she could trust this man, regardless of all that had happened between them, and, somehow, not being honest with him seemed a more terrible crime than exposing her folly to his censure.

'Oh Captain!' she said at last. 'Captain, I fear that I have made a grave error. Can you find it in your heart to forgive me? Is there any honour in me worth preserving?' he looked down at her, at first disapprovingly, but then with a wry little smile and a raise of his eyebrow.

'That remains to be seen' he said to her, unsmiling. 'However, not all men are unfeeling brutes who will not forgive an impressionable young lady the slightest indiscretion. Passion is a strange and powerful force, and there are still some willing to fight to excuse it, and to restore some honour to a lady's reputation.'

'You have found me out, sir' she said, although by this point she did not really need to. 'I did allow passion to overcome me with Mr. Blackwood, in a most inappropriate manner. I fear that his experience at raising passion in women was too much for me. I regret it profoundly, but he has taken most unseemly pleasure in making me aware of the fact that if word ever gets out I, and my family, will be ruined in the eyes of society! He…. He…. He has used that fact to compel me to further intimacy with him, whenever he has been able to make the opportunity.'

Her breathing was coming hard, her face had gone white with fear as she spoke, and her hands clenched in the folds of her beautiful gown.

'Egads!  Blackwood is more of a cad and a bounder than even I had thought. Well then…' he spoke with a new found sense of purpose. 'There is only one thing for it. For your sake, and for the sake of all happy and decent futures, I will do what I must.'

She looked up, confusion in her eyes, as he turned from her, and strode purposefully over to where Blackwood stood, looking barely interested in the young men's talk of hunting and gambling.. She watched him tap Blackwood on the shoulder, draw him aside, and then say a few words to him discreetly, in his ear. Blackwood started, looking very displeased, then stilled.

The pair left together, but not before each of them threw her a glance, Blackwood one of malice and hate, Westbury a steely look that seemed determined to convey some sense of hope. She slumped into a chair, hiding behind the potted palms, feeling very confused and very conflicted.

# Chapter Eleven

As she pored over her journal, trying to get all of these thoughts out without spilling ink all over herself, there was a knocking at the door, and Smithers, the family butler answered when she asked who was there. She unlocked the door and he entered, looking slightly askance at the fact that the door had been locked, but much too reserved to enquire about it.

He was a tall and grave looking man, with the tact of a veteran servant. He held out a small tray, with a note on top.

'A correspondence for you, my Lady, from young Captain Westbury.'

'Thank you Smithers, that will be all.' She lifted the paper from the tray, cautiously, almost as if it might burn her.

With a slight bow the butler left, leaving her feeling mightily confused. What could the note possibly say? Was the Captain also proposing a salacious liaison?

Would that be a terrible mistake, or was that secretly what she desired? NO!  That was her wanton nature speaking – she refused to think that way. And surely, after the way that he had left her tonight, he would no longer desire her in any way – she had seen the disgust in his eyes – there was no hope there.

She locked the door again, then, hands shaking with nervous energy, she opened and read the short note, scribbled in the hand of a man more used to writing hasty notes on a battlefield than to writing sentimental or poetic verses:

*I have pledged myself to your honour, and it is to be pistols at dawn. We shall be down by the old pine tree in the grounds.*

*Yours,*

*H W*

A strange blend of excitement and horror ran right through her. A duel! And all on her account! She could not but feel moved by Captain Westbury's gesture, and yet feel awkward that it should be happening at all. That he should so choose to defend her honour, knowing how sullied that honour was, even after she had pushed him away this afternoon in the gardens, amazed her, she did not understand at all. Unable to decide what on earth she could do, beyond rising before dawn to sneak out to see the result of her terrible mistake, and more conscious than ever of the strange and foolish ways of the heart, she lay down and tried as hard as she could to get a little sleep.

The conciseness of the Captain's missive brought a faint smile to her face as she gazed at the ceiling, waiting for sleep to arrive.

It seemed to have the tone of a military directive. *It is to be pistols at dawn. Ready yourselves.* Stoic and unshakable. And yet she couldn't help speculate, as she dozed off, what chimaera of hopes and fears breathed life into these words. Was he not apprehensive *at all*?

Perhaps the message was merely functional, and he gave no consideration to the artful communication of feelings. Perhaps, as she briefly recalled him mentioning earlier in the evening, his emotions had been numbed and tamed by years of warfare.

But speculations tempted her, and she pictured him frowning as he wrote the message, without prevarication; without anxiety, but with just a hint of sentimentality, just for her. But for all its confidence, were there not some whispers of a gentle, hopeful soul that could be inferred?

What hadn't he written, and why? *I have pledged myself to your honour*, she heard over and over as she drifted in and out of sleep. How dependable and safe words seemed to sound when they came from his lips! One could almost touch and embrace his utterances for how solid they were, she thought. Every so often, the initial element of horror she had felt when she first received the correspondence surged back up through her, from where she had tried to swallow it down. She struggled to sleep despite the tumult of emotions, yet it was nigh on impossible, so vertiginous was the excitement of a pledge to her honour; so deep the fear of gunshots at sunrise.

After what could have been minutes or hours, she heard the first lark, and struggled to work out whether she had managed to sleep or not.

But as the pale half-light of pre-dawn edged through her window, and as the events of the previous night crystallized into focus in her mind, she realised what she had to do. It was but a ten minute walk to the pine tree that Captain Westbury had alluded to in his message, which, she noticed with a start, was scrunched up in her exertion-blanched fist where she had clutched it anxiously all night. It would be less than half an hour until dawn. The men would doubtless already be there by the time she arrived, checking their firearms.

She would have little time to adequately prepare herself for the coming rendezvous, and people would utterly disapprove of her presence at the duel, but in that piercing clarity that only fatigue seems to proffer, she knew that she had to watch it happen, had to take at least that much responsibility for the consequences of her actions.

Had to be there – because she could imagine only grief resulting – her heart clenched at the thought of either of them hurt or killed. No matter how much she might despise James Blackwood at this moment, he did not deserve death, just because she had been overcome by her own lust.

She rose, resolved to escape the house undetected and to observe the conflict from the hillock that overlooked the expanse upon which that Scots pine towered and brooded.

She hastily dressed in a simple day dress and thrust her hair under a shawl, hoping to be taken for a maid if she were to be spotted, and exited the house through the servants' door. As she rushed through the dewy, crepuscular morning, stifling groans as she stumbled on tufts of grass, near invisible in the pre-dawn light, nightmare images of the possible outcomes of the impending scene danced through her thoughts.

How could she be expected to react to the news of a defeated, perhaps slain, rival for her affections? Was this not a rather joyless affair, no matter the result?

Did Captain Westbury expect her to come? Did Blackwood know of this message? Was this merely some strange masculine ruse to test her interest?

She reached the hillock and crept up through the bracken, and, sure enough, she saw in the dim dawn light, across an expanse of lawn, five figures standing rigid under the branches of a pine tree, as if extensions of its brittle limbs.

She could not, however, pick out who was who. Who were the seconds, who the fifth figure?  A doctor, she supposed.

She became aware of a rising wind, still chill at this time of year, and began to shiver, so she ventured to move down the slope to escape the wind, and find a better vantage to view the scene, supposing that she was unlikely to be seen among the foliage. She crouched behind a shrouding bush and saw the gilded epaulettes of Captain Westbury glint very briefly, and a few yards from him, Blackwood whispering something in his Second's ear.

She could now see who was there.  It seemed that the staff had been pressed into duty as Seconds, and rightly nervous they looked as a result. The tired-looking head gardener, Mr Blyth, a stout Cheshireman, was standing as Second for Blackwood, and Jamison, the Stablemaster, was standing as Second for the Captain. That, at least, gave her confidence that this would be a fair contest – neither of the longstanding and loyal servants would permit anything underhanded.

The village doctor was the fifth man, and he looked extremely disapproving about the whole process, but she knew him to be a good man, who would heal any damage if he possibly could.

Blackwood's lips were moving, but Blanche could not hear what was being said. She suspected he was discussing the rules of engagement, since Captain Westbury stood still and calm, listening respectfully, while Mr Blackwood paced to and fro in agitation. After perhaps five minutes, pale dawn had arrived. Mr Blyth and Jamison nodded at Blackwood and the Captain.

Blanche then jumped as Mr Blyth suddenly yelled, 'Back to back, gentlemen! Ten paces on my count, then turn and fire!' The duellists approached and faced one another, their guns now behind their backs, and abruptly turned around.

Captain Westbury was now facing Blanchette from some thirty yards away. In time to Blyth's count, he took ten deliberate paces towards her, his body carried with physical eloquence; his firearm behind his back. But she became suddenly aware that he could now easily see her among the glistening wet leaves. His eyes narrowed for a moment and his lips made the unmistakeable shapes of the word, 'Blanchette…' Their eyes connected after Westbury's sixth step. They gazed at each other as he moved toward her, and Blanche now felt the strong desire to rush through the clear air, risking a wayward bullet, just to embrace this man, whose eyes rested warmly on her chill-pinched face.

At the tenth pace, Mr Blyth roared, "Turn and fire!"

Blackwood had turned and shot before Blyth had finished the first word.

But the bullet sailed past its target and produced a loud crack in the bushes but a yard from Blanche's crouched vantage point, in response to which she could not control issuing a sharp scream which reverberated across the clearing.

It was the first time that she had noticed fear in the Captain's eyes, as he took a pace forward and called.

'My Lady!'

Blanche stood, now blushing, and called out shakily.

"The projectile missed both you and I, sir, and has found its resting place in the trunk of this unfortunate sapling."

She thought that she saw a flicker of a smile pass over Westbury's lips, as he turned and faced his opponent.

"Captain Westbury, you must fire, sir." Jamison announced, eyeing Blanche warily as she walked towards the assembled men.

Blanche looked past the Captain's unwavering frame, to see a fuming Blackwood.

Captain Westbury raised his pistol and pointed it at Blackwood, his arm straight and unmoving. Blackwood squirmed, but held his ground.

Blanche stopped in her tracks and held her breath.

"Ladies should not be present at duels! It is a most scandalous distraction! Did you invite her, sir? May the devil take you, Westbury, for this sabotage! Go on, you dog," Blackwood called out, from his position twenty paces from the Captain, "show us your mettle, you cowardly saboteur!"

"I am inclined to remind you, Mr Blackwood," Mr Blyth said sternly, and without bothering to affect a more genteel accent, "that gentlemanly and civilised manners comprise the soul of this activity…"

"To Hell with you, cur," Blackwood raged, as he stood, shuddering in the wind. Or perhaps shaking with fear.

The Captain, slowly but decidedly, then lowered his firing arm a little and, with telling accuracy, fired his shot straight into the earth a yard from Blackwood's right foot. Blackwood had been spared – it was very, very obvious, however, that it was by the Captain's choice, not from any lack of ability to make the shot.

"What unconscionable cowardice and hypocrisy!" Blackwood shrieked, beginning to look desperate.

He then saw the look of distaste on Blanche's face and attempted to recover from his fit of anger.

"I feel it would be only fair," he began with serpentine composure, "that this duel be restarted, since the delightful, but unwitting distraction of Lady Blanchette…"

'  happened after your shot had been fired, and can in no way be said to be responsible for your failure to hit me'. Westbury responded at exactly the same moment that Mr Blyth said "I'm afraid, sir, that would be most irregular".

Blyth, to Blanche's amusement and astonishment, appeared to be stifling a yawn as he responded to his superior, the vexed and reddening Blackwood. Clearly keen to regain his bed, Blyth gathered the two pistols in discreet silence, and headed back inside.

'Rest assured Blackwood, should I ever hear of you speaking ill of this Lady, or of you doing anything to her detriment, in any way, I will hunt you down.  And next time I will not be merciful, and I will not miss.' Captain Westbury's voice was cold and hard as he spoke.

Blackwood, fuming, acknowledged this statement with a curt nod and turned, throwing her a covetous and furious glare, before disappearing over the hill, ranting and mumbling to himself, his nerves clearly shot through.

'Your courage and dignity are an example to all Englishmen, Captain Westbury. I cannot thank you enough for choosing to champion my honour, especially as you know just how sullied it is.'

'Please' replied the soldier, still impassive and unflappable '- do not flatter me unnecessarily, it is not what I require. I had merely hoped to prevent a young lady from becoming disgraced in the eyes of society. I trust that my efforts were not in vain.'

'Not at all sir! I must trust that Blackwood will heed your words, and not speak of this again.  You have saved me from despair and my family from ruin in the eyes of society.'

She rushed towards him, carried forward by an unseen force that swelled within her, beneath that modest dress, and plunged her into his arms. He caught her to him, and very deliberately bent to kiss her. The kiss began gently, but rapidly escalated in intensity, as the fear of the last hours dissolved in the certainty that Westbury was here, alive still, and in her arms.

Blanche knew suddenly that this was the man whom she truly loved.

The James Blackwoods of the world could keep their sordid seductions and uncaring attitudes - to find herself in the arms of a man of integrity and honor, whose word she could trust, was what she had, deep down, always desired.

Captain Westbury's composure was, finally, disrupted.  His breathing was fast, and he looked at her with undisguised hunger in his eyes. It seemed at last that his bluff, soldierly façade was cracking, and she was at last getting some glimpse of the man beneath, who felt and dreamed and throbbed, just like anybody else.

He returned her kisses manfully, as he had returned fire in the earlier duel, his tongue more direct than James Blackwood's, but no less stimulating to a young lady on a chilly May morn. She was swept up in his powerful arms and felt that this moment ought to last forever.

Blanche hesitated at first, to do more than simply melt into his kiss, but as the arousal rose in her body, his kiss seeming to spark reactions everywhere, felt confident enough to provoke her handsome Captain further, to allow herself just a little indulgence of her own desires, knowing instinctively that this man would never use her the way that Blackwood had.

She allowed her hand to stray a little below his strapping waistline, towards his breeches and the hard ridge of his manhood, pressing so delightfully against her body as he held her.

She slid her fingers against him, feeling his shape through the taught cloth of his breeches, and knew at once that she had him entranced, as his breath came on a gasp and his lips came down on hers again, plundering the softness of her mouth, as she drove his body to distraction.

The solider stood to attention, tall and firm, inflated with pomp and ceremony, ready for action – she was amused at the image in her mind, even as she was aroused by it.

It took only a little of her intuition to sense forces swelling up inside him, as they were swelling in her, hot need and almost animal lust, fluids and feelings desperate to burst forth between them.

As she had intended, Captain Westbury pulled her harder against him. She was happy now to have brought these instincts out in him, and the lustful wanton in her wanted to submit to this need, to be taken by him, right now. The cold wind had ceased to matter, and all she wanted was his touch.

She had, she thought, managed to bring out this whole new side of his nature, and she rejoiced in knowing that he felt about her so strongly.

She needed this in a man, she now realised, this intensity of physical desire for her, but she needed it accompanied by true care, by love, not as just a sating of the body's needs.

He brought her whole body to him, pressing his maleness against her, hard and forceful. She could feel it through the layers of their clothing, the bulging, turgid shape she had called into service between the Captain's legs.

His kisses, mixed with little nipping bites, brushed down her neck with an energy and passion that she had presumed was the monopoly of more polished lovers, but she realised, perhaps he was in that category – she knew so little of his experience! His bluff exterior may cover hidden depths, which she could not wait to explore.

Regardless, his kisses stirred in her the same bubbling, trembling warmth and wetness that she had experienced with her roguish seducer that first evening in the Library, before his true nature had been revealed. She felt no fear of him, no revulsion for any part of him. Her entire being yearned for his touch, longed to obey his orders.

Westbury, her Henry, the man who had addressed that note to her, fought for her, dazzled her with his looks and grace, was now providing her with greater pleasure than she had ever imagined, just from his kiss.

She wrapped her arms around him, like ivy climbing up a tall, strong tree, surrendering herself to his touch. His hands roamed over her body, caressing her softly and sending tingles up to her breasts and down to her womanhood. His hand hitched up her skirts, as the need to touch her more intimately drove him.

She let out a gasp 'Henry...' and lifted her head back from their kiss to look him directly in the face. He was all so perfect - his sculpted face, golden hair and broad shoulders. His hands already under her skirts, he grabbed her firmly by the buttocks and pulled her close again. She was shaking, not with the cold but from the sheer anticipation of what she knew surely was to come.

He surprised her.  With a deep shuddering breath, he dropped his hands from her, and moved back a scant few inches, and stood, breathing hard. Looking deep into her amazing cerulean eyes, he spoke.  So dazed was she with passionate need, that it took a few moments for his words to sink in.

'I will not continue any further, no matter how deeply I desire you.' He said, his face touching hers. 'It is not my intention to risk life and limb for a lady's honour and then to violate it myself. I shall do what I had hoped I might eventually do, when I received an invitation to this very party' and then, with a look of regretful determination, he took a further step back.

For a moment, Blanche was bitterly disappointed.

She did not care for any silly notions about 'honour' any more, what she wanted was to feel, and to love, and to experience the highest of pleasures with her dashing officer of the guards!

Had she done something wrong? What on earth had come over him? Or was she being terribly foolish again, and letting her lusts overcome her?

The very next second she had all of her answers in one. Captain Westbury dropped onto one stout knee and his face finally cracked into a pure smile, clean and pearly:

'Lady Blanchette, will you be my bride?' she almost swooned with shock and awe. At last!

'Oh yes! Yes I will!' she declared, tears of joy swelling in her eyes. What a man! Heroic, strong, romantic and capable! He was what she had always wanted, needed, even. As he rose to his feet, he kissed her again, with loving passion, and she allowed him to pull her into his arms.

She looked up at him; he looked just as good from this angle as from every other. Her head rested perfectly against his shoulder, and the strong beat of his heart echoed in her ear.

'Now my dear', he said, full of joyful confidence and with a twinkle in his eye, 'we shall find a little tea and some breakfast. But first, perhaps, we should find somewhere discreet to relieve each other's need, at least a little....'

His very words brought her almost to a quivering climax, and she walked up the hillock, back towards the house, with him, happier and more satisfied than she had ever been in all her life.

They snuck in through the servant's door, and she led him to an unused guest room, at the furthest end of the least used wing of the house.  Laughing, they slipped through the door, and locked it, to fall onto the bed, already kissing. There was nothing manipulative or posed about Henry's response and actions – it was abundantly clear to her that he wanted her with the same desperation as she wanted him.

Their hands roamed each other's bodies and she revelled in how different this felt from anything that she had experienced before.

She could stand it no longer – her fingers slid under the edges of his jacket, and down over his muscled abdomen to where the buttons of his falls stood strained by the pressure that his hardness put on them.  Undoing them as fast as she could, she gasped as his kisses moved down her neck, to tease her hardened nipples through the thin fabric of the day dress.

At the same time, his fingers found the laces of the dress, and deftly undid them, allowing it to a slide from her shoulders and reveal her beautiful breasts to his gaze.

She gasped as his tongue delicately traced the edge of her nipple, and reached for him again.  He moaned his pleasure against her skin as her fingers finally found his cock, and stroked along the silken skin of its hard length.

His hands grasped her skirts, drawing them up to her waist in one quick movement, as they slid to lie fully on the bed, and she gasped again as the cool morning air touched the wet folds of her most intimate flesh.

'Oh Blanche, you are so beautiful.'

His words drifted warm breath across her, bringing her to a quivering height of sensitivity, just before his skilful tongue found the nub of her pleasure and began to work gently to drive her need even higher.  She clung to him, pulling him to her, as her hips lifted and drove her against his working tongue.

In all too short a time, she found herself cresting the wave of her pleasure, crying out his name as she came apart under his touch.

He held her to him as she came back to herself, watching her with such caring and love in his blue eyes that the contrast to her experiences with Blackwood was enough to make her almost cry with her relief.  Gently, she reached for him again, her fingers finding his cock again, and stroking over it wonderingly – he felt so different, and she wanted him so much.

The difference, she realised, with sudden clarity, was that she loved this man, as well as lusting after him most intensely.

He went to pull away a little, but Blanche drew him to her, pulling him down over her, kissing him.

'Love me, Henry, please. I want you with all my heart.'

He needed no further encouragement, and shifted to slide himself into her, with one long slow thrust, a moan of deep pleasure forcing itself through his lips as he did, echoed by her own cry of delight.

Their eyes locked as he began to move inside her, and she marvelled again at how wonderfully different this was, at how much she wanted to give this man pleasure in return.

Then all thought fled as her pleasure built again and the world shattered, his cries mingling with hers as he pulled from her at the last moment.

They lay in each other's arms, content and happy, until, after some time, Henry raised himself on an elbow, and looked at her smiling.

'That, Blanche, was quite the most intense pleasure that I have ever felt, although I must apologise for the rushed nature of this today. I fear that my desperate need for you led me to not spend as much time as I should have on your pleasure. I will do better next time, I promise you my love.'

She looked at him, wonder in her eyes, that he should want her, love her, even knowing what she had done. And that with him, this intimacy should be so different, so very much more, than it had been before, with either Charles or Blackwood. He shifted, almost uncomfortable at the intensity of her gaze, then smiled.

'Shall we go and find that breakfast now, my love?'

They left the room hand in hand.

# Chapter Twelve

'I say Blackwood' said Lord Derbyshire a little later that day, chewing his way through a scone over tea in the breakfast room. '- I must say you look as if you haven't slept a wink! I trust the room and bed are to your satisfaction, I can have you moved if you'd like?'

'They are most satisfactory sir, fear not' replied Blackwood, distractedly. The rogue did certainly look worse for wear that afternoon, with grey-black bulges under his eyes and his hair quite out of place, despite the best efforts of his manservant.

Derbyshire's questions demonstrated that word of the duel under the pine tree had not yet got out. Hopefully, he pondered, it would stay that way.

'I regret that I am only a light sleeper, as the Sultan of Aleppo once found to his cost. My slumber is easily disrupted by birds you see, I can often hear them twittering in the small hours, distracting me...'

'Well we can't be having that!' declared Derbyshire at once. 'I can send Blyth out to scare 'em off if you'd like! He's rather a good shot I believe!'

'That will not be necessary.' Mumbled Blackwood, already bored by this dialogue. He did not bother to point out to his host the futility of trying to improve his guests' sleep with the noise of gunshots. 'I am quite used to sleeping little. Indeed, rest is not, in my humble opinion, the principle purpose of the bedchamber.'

'Ah, I quite see what you mean sir!' Derbyshire replied, with a wink and a knowing pat on the shoulder. 'Precisely what you mean! Reading, of course! There is nothing like the pleasure of a good book before bed, good stirring stuff that stimulates the senses. I have often seen fit to sacrifice sleep myself for the sake of an especially riveting chapter!'

'Yes, my Lord' Blackwood replied, suppressing a sarcastic groan, 'that is precisely what I meant.'

"Well Blackwood, get some food into you, I assume you will be joining us for the hunt this afternoon?   I'm off to see that everything is in readiness.' Lord Derbyshire rose, smiling, and headed for the door.

As he stepped into the hall, he almost collided with Blanche and Captain Westbury. They were considerably better turned out than Blackwood.

Blanche had changed into a sumptuous yellow-cream dress for the morning's conversation, while Westbury had managed to buff up his hair and uniform perfectly. For two people who had also slept very little last night, they looked positively radiant, and were rather pointedly holding each other's hands.

'Pardon me for interrupting Lord Derbyshire.' Westbury said. 'If we might have a word with you, in your study?'

"Of course, of course, what's this all about then?" Lord Derbyshire led them through the study door, and turned to them enquiringly.

'Sir, I have asked Lady Blanchette to marry me, and she has done me the honor of accepting.  I hope that you will grant your approval.'

The old earl seemed quite taken aback, and looked at them both consideringly.

'Why…' he blurted. He couldn't refuse them, could he? 'This is rather sudden! Blanchette, are you certain?  Is this what you want?'

'Oh yes, father, yes, it is everything that I want' replied Blanche in a clear voice that trembled with happiness at the edges.

"Then of course! Of course you can marry, a most suitable match!  Certainly, you have my blessing.  And you and I shall have to get better acquainted, Captain Westbury. Tell me my lad, do you hunt often?"

'Why yes sir, it is one of my principle diversions.'

"Capital, capital!  But I think that you had best go and tell your mother and sister now, Blanchette.  They will never forgive you if you don't tell them straight away!"

They left the room, Lord Derbyshire back to arranging hunting parties, and Blanche and the Captain to seek out her mother and sister.  They found them in the drawing room, conversing with a number of guests. Blanchette could barely wait to speak.

'Mama, Captain Westbury and I have an announcement we wish to make.  The Captain has asked me to marry him, I have accepted, and Papa has approved the match. We are now engaged to be married.'

There were a few sudden gasps around the room, followed by a courteous but genuine applause. Blanche could not help but notice a few envious glances, from the young ladies present, at the sight of her handsome fiancée in his splendid uniform. He was everything that most young women wanted – handsome, heroic, and the heir to the Bevington fortune as well.

'We shall start making the necessary arrangements at once!' Lady Derbyshire cried. 'It shall be the finest wedding the County of Derbyshire ever saw, and no mistake. She's always had an eye for a good fellow, my Blanche. You've made no mistakes this time my dear... How delightful!  Now this evening's ball can be your betrothal ball as well!'

Blackwood edged his way into the corner, and threw Blanchette and Westbury a bitter look.

Lord Derbyshire came through the door at that point, and came to a halt beside his wife, who was continuing regaling the room with her happiness about Blanche and Henry's announcement.

"I can't imagine anything that could be better – I am so happy for you.  Nothing can make today less wonderful!'

'I can think of a few things' said James Blackwood, cynically. He had stepped forward into the conversation as if from nowhere, the ghost at the feast. Everyone present suddenly felt a little muted in their happiness.

'I can think of a few reasons why this wedding should not occur. This couple I fear, have a few tales to tell and no mistake. This whole thing is a sham.' Blanchette felt a sudden hatred for this man prickle within her. What a cad! To try and disrupt their happiness like this and ruin the mood of the day, it was absurd!

And yet she could not but feel deeply anxious at the same time. She had felt sure, just a few hours ago, that he had taken heed of Captain Westbury's words, and would not be a threat to her any more. What if he chose to defy the Captain? Would he tell her father what had taken place between them? Would he rob of her handsome guardsman and her chance of happiness?

To think that she had felt some attraction to this man, and had allowed him to seduce her, nay had even acted to seduce him, in her very own house! She felt a little queasy and had to turn away, as the events of the last few days came rushing back to her. Her feelings must have shown clearly, Blackwood spoke directly to her, bitterness in his tone.

'Now you shrink back, Lady Blanchette – yet you were quite willing to entertain my company this last few days. Quite willing indeed...'

'What are you...' Lord Derbyshire started muttering a confused response, but Westbury stepped in, tall and proud, feigning ignorance.

'To what exactly, are you referring Mr. Blackwood? What is the substance of your allegation?'

Blanche was filled with admiration for him. He had skilfully turned the glare of suspicion onto Blackwood himself.

'Well...' Blackwood stuttered, backing away from the Captain, who was bigger and younger than he. 'I mean, isn't it obvious?'

'Not to me' said Westbury.

'Nor I' said Lord Derbyshire, finding his voice again. 'My dear Blackwood, I should like to know exactly what it is you are referring to here.' Blackwood paused, eyed the room, took in the disapproving, hard faces staring at him. He was not a brave man, when confronted by so many disapproving eyes, and he backed away.

'Oh dash it!' he exclaimed. 'English girls are all just whores and harlots at heart! No good will come of it!' and with that he stormed out, and was not seen in Amfield House, nor heard from by the Cavendish family for quite some time to come.

'Good heavens!' said the Earl, still confused. 'What a remarkable outburst. Do you have any idea to what he is referring?' Blanche and Westbury shared a glance. Charlotte fixed her curious gaze on her sister. Blanche and Henry smiled as one.

'I have absolutely no idea' said Captain Westbury at last, lifting Blanche's hand to his lips and kissing it.

# Chapter Thirteen

That evening's ball was a glittering affair. The staff had outdone themselves with decorating the room, and preparing a magnificent feast. Flowers filled the huge urns around the room, and a larger orchestra than usual had been persuaded to be available, even on such short notice. Invitations had rapidly been sent to all of the local aristocracy, and many had come to join the house party guests in celebrating Blanche's betrothal.

Blanche had been surrounded by well-wishers from the start, only finding relief when the Captain carried her away from them to dance. Charlotte had watched it all, while dutifully trying, yet again, to hold something approaching a sensible conversation with the young gentlemen who sought her out.

Her conversations were as unsuccessful as always, and seeing Blanche so happy made her wonder if she would ever find someone to be happy with, herself.

She had hoped, with all of the extra people in attendance tonight, that there might be some new gentleman to meet, who might, just maybe, be of interest to her.  So far, that was not the case. Her mother's mysterious promises of important special guests appeared to be unfulfilled, and generally, of all those present, she seemed to be the only one who was not happy, not having a wonderful time.  She was glad that Blanche was happy, but, try as she might, she could not feel happy herself.

Charlotte made her way towards the door, where her parents stood, greeting some late arrivals.  She had nearly reached them when a large gentleman bumped her as he passed, and she spent a minute dealing with his profuse apologies, and his insistence on fetching her a glass of ratafia, in apology for his boorish clumsiness.  Finally rid of him, she turned and was suddenly arrested in place at the sight of a new arrival - tall, dark, and devilishly handsome.

'Don Diego Sanchez-Zapata' the doorman struggled to say in his Derbyshire accent 'Count of San Pedro, Estanciero of Buenos Aires Province in the Rio de la Plata'.  The man nodded approval at the servant's efforts, and surveyed the room, which had fallen silent as everyone gawped at this exotic intruder. An Argentine! Here, at Amfield House? This was most unexpected. Charlotte immediately moved closer to her parents, who were greeting the Don by the door.

'Don Diego!' said her mother, as he kissed her cheek in his sensual, Latin manner. 'We are deeply honoured that you could make it.'

'There is no place that I would rather be on a fine evening in May' he said, in a dark and whispering accent that nevertheless seemed to be used to conversing in English. 'It is so profoundly generous of you to host me, on my return to your fair country.'

'Please, the pleasure is entirely ours! As a bachelor, I am sure you will be pleased to learn that there are many fine young ladies here, who would be more than grateful for the opportunity to converse with an Argentine of your pre-eminent quality! I am sure that they will all be full of questions about your exotic homeland.'

'I am grateful for your generous hospitality. As you know, business compels me to London next week, but for tonight I will be happy to avail myself of your magnificent hospitality.'

'*Mi casa es su casa*, as I believe you Spaniards say!' said her father the Earl, pronouncing the words horribly.

The Don chuckled politely.

'We do indeed, though I regret to inform you, my Lord, your inflexion was a little flat!'

'Ha! Languages were never my strong suit old boy, had to have Cuthbert here look that one up for me as it is!' as the two men were laughing and slapping each other on the back, Charlotte's eyes met those of her mother, who had not realised how close by she was standing.

They exchanged a glance, and with a nodding gesture that seemed to say 'would you like me to…' she interrupted the conversation:

'Don Diego, might I present my daughter, Charlotte.' He turned in a single, neat swivelling motion and their eyes met at once.

Up close he was even more handsome than she had anticipated. His face, hardened from riding across the Pampas, yet with soft edges and contours that seemed to invite the viewer in, was immediately compelling.

He had a strong profile with an elegant Roman nose and cheekbones that were high enough to give his face a heart-like shape. His eyes were dark and his skin was the colour of pale liquid caramel. He was dressed in a manner rather exotic for Derbyshire society, with a great red sash running across his navy blue and gold jacket, with its glimmering golden epaulettes. Charlotte could not take her eyes off him, and could almost hear an enticing Latin rhythm playing out in the back of her mind. She knew at once that she must have this man, by any means necessary.

'A pleasure to make your acquaintance, Don Diego' she said, trying to suppress the quaking of her heart.

'The pleasure is entirely mine, Lady Charlotte' he replied, laying a delicate kiss on her hand without breaking eye contact. 'Indeed, it pains me that I have not made your acquaintance sooner. Had I know what an intensely beautiful daughter the Earl of Derbyshire had, I would surely have left Buenos Aires sooner.'

The compliment was delivered with such sincerity and clarity that it was all Charlotte could do to keep her pale English skin from breaking out into a blush. This strange and exotic man had aroused something quite new in her.

'If your mother and father permit it' he added, still holding her in his burning gaze 'it would bring me great joy to share a dance with you.'

Charlotte broke eye contact with the Don for the first time to look over expectantly at her parents. Her father, smiling approval, made a permissive hand gesture. He knew what balls was for, and had enough of an idea of what forces moved the hearts of young ladies.

He was glad to see Charlotte receive some attention, at this point when she had been in Blanche's shadow for so long.

'Of course, Don Diego, I would be very happy to' she said warmly. 'Although, I fear to admit I do not know of any South American dances, having never travelled more widely than England before.'

'Please!' he said, with a steely inner strength. 'There is time enough for both of us to learn more of one another's cultures. I, fortunately, do know some English dances, although I fear that my style is a little more flamboyant than you may be used to. Allow me…' he lifted her hand to his arm with his swarthy hand, and without pondering or apology led her straight to the centre of the dance floor, just as the orchestra began playing a waltz.

Charlotte was both pleased, and nervous, to dance such an intimate dance with the Don as a first dance.

He took her in his arms with much more firmness than any English gentleman, and drew her closer than was seemly. Such closeness only excited her more, so that her heart pounded so loudly she wondered that he did not hear it.

His scent invaded her nostrils, and wrapped itself around her – complex and subtle, with something exotic and very un-English about it. She could not identify it – she only knew that she loved it.

Held in a firm pose, she found his approach to dancing already much more passionate than the genteel English dancing going on all around them. They began to move, and it was obvious that the rhythm of the music was something that he connected to, very strongly.

Charlotte was immediately smitten. Feeling the Don holding her close against his lithe body, she could feel her heart hammering even harder, and a great arousal bubbling and boiling up within her. Perhaps this ball was not going to be such a disaster after all. Maybe, for once, others would even envy *her*.

Captain Westbury managed to extricate Blanche from yet another group of well-wishers, and let her towards the dance floor, already anticipating the delicious pleasure of holding her close in the waltz.

Blanche was surprised to see her sister, dancing with vigour, and a passion unusual at occasions such as this, with a tall, dark fellow in a strange sort of a uniform, right in the centre of the room. Many of the eyes at the ball were trained fixedly on this rather odd couple, including the prying and suspicious eyes of the chaperones.

Nevertheless, there was little that anyone could do, with the hosts having given consent to this dance, and surely certain allowances could be made for the gentleman obviously being a foreigner. Blanche, still a little giddy from her very intense day, and the joy of her betrothal, was filled with a strange mixture of emotions on seeing this. A huge part of her was delighted for her sister, who she was well aware was waiting in line behind her, as far as the strictures of the marriage market were concerned. Nevertheless, despite their sisterly love and affection, she could not but feel a tiny pang of worry on seeing Charlotte in the arms of so handsome a stranger.

As Blanche and Henry stepped onto the floor, joining the swirl of dancers, they looked to where Don Diego was still holding Charlotte close to him as they circled each other dramatically.

'Your sister appears to be quite taken by this Argentine fellow' Westbury commented, clearly amused, like many of the onlookers, by the unrestrained passion of their dancing.

'Yes, I hope that he behaves respectably towards her. I would not want her to be tempted to be as foolish as I was.'

'I am certain that he will be, darling Blanche. For tonight, do not worry – let us just enjoy being together. And let us make sure that your mother plans a fast wedding – I do not think that I could bear to wait very long to have you with me at all times. So much so, that I suspect I may feel the need to sneak into your room very late tonight....'

Her face lit with a brilliant smile at his words, and with that he swept her into the dance, holding her just as close as the Don held Charlotte, letting their betrothal be the excuse for such an intimate hold.

Some hours later, after their betrothal had been formally announced to the room at large, and much of the rather delicious new champagne wine had been consumed, the party, as all parties must eventually, began to die down for the night. First as a trickle, then as a torrent, the guests began to leave the ballroom and retire to their quarters. Almost all were staying at least one night at Amfield House, and might yet stay longer.

There was still food to be eaten, wine, punch, and port to be drunk, conversations to be carried on, hunting for the gentlemen and indoor games for the ladies. And most importantly of all, especially for the young ladies and gentlemen who were here really only for one thing, love affairs to be pursued, and matches to be made.

Many retreated to their beds disappointed by the night's encounters, but many more would struggle to sleep tonight, excited by the promise of passion and future happiness in the arms of a favoured dance partner.

One such sleepless guest, though she was not really a guest at all, this being her own house, in which she had grown up, was Charlotte Cavendish.

She had spent part of the night dancing in a manner and style she had never dreamed possible, and certainly not seen or attempted before, with her Don Diego. In intermittent moments they had stopped to catch their breath and converse, and she had learned much about him. Her fascination with the dashing Argentine had not been dimmed by getting to know more about him - indeed it had been quite further aroused.

So often in her former conversations with young gentlemen, she had been quite bored by their incessant talk of hunting or gambling, of guns and horses and cricket, but here she had found a man who genuinely interested her, and who she was quite happy to simply listen to. He had spoken with such eloquence, even in a language that was not his own, of his country, its great Pampas plains stretching for thousands of miles in every direction, of the Andes Mountains and the Rio de la Plata, of the raw energy and humanity of the city of Buenos Aires.

Charlotte was quite fascinated, and willing to hear about all of his interests. Don Diego was a great reader and thinker, and had many original ideas, especially on the subject of love.

'To feel love, is to be alive' he had said in his beautiful husky voice. He spoke like no Englishman she had ever met, and not merely on account of his accent. 'Whether that love endures and goes on and on, beyond the realm of our physical lives, or whether it burns out, bright and sudden like a candle lit at both ends, this matters not. What matters is to feel, to have that swelling passion within you and to express it with all your heart.'

'Yes, I had never considered it like that, but yes, you must be right.'

'You English, I have a lot of affection for you and your country. I feel you understand this, somewhere deep down inside' their eyes met and it was all she could do not to gasp out her attraction. It rumbled deep within her, anticipating him, penetrating her, from the top of her head to the tingling tips of her toes.

'- and yet I fear you are uncomfortable to express these sorts of things, these sentiments, these, how you say? Emotions. This saddens me. All life is feeling, and love is the prince of feelings.'

As all the other guests were drifting away, to find their beds, or for quiet conversation, including, Charlotte noticed, her sister Blanche, looking exhausted but happy, when they finally decided to end their long conversation and each retire for the night.

At the top of Amfield's grand staircase, beneath the nose of Alfred Cavendish, one of the family's most esteemed ancestors, whose portrait had pride of place, they paused, and Don Diego drew her gently into his embrace.

She shivered with delight as he bent his head to place a gentle, sensual kiss on her lips.

Charlotte had never kissed a gentleman before, but immediately felt as if it were all she ever wanted to do henceforth in her life. The Don's lips were sweeter and softer than she had ever imagined human lips to be, and his tongue made swift and skilful motions, playing delicately across her lips, that stimulated a powerful feeling within her, right in her loins.

She felt a tingling all over and an urge to cry out with happiness, but then, Don Diego released her, stepping back, retaining her hand only long enough to place a genteel kiss upon it, and turned towards his allocated guest rooms. 'Buenas noches, mi querida' – his soft parting words reached her ears.

Just as he was leaving though, she felt a desperate wish to not let him leave, to have him stay with her, even if only for a few moments longer, and she reached out her hand to stay him a moment, saying:

'Will you be staying with us long, Don Diego?'

'Alas, Lady Charlotte, I must leave early on the morrow, as I have business in London that cannot wait.'

Her heart fell at his words. She had so hoped to spend more time with him!

'I hope, Don Diego, that you will see your way to find the time to visit us again soon. I have found your conversation most... stimulating...'

'Of course Lady Charlotte, I give you my word that I will return to your charming home soon – I could not refuse such a beautiful Lady. You flatter me. But for now, Good night.'

He bowed again and left her, to seek his bed.

Charlotte stood for a moment, watching him walk away, feeling somewhat lost and bereft, then shook herself and set off to her own room, firmly telling herself that she should push aside her fantasies. What could she possibly have to offer such a well-travelled and sophisticated man?

The next morning she felt much improved, and the events of the previous evening seemed like a fantastical dream. The day proceeded with a whirlwind of activities, as her mother set about organising Blanche's wedding.

Captain Westbury had persuaded her parents that he and Blanche should wed with all speed, and her mother had been only too happy to launch immediately into wedding plans.

It was late afternoon when she stood in the entryway, watching Blanche bid farewell to Captain Westbury, who was off for a few days to make his own part of the arrangements. The Captain drew Blanche to him, and, regardless of who was watching, kissed her deeply and passionately. Blanche melted into his arms, and sighed.

'Godspeed Henry – come back to me soon. I fear I am missing you already.'

Everyone laughed at Blanche's words, which she ignored completely.

"Believe me my love, if there was any way to have things arranged without me leaving you at all, then I would never leave!" He bent to kiss her again, then turned for the door. Only to almost collide with a messenger, who had just arrived. Henry bowed, and stepped around the man, striding to his waiting horse.

Blanche stared after him, looking just a little lost.

"Message for Lady Charlotte Cavendish" announced the messenger, looking hopefully at the ladies present. Charlotte, shocked, stepped forward to take the missive from his hand.

'Thank you.'

She never received letters. All her true friends lived close and spoke in person. She wondered who it was from, all the while hoping desperately that she knew.

Heart racing, she ignored the curious onlookers, and removed herself to her room.  Once inside, Charlotte dared to look at the letter.  It was from him!  Don Diego's handwriting was as flamboyant as his person, and she could just imagine him sitting down to write it.  His exotic scent clung to the paper, and she clutched it to herself for a moment before she gathered the courage to read it.

It was short, but so exciting.  He professed his desire to see her again as soon as possible, to spend hours, days, in her fascinating company, and, to that end, he had decided to purchase an estate in England, that he might be nearby.  He would see her at Blanche and Henry's wedding, and hoped that she might save more than one dance for him.

Charlotte quivered, her heart bursting with joy! – He wanted to see her, and would soon – the wedding was but two weeks away!

When Henry returned a few days later, and swept Blanche into his arms for a long kiss, Charlotte was no longer envious at all, and was quite certain that she awaited their wedding as fervently as they did.

The Derbyshire Set - Book 3
Regency Historical Romance
The Viscount's Unsuitable Affair
AMAZON BESTSELLER CATEGORY
Arietta Richmond

The Derbyshire Set ~ Book 3

Regency Historical Romance

# Arietta Richmond

ARIETTA RICHMOND

For everyone who had the grace to be patient while this book, and the ones before and after it, were coming into existence, who provided cups of tea, and food, when the writing would not let me go, and endured countless times being asked for opinions.

For the readers coming to know these characters well, and who inspire me to continue, by buying my books!

And for all the writers of Regency Historical Romance, whose books I read, who inspired me to write in this fascinating period.

ARIETTA RICHMOND

Anna Perkins' hands were shaking along with the jellies on top of the tray. This was the first major occasion since she had been promoted to housemaid, and she desperately wanted to make a good impression. The demands of a huge occasion such as this - the first large house party after the rather scandalous wedding of the houses' master, the Earl of Stanningfield, required input from every single person employed in the household, preparing the feasts and the rounds of drinks or teas that went between, keeping the house neat and orderly without disrupting the guests, and serving everything up in a tidy and efficient operation.

This was how she found herself nervously picking her way along one of the principal corridors of the main part of the house.

A part of it so grand and smart she had barely even seen in her previous role as a scullery maid. She was, despite her protests to the housekeeper and her lack of upper body strength, quaking under the weight of a platter full of jellies.

She rounded a corner and bumped straight into something remarkably solid, which turned out to be Richard Maitland. Viscount Bellham. He was striding up the corridor purposefully, away from the rest of the house guests, and walked straight into her. There was nothing she could do. Within a clattering instant, the elegant young nobleman was covered in jelly.

'Good grief!' he was just in the process of saying, making a rudimentary effort to scrape the stuff off his jacket, when their eyes met for the first time. Anna had not had the chance to see many of the guests as yet, and certainly hadn't spoken to any. It had not been her place to look out for handsome young gentlemen, but if it had been, Viscount Bellham would have been the first she noticed.

He was tall and well-built, filling out the superbly tailored and arranged clothes she had just spilled red and yellow fruit jellies all over. He wore a rich golden waistcoat over a glistening white shirt, with an elaborate cravat, in the manner fashionable in London society, and an elegant dress coat in navy blue. His stance and posture belied an easy confidence, a swagger even. He moved forcefully, as if he always had somewhere important to be, significant things to be getting on with, and would not allow any man, woman or beast to detain him in his endeavours. His breeches clung tight to his well-formed calves and thighs, bringing tight definition to his muscular masculinity.

He had a wild look in his eyes, like a celtic druid or a warrior king, a face encircled by dark, compelling shadows, full red lips and a robust jawline. Atop his head was a beautifully coiffured mane of a rich, golden brown. As she stood beside him, her eyes meeting his, ashamed in an instant of her low status and her error with the jellies, Anna felt quite plain in her servants' uniform, and yet he seemed to be peering deep into her soul, communing with her, in some profound, impossible way, via their two sets of eyes.

His face quickly turned from angry disbelief to soft contemplation of the woman in front of him. She was completely fascinated by this man, whom she knew she could never hope to know more of than she saw in this instant, and wanted, for some reason that she did not understand, to reveal all of herself to him.

'Richard! What is going on!' the voice came from a young woman, Lady Duckington, one of the few aristocrats present whom Anna had had any contact with.

She had requested, yesterday, whilst taking tea in the drawing room, that Anna pick up a handkerchief for her. Anna had obliged, but Lady Duckington had not said even a word of thanks. Anna supposed it was to be expected - most of these upper-class ladies took their own servants entirely for granted, let alone those of other households.

She was a very attractive lady, quite beautiful to look at and extremely well-dressed and well-bred, but she had a coldness of manner that made Anna find her immediately hard to like. Her voice was piercing and harsh, like a January frost.

"Are we going to take this walk in the grounds, or aren't we…" her voice tailed off as she saw the scene before her. She did not bother to disguise her disgust. Ladies of her station could afford to be disgusted at servants, especially when they were, as Anna seemed to be here, in error. Richard, covered in sweet-smelling slime, turned to face her, breaking eye contact with Anna for the first time in what felt like ages.

"It's quite alright, Lady Duckington," he said, in a warm voice that almost glowed with its own attractiveness "I've merely had a little altercation with a tray of jellies". Without a second for pause or thought, rage spread across Lady Duckington's face.

"What in God's name did you think you were doing?!" she exclaimed, partly at Richard, mostly at Anna. "Idiotic girl! Can you people not even carry jellies correctly?"

"I'm very sorry, my Lady" said Anna, trying to curtsy, blushing with embarrassment, as a sense of desperation rose in her.

"Sorry? You're sorry, are you? Do you have any idea what this gentleman's dress coat cost, or how long the labour of the tailors on Saville Row? I expect you have no idea, but it would be more than thrice your paltry salary! I've a good mind to summon my manservant and have you soundly thrashed in front of us, insolent girl!"

"It's quite alright, my lady" said Richard at last, intervening, to Anna's shock, on her behalf. He remained calm, even in the face of Lady Duckington's mad fury. Anna, feeling more ashamed and exposed than perhaps she ever had before, was filled with a sudden gratitude towards this man.

Would he speak on her behalf? Was he coming to her defence, her, Anna Perkins, the most junior housemaid at Havisham Hall?

"The fault was entirely mine. I have this unfortunate tendency to not look where I am going in great houses, and to stride around foolishly as if the place is my own. It must come from my father, do not blame this poor girl for my error, it is most unseemly"

"Unseemly?" Lady Duckington all but spat, her fair, round face colouring with her anger, the red of her cheeks clashing horribly with her intricately coiffed golden hair. Anna could not help but think that the Lady brought dishonour to her title by behaving like this and that her fine garments perhaps clothed a character not so fine, but could never have articulated such an insubordinate thought.

"What is truly unseemly Mr. Maitland, is that you, nephew to the Earl of Wiltshire and heir to one of the finest estates in England, should have your best clothes drenched in jelly, and then feel a strange desire to speak in defence of a low-born servant! I ask you! You can quite forget about that walk around the grounds! I'm off to seek out the company of someone a little less..." she looked him up and down in disgust. Her face seemed oddly well-used to contorting itself into contemptuous glares "...eccentric". With that she was off, leaving the two of them alone. Maitland turned to face Anna, smiling, a laugh forming at the back of his throat.

"She isn't always like that" he said, seeing the funny side of the entire situation. "On occasion she can even be quite charming. On occasion that is..."

"Oh sir!" Anna said, stepping forward in desperation and trying, almost without thinking, to soften her country girl's accent, in the presence of this prominent gentleman. "Words cannot express how sorry I am! I thank you kindly for accepting some measure of blame in front of Lady Duckington, but really the fault was all mine, however can I make it up to you?" she realised that in her unguarded moment, compelled by some intense attraction swelling inside her, she had reached out to take one of his hands. Rather than pulling away and chastising her for this completely inappropriate action, Maitland threw her a dark smile, wry and fascinating.

"Well you can start by ceasing this ridiculous grovelling" he said lightly. She drew back, fearing at once that she had made herself foolish and vulnerable before him.

"- and then when you are quite restored to your senses, you can accompany me to my quarters to help me change into something slightly less…" he sniffed his coat, glistening with the spilled jelly. "- fragrant." Despite herself, she giggled a little at his remark, and they set off together up the main staircase of Havisham Hall towards the guest suites.

# Chapter Two

As befit a man of his status, and his friendship with Charles Rockingham, Earl of Stanningfield and master of this house, Richard Maitland, Viscount Bellham, was staying in one of the finest of Havisham's many chambers. It was, in many ways, a hang-over from Havisham's past, and had not been comprehensively refurbished by the new Earl in a fashionable, modern way, like so much of the front of the house.

A seemingly ancient four-poster bed dominated the room, carved, back in the 16th century, in rich mahogany and draped in tapestry hangings, which had faded a little with time, but upon which the finely stitched scenes of hunting and feasting were still visible.

Only one of the walls had been re-plastered and painted in a light shade, as had much of the rest of the house, to give it a sense of airy lightness, the rest remained wood panelled, with a heavy, stately air.

There were two landscape paintings facing each other on the west and east walls, an enormous wardrobe and dresser, and the stuffed head of a small deer, shot by the previous Earl, mounted next to the bed. The whole room conveyed a certain antique luxury. Anna did not think she had ever been in this particular room before.

"Ghastly bedchamber really" said Richard as they entered. "I've no idea why Stanningfield is always so keen to put me up in here, although, I suppose, having never complained, I can only really blame myself".

"The room seems quite wonderful to me sir" she said, still awestruck by its grandeur.

"Yes, I can see why it might, but I can't abide all this old stuff" he replied briskly, tapping at the varnished oak panelling around the walls.

"Don't really like sharing my sleeping space with that old boy, either" he gestured at the deer's head "- but then I suppose it wouldn't be an English country house without some severed animal parts. We of the gentry have a certain image to keep up, don't we?"

Anna had no idea what to say in response to all of this upper-class irony. She was gaining insights here that she had never thought she would get, glimpsing a world that had not ever been her own. It was overwhelming and fascinating in equal measure.

"What is your name, girl?" he turned to face her again. The fine hairs on her arms lifted, and a jolt of nervous energy ran through her the instant their eyes met.

"I hope I have not bored you into submission with all my talk of great houses?"

"No sir, not a bit"

"Good. Then you won't mind me asking what your name is?"

"Of course not sir, it is Anna Perkins" she said it with a curtsey and a practiced look of innocence and modesty. It was good for servants to pretend that they had no personality at all, when they spoke to the upper classes. As far as their employers' were concerned, they were there to fulfil their duty and nothing more. She thought to add, unnecessarily: "a simple name, for nought but a simple housemaid."

"Not a bit! It is quite a charming name, in its own way. You need not assume all of us gentle-folk have no interest in our servants as people" he was coming closer to her now. She tried to contain the nervous, quivering sensations inside her, as he came so close that she could almost feel his breath mingling with hers.

"We're not all like Lady Amelia Duckington, thank Christ!" he laughed, and she smiled at him nervously, unsure where she stood.

Softly, gently, his finger stroked her chin, tilting her face closer to his. She was struck by surprise, unsure how to respond to this man, who actually saw her as a person, but at the same time a huge part of her knew that she desired this, desired him.

She consented to his touch, allowed him to move her as he wished, enjoying the sensation of his hand on her as he ran his fingers across her skin, silently encouraging it.

"You are a rather fair young lady, Miss Perkins" he said. She instinctively looked away, concealing the redness spreading across her face at this unexpected compliment. "I am disappointed that I did not have the chance to make your acquaintance sooner."

Then, in a single movement he turned away from her, and gestured down at his clothes, still covered in the sticky evidence of their earlier run-in. The jelly was already beginning to smell quite strongly, as the heat of his body warmed it through his clothes, thought the practical-minded servant in Anna.

"Come, help me out of these clothes. You cannot deny it; you played some part in their ruin, you can assist me in their salvation."

"Of course sir!" she said, hurrying over to him at once. He had all but taken his coat off himself, but the jelly had spilled all over the rest of his clothes as well, from his collar, right down to his breeches.

Despite her lack of experience with gentleman's clothing, and the fact that she knew that really Viscount Bellham ought to have summoned his valet to perform this duty, and therefore might only have employed her to assist him with some salacious intent, she began at once to undress him.

It was most rash of her to do so, but in his presence she seemed to have lost all caution.

Her nimble fingers worked at his cravat, untying the elaborate knot that had no doubt taken quite some time to tie to its perfect, fashionable state, and then easing it away from his neck.

She was forced to press herself very close to him to do this, their faces almost touching.

The temptation to steal an upwards glance at his face was, at one stage, too much but she noted, with more than a hint of disappointment, he was staring imperiously into the middle distance, aloof, clearly used to the attention of servants in this manner.

She then began to loosen the buttons on his waistcoat. The tight definition of the muscles in his chest and abdominal region was clearly visible beneath his well fitted shirt, and she felt a strong desire to run her fingers over the cloth, to feel that hard warmth beneath her hand.

She resisted the temptation.

The more of his clothes she removed, the more she felt a swelling inside her, a heat rising from her lower body, a desire to feel him, and for him to feel her.

It was more than a year now, since John had been killed in the war, and she had not been with a man since, nor wanted to be. Until now.

The demands of her position, the need for her to keep at her duties and perform as required, to in no way act above her station, made these sensations all the more acute – how utterly impossible of her, to want a man like this, a Viscount!

Finally, the waistcoat removed, he pulled his shirt over his head and, tossing it carelessly aside for his valet to clean up later, he turned to face her, shirtless, standing tall and proud, awaiting the attention of her hands on his breeches. She took a deep breath, and considered backing out of this situation, fleeing the room, but instead, found herself stepping forward.

"... with sir's permission" she said, as impassively as she could manage.

"Granted, of course" he said, with a grin. She nodded, and began to delicately undo the buttons of his falls, her breathing coming harder as she did so.

What would it be like, to run her hands over his hips, to touch his manhood, to bring him to full arousal, to sate her desire with him ?

She pushed the thoughts aside, and focused only on easing down his breeches, over those tempting hips, in such a way as to avoid smearing jelly on his skin. Once the breeches reached his knees, he sat, with care not to spread jelly onto the brocade of the chair, and waited for her to pull of his boots.

She did so, with her eyes carefully averted, no matter how much she wished to look, as nothing now preserved his modesty. The boots removed, with a final, faltering pull she slid the breeches from his feet and cast them aside to join the shirt.

Turning back she was met immediately with the sight of a throbbing, pulsing manhood, turgid and magnificent. Her nipples hardened, and a pulse of hot need shot between her legs.  It had been so long!

"I appear to be rather exposed" he said, still smiling. "I was not expecting so close an inspection of my intimate areas."

"Sir…" she could not think what to say in response, but she did not have to. Before she could utter another word their mouths met and he was kissing her, with demanding passionate lips, penetrating her mouth with a tongue as stiff and proud as the instrument between his legs.

The heat of intense desire pulsed in both of them, a shared need making them lean into each other, his strong arms wrapping around her.

She was overcome with sensation, with the memories of how good it could be between a man and a woman.

Her desire rushed through her body, making her mouth even more heated on his and the wetness of her intimate flesh spread against her simple servant's petticoats. Could this really be happening, here, with the nephew of the Earl of Wiltshire?

It was. Unlikely as it seemed, this was really happening to her, sensations overwhelming her, desire rushing through her in waves as their tongues jostled and jousted, tangling together in their mouths.

He stroked her body lightly, ran his hand over her breasts and nipples, where they stood proud against the thin fabric of her worn servant's dress, sending great tremors of desire all through her. Her entire being seemed to be in thrall to him, she could feel every hair on her body standing on edge, her skin prickling at his touch, sense forces greater than either of them pulsing through their two bodies, compelling them together.

She seemed to lose herself in his embrace, strong, firm, warm, the room around her, with all its panelling and decoration, fading away into a blur.

Sensation was all there was, and she ceased to consciously be aware of where they were or who they were.  In that moment, he ceased to be Richard Maitland, Viscount Bellham, and became only a beautiful man, naked in sensual communion, with her, a woman, clothed.

They would have made a rather odd sight had anyone had cause to enter what had turned from a sombre bedchamber into a dangerous boudoir, but Anna was too caught up in his kiss to think such trivial thoughts. The world outside meant nothing in comparison to this sensation, this intensity.

She felt his hands straying, delicately but with a certain force, down towards her most vulnerable area. He worked his way under the outer façade of the drab dress, into the plain and practical underclothes, towards that area which promised so much to both man and woman, and which was now throbbing and beating in time with her racing heart.

His hand brushed aside her modesty and felt the wetness down there, the little bundle of hair above her aching femininity, and he groaned against her mouth. Then slowly, deliberately, he eased a finger into her, so that she bucked her hips against his hand and whimpered her pleasure at the sensation.

He nibbled and kissed on her neck as he did this, biting her softly, more delicate and arousing than she had thought possible, in a way that she was not used to but immediately liked.

She was prepared to give herself to him, to feel more than just his hand in her, her desire overriding any concerns that she may have felt, but then he stopped. She rocked on her feet, unsteady and confused as he pulled his hand out from beneath her skirts, and stepped back, almost embarrassed. He gave her a little kiss on the top of her head, and turned away.

"I'm sorry. We should not do this."

"What? Why?" she said, momentarily forgetting her station, and the scandalous nature of this encounter.

He had no way to know that she was a widow, that she knew what went on between men and women, and might desire this for herself.

"I did not wish to take advantage of you in this manner. I apologise. I should have summoned my valet for this task. I shall attend to changing my attire in my own turn." He looked at her with a compelling compassion wrought across his face. He seemed oddly vulnerable there, completely naked and looking at her with sympathy.

She felt strange. A huge part of her simply wanted this handsome gentleman to grab her and ravish her and share the pleasures that she knew they both wanted.

But on the other hand, it was right that he had done this. She was perhaps more worldly than he assumed, but his concern for her honour and her welfare was flattering. He started to move towards his wardrobe.

"Before you leave however, it would be remiss of me not to make use of the practised and no doubt tasteful eye of a young lady in assisting me with selecting my attire."

He beckoned her over, throwing the wardrobe open to reveal several ranks of finely tailored shirts and coats, and beautifully pressed breeches. She was entranced by them, the range of colours and cuts greater than any she had ever imagined possible.

"How do you feel Viscount Bellham should dress himself?" he said, squeezing her hand lightly and smiling at her. She looked up, still in awe.

There was such a broad selection here that she was not at all surprised that he wanted a second opinion. It was unusual indeed for her to get such an intimate insight into a man's private life, especially a man of such breeding and distinction, and she rather liked it.

Glancing across the many options in front of her, her eye, and her small servant's hand, came to rest on the sleeve of a charming jacket in a sky blue.

"With sir's permission?"

"Granted, of course"

"Though little versed in the arts of men's tailoring, I feel that this one would suit sir's complexion and hair very handsomely."

"Yes, yes I think you might be right" he said, taking the jacket from the wardrobe.

"I usually have my man Thompson take care of such sartorial questions, but I can see that you have quite an eye for clothing."

She blushed at the compliment. As he held the jacket up against his muscled torso, she could see that she was not wrong. The light colour of the jacket seemed only to lend the dark, enchanting richness of the Viscount's eyes an extra glimmer.

"Perhaps in concert with a fine cream shirt and cravat, and darker buff breeches?"

"Certainly sir, an excellent selection."

"Very good, very good" he said, gathering the necessary clothes. "I feel it would be best if I dressed myself now, my servants would be most confused were I to summon them at this juncture and they were to walk in on me unclothed. I have little experience of these things but I shall do my best to make myself presentable."

She laughed at this. It had never entirely occurred to her just how much gentlefolk depended on their servants, but now she was confronted with the notion it made perfect sense. To think that this fully-grown young man, intelligent, fit and lively, had little idea of how to dress himself in the morning without the assistance of another! She giggled inwardly, imaging him struggling with his button holes and fumbling at the edges of his cravat. How ridiculous the upper classes were, up close and behind closed doors!

Her thoughts drew a smile to her face, causing him to exclaim, wryly "I can see that you find my predicament amusing" as he pulled on his undershirt.

"I suppose it is to a more practical minded person. We nobles really would be quite lost without our servants, we depend upon you entirely."

She laughed again, this time out loud. His self-awareness was very attractive. He was neither a snob nor a prude, but merely a man who happened to have a lot of money and a good family. She felt even more drawn to him, and she hoped, he to her.

"You'd best leave now, we don't want to generate any unnecessary gossip.

You should hear some of the mother hens Stanningfield invited to this party, they have nothing better to do than whisper to each other about scandals concerning people they barely know. I could not stand to give them any more fodder. Good day, Miss. Perkins" and he leant in and kissed her softly and affectionately on the cheek. Anna left the room, struggling to repress the urge to turn around and beam at him, feeling like an entirely new person.

Edward Greenidge was a scholar, and it was his opinion that large balls, house parties and the like were no place for scholars. It was not that he did not like the company, or that he considered it to be in some way alien to him. He was here for the same reasons as everyone else of course, on account of his ties to the great and noble families who were here to enjoy the Earl of Stanningfield's hospitality, and to get a closer look at the woman whom he had married, in that rather delightfully scandalous wedding.

Like everyone else, he had been at first shocked, and then stunned into silence, and then finally delighted at the wedding ceremony itself, when the Earl had spurned his pre-arranged dynastic match, to the Earl of Derbyshire's daughter, for the love of a humble governess.

Along with all the others, he had spoken about nothing else now for two whole days. It was like a fever that had come over the entire party, and the only way to sweat it out seemed to be through constant gossip and speculation.

"Well of course this will be the ruin of the Stanningfield name" one Lady had said. Greenidge could not now recall her first name, if he had even bothered to learn it. Such trivialities did not concern him, but what was of interest to a scholar of the Royal College of Arms had been her title and position. She was the wife of Phillip Grey, Marquess of Tewkesbury, and that made her by marriage (he recalled instantly from memory) the great, great, great, great, great, great sister-in-law of Sir Thomas Fairfax, victor of Marston Moor and Naseby. These were the sorts of details that did exercise his academic imagination.

"I wouldn't be quite so sure" another lady, the Dowager Baroness of Wycombe, had said. "Loath as I am to repeat idle servant's gossip, I have heard that Lord Stanningfield's new bride is in fact a descendent of the de Quincys." Greenidge's ears had immediately pricked up at this. He believed he may have slurped his tea, drawing disapproving looks from the great ladies nearby, but this did not concern him. A descendant of the de Quincy line was quite a discovery! They were one of the oldest lost houses of England, one of the great medieval dynasties, and the thought of them being revived through a love marriage was remarkable enough to exercise his imagination. Perhaps he could investigate the subject further, possibly put a little treatise together for the college?

"Even if that is the case, no good will come of it" the first woman had said. "Even if she is a de Quincey, they are a spent force. They have no money, no estates, their title is quite meaningless."

"Meaningless?" Greenidge had cut in, surprising all and sundry. "I think not, er, er, er, even without any tangible claim to er, er, as you, say, monies, er, lands, er, er, houses, etc. er, the name of de Quincy should not be considered a trifle. Why they were er, er, one of the greatest of the Norman houses, er, er, on a par with say, er, the de Montforts, who have the focus of much of my later, er, er, er, research as you might put it, and…" but the ladies, little interested in what the renowned man of letters had to say, had cut him off and carried on their gossip.

Such social occasions had never really been the scholar's natural habitat, and he was quite used to such indifference. Now, bored with the company and used to the guests' lack of interest in his insights on questions of inheritance and titles, he was making his way off to the library, confident that there he would find diversion more to his liking.

The library was certainly a splendid room, fit for a great house like Havisham. From what Greenidge knew of the Earl, he suspected that its master was not much of a reading man, but whether he had assembled this collection of books and manuscripts for his own purposes, merely for showing off to guests, or if he had come into them via some other means (presumably inheritance) did not matter. The Earl's excellent collection covered a wide range of topics, and included a few rare volumes that he absolutely must read whilst here.

Organised over more than a dozen huge shelves, all of them stretching from floor to ceiling, every type of book under the sun seemed to be present, from the ancient classics to modern texts on science and philosophy, via books of medieval and Tudor poetry and plays, and even a variety of different novels.

The escritoire on the far wall commanded excellent views of the grounds via one of the defining features of this house, the tall windows, so clear and well-wrought that, at first glance, they seemed open, looking out towards a spinney of trees the other side of a meadow, laid out discreetly in the English fashion. Greenidge lost all sense of time, wandering slowly around the perimeter of the room, glancing at the titles, making his selection.

He was filled with the same feeling he always felt when confronted with a well-stocked library - an erratic desire somehow to read all of the hundreds of books here, all at once, and soak in the knowledge that they held as rapidly as he could.

Despite being the third son of a Viscount, ordinary aristocratic pursuits had never interested him much. Hunting was tiresome, shooting rather over-stimulating, gambling a waste of money, parties and balls a bore, riding and driving fast frightening and fishing a total waste of everyone's time. Ever since he was a small boy all he'd wanted to do was find a quiet corner in which to read, and, as a professor of the Royal College of Arms, that is how he spent his days. He was rather proud of having found a solution to being a third son, which did not involve going into either the army or the clergy.

Noting with pleasure that the books were arranged by genre and type, he made his way over to the section on the history of the heraldry of the nobility, his favourite subject. Pulling a book with an intriguing title, *Arms and Mottos of Angevin England,* by one Harold Jenkinson, from the shelf, he sat down in a plump leather armchair and began to read.

However, just as Greenidge was settling in to absorbing the wisdom held therein, he was disturbed by the sound of a servant entering with a feather duster. He did not know it just yet, but the girl in her modest black uniform was Anna Perkins.

"Oh, hello there!" he said at once, startling her for a second with his sudden speech. "I'm afraid you've er, er quite caught me! I slipped away from the, er, main body of the party as it were to make a, er, er, er, perusal of some of the volumes. A most interesting selection you have here at Havisham, it must be said!"

"Begging your pardon sir, I didn't realise there was anyone here." Anna curtsied automatically, doing everything that she could to conceal the flushes that were still running all up and down her body from her earlier encounter with Viscount Bellham. "I shall leave you in peace."

"No, no! No need for that, don't be silly, girl!" Greenidge replied. Despite his eccentricity, and clear dis-ease in the company of people, as opposed to books, he had a warm and open manner that Anna took an immediate liking to. Unlike so many of the snooty toffs present at the wedding celebration she thought, this old chap seems to be genuine, good-natured and honest in his intentions.

"I would not wish to er, er, disrupt your no doubt vital domestic duties! A house like this must require daily labour, do what er, er, you will."

"Thank you sir, that is most kind of you." Anna smiled, turning to carry on her with her dusting. She noted, as well, a selection of used china tea cups on one of the tables that would need to be cleared away. Evidently this fellow was not the first to be attracted to the tranquil atmosphere of the library, away from the other guests.

"I'm so sorry!" Greenidge added suddenly "- where on earth have I left my manners today, er, permit me to introduce myself, Professor Edward Greenidge, er, er, scholar-resident at the Royal College of Arms in London." Anna turned and curtsied again.

"A pleasure to make your acquaintance, Professor" she said, hoping that she had used the correct term of address. She had never met a professor before. This role as housemaid certainly beat slaving away down in the pantry and kitchens! She seemed to be meeting all manner of interesting gentle folk. "Wait 'til folk back down in Harteston hear about all this!" she thought.

"As a scholar of heraldry and familial ancestry, I make it er, er, my habit to ask the names of all those who's acquaintance I, er, make. Tell me, girl, what is your full name?"

"Why it is Anna Jane Perkins, sir. That's my married name – my husband's dead, like so many others in the war.  Anna Jane Winton is what I was christened as, if you'll pardon me, er, Professor."

"Oh yes, yes absolutely!" he replied, seeming oddly enthused all of a sudden. He was so enthused in fact, that he rose to his feet and seemed about to start pacing contemplatively. He then turned to her in an instant, with a serious, startled look on his face. Anna was worried that she had made some accidental digression and offended this scholar, and was about to start apologising profusely when he began speaking again.

"I'm sorry, did you say Perkins, by any chance?" he said with a new energy, his usual stammer completely forgotten.

"Yes sir, I did. It was my husband's surname, if you take me correctly."

"I do, I most certainly do!" he said forcefully, almost seeming to jump into the air. "And you are a native of this fair county, born and raised in one of the villages proximate to this house?"

"Most certainly, professor. I've lived my whole life in Harteston parish, as far as I am aware. All of the records are, I believe, in order down at the church registry. My husband was born and raised here too." She could not quite understand his interest. Why was he scrutinizing her like this?

"Tell me" continued Professor Greenidge, serious all over again "- did your husband have a father by the, er, forgive me, rather unusual Christian name of Franklin?" Anna was astounded. In fact she was suddenly a little frightened, and began to back away from this strange man of letters.

"Why, yes sir, he did". She confirmed, trying to conceal how startled she was. "That was my husband's father's name, all of his life."

"Most interesting." Greenidge muttered to himself, his manic energy subsiding as he returned to his book. "Most interesting indeed. You will forgive me, Miss Perkins, I will detain you from your er, er, er, duties, no further. I have er, ample reading to be getting on with. But er, thank you er, er, most kindly for your co-operation in my little er, er, cross-examination." He stuck his nose firmly back into the book, and left Anna, confused and a little worried for the clever fellow's sanity, to carry on with her allotted chores.

Only a few short hours after finishing her duties in the library (ignoring the muttering and somewhat frantic reading habits of Professor Greenidge as best she could), Anna was back in the pantry receiving orders from the housekeeper, Mrs. Cartwright. She was a stern and doughty woman who seemed at times to be running Lord Stanningfield's household like a military camp. Her twenty-something years of dedicated service had made her fiercely loyal to her lord and employer, and she didn't care who knew it:

"Ah Miss Perkins!" she boomed as Anna slipped in, hoping in vain not to be noticed by her superiors. "I have about your little encounter with Viscount Bellham in the west wing! You ought to bloody well look where you're going, lass!"

Anna was immediately conscious that her face might be turning red at this mention of the Viscount. Certainly her heart fluttered uncontrollably, in a way she was not used to. The flush of infatuation immediately turned to anxious panic though, when she thought about exactly what Mrs. Cartwright might have heard.

Could she possibly have heard about her accompanying him to his own private quarters, and what had transpired after that?

"If you don't wish to be demoted back down to scullery maid you'll mind where you're going! There's plenty of little nooks and crannies and blind corners about this great house, and it's your duty as a servant to see that you don't disrupt the activities of Lord Stanningfield's guests, not the other way around. See that you are more discreet in future!"

"Yes, ma'am" Anna said, demurely. Part of her wanted to object, to complain that it had not been her who'd come running around the corner of a corridor in an unfamiliar house, pursued by someone she was not married to, but she held her tongue.

She knew what her job was worth, relative to questions of truth and justice.

As a servant, it was often best just to put up and shut up. And, as it seemed that Mrs Cartwright had heard nothing more than that there had been an unfortunate collision, involving the tray of jellies, she was certainly not going to do anything to encourage further questions! She took a deep relieved breath, and waited to see what came next.

'Now my dear' continued Mrs. Cartwright, warmer and more affectionate all of a sudden.

"Upstairs, in the principle drawing room, many of the guests are taking another round of tea. Not my place to question how much of the stuff these ladies and gentlemen like to drink, though you may have noted, it is rather a lot. Here…" she gestured to a few platters assembled on a simple wooden table "- are some additional refreshments, cakes, scones, fondant fancies and the like. See that they reach their intended recipients unspoiled this time, and you shall find your way back into my good books".

Anna nodded purposefully, in the way one gets used to doing as a servant, and, taking two platters of little cakes in her arms, started up the stairs towards the main body of the party, and, though she did not know it yet, but already sincerely hoped, towards Viscount Bellham.

Unfortunately, from her perspective, the first person that Anna came to as she entered the sumptuous drawing room of Havisham Hall was Lady Duckington. As usual she appeared to be avoiding the company of her husband, who was more than twice her age, in favour of a gaggle of admiring upper-class girls, most of them plain and unwed, who seemed to cling to the hems of her richly tailored dresses like children.

Lady Duckington was just holding forth as Anna quietly picked her way over to them:

"Of course the Haymarket theatre isn't anything like as good as it used to be" she pronounced in her arrogant manner, all eyes fixed on her.

"I saw a marvellous production of *Julius Caesar* there when I was but a girl, and it was the first time I really fell in love with the theatre, do you remember that, the first great awakening of a love of the stage?" her onlookers all nodded as one, sycophantically.

"But since then the place has become a complete and utter dump. I mean no-one who is anyone in London society would be seen dead in the place these days. They turn out a lot of rot- Gay, and Bacon and all of those absurd little fellows - and employ some of the most disreputable players this side of Samarkand to boot. As I say, no-one with any sense of taste or decency would be seen dead in the place."

Anna slipped in among the assembled young ladies, and started delicately placing cakes on their saucers.

The intention was to do so without being noticed at all, as if to maintain an illusion for the nobility that servants and working people did not in fact exist, and that their tea and cakes and meals all appeared out of thin air. Unfortunately, being still quite new to the domestic arts, she did not seem to have succeeded:

"I say girl!" Lady Duckington said to her directly, in a manner unbecoming to anyone, let alone a lady of her standing.

"Are you the coarse little servant who spilled jellies all over Viscount Bellham earlier?"

Anna looked up. She stammered. What should she say? Ideally she ought to say nothing, but when engaged directly in this rather unorthodox manner, by a guest, she had to respond somehow.

Yet she could not seem to get her lips or tongue to work, and she had a strange, sticky feeling already at the back of her throat, as if someone had poured glue down it to prevent her from ever speaking again.

"You are aren't you?" Lady Duckington said, with a malicious glint in her eyes. Her admirers tittered pathetically along.

"You are that idiot girl who ruined the Viscount's finest dress coat! I'm surprised they kept you on at all after that, you people have one, simple job to do and you botched it entirely! You ought to go back to pulling pints for farmhands! Present company is far too good for you!" The company laughed again, with Lady Duckington, at Anna.

The poor serving girl carried on with her duties, laying the little cakes down as diligently as she could, but she felt an overwhelming urge to run away, and cry, and never come back to Havisham Hall, or these cruel noble folk, who assumed that they were better than her, just because they had titles, money and big houses!

Oh if only she were a Lady and could give this stuck-up madam a piece of her mind, but she was only the daughter of simple James Winton, the ploughman, and wife, once, of plain Franklin Perkins, and it was not her place to share her thoughts with the great and the good.

"And whilst I have your ear…" Lady Duckington was relentless! She could not help herself, some horrible instinct deep inside her seemed to compel her to be cruel! *What on earth was wrong with her?* a more self-assured person might have allowed themselves to think.

"I have to ask you, maid, why the dreadful quality of cakes in this house? I had thought better of Lord Stanningfield quite frankly, his staff appear to be nothing but clumsy dullards and dribbling village morons!"

Her followers seemed very amused by this latest quip, falling about in laughter as they crammed cake into their over-privileged mouths. Anna was quietly seething, and was about to draw away from them, towards what she hoped would be a kinder party on the other side of the room.

"Why only the other day I had a fondant fancy that was harder and staler than the Rock of Gibraltar!" She drew more laughter, but it was suddenly silenced by a new arrival, a different presence on the edge of the conversation.

All at once the silly unmarried girls stopped their laughing, remembered to cover their mouths as their nannies had taught them, and looked up at the handsome bachelor who had stepped, without a moment's pause, into their conversational circle.

Anna looked up from her platter to see the Viscount, looking right at her, with a warm smile on his face, still wearing the same sky blue coat and cream cravat she had helped him into earlier.

"Are you harassing the staff, Lady Duckington?" he said boldly, in a light-hearted tone that took all of the malice out of the situation at once. "Come, come, this poor girl has had more than enough grief from me over her earlier error, haven't you Anna? She needs no further reminder of her simple mistake, it could have happened to any of us."

"Any of us who are forced to carry trays around for a living!" Lady Duckington said, her sadistic wit muted a little by the Viscount's presence. "Some of us have the means and breeding to avoid so lowly a fate!"

"Indeed, but we would do well to demonstrate that breeding better by treating our spiritual equals with a little kindness." he gazed into Anna's eyes with an intensity she had never seen in any gentleman before.

He had come to her defence, this charming young gentleman! She was astounded, and felt a renewed desire for him, as acute as it had been before, barely suppressed beneath her serving girls' attire.

"Without staff, we of the gentry are nothing, and we would do well to remember that. As to the quality of Havisham's fondant fancies..." he said, cheekily plucking a cake from Lady Duckington's saucer and taking a bite.

"- I fancy that Miss Perkins here is not responsible for such matters, and that their fondancy, along with their freshness has been dimmed somewhat by the length of our stay as guests. I expect that the household has good reason to wish for our swift departure back to our estates so that they who actually know a little of baking and hospitality may return to a less hard-pressed mode of existence. You will excuse me..."

And with that he left the company to sip their tea and nibble their cakes in stunned silence, quite trumped by his logic.

As he passed by Anna, he slipped a small note into the front of her pinafore in a single, deft movement, threw her a warm and friendly wink, and passed on out of the room to attend to his own business.

Anna continued her duties glowing inside, concealing her blush and fairly throbbing with her new desires.

By the time Anna had finished serving up her cakes, her entire body was fairly swollen with excitement and anticipation. The note sat in her pinafore, exercising her imagination, compelling her attention. She could not help but glance down at it a few times; the humble piece of crumpled parchment that she had already invested with so much wonder and hope, the vessel bearing her into what she prayed would be a better, happier future.

What could he possibly have to say to her, the young noble who had just come to her defence in the presence of his peers? She did not, and could not, possibly know, until she had opened it up and read it, and she could not do that until she had served all the cakes, as she was required to.

Despite her trembling hand and blushing, sweaty brow, she went about her duty as diligently as she could, until she could finally get away, return the platters to the kitchen, sneak into the storage rooms a minute, and read what he had written to her.

The note was small and brief, but it was written in a flowing, elegant script. She immediately noted the excellence of his handwriting, so much finer than her own. She was grateful as well, for her simple village schooling, received as part of the bequest of Harteston Parish and the charity of the local gentry, a privilege not afforded to many ploughmen's daughters in the Kingdom of England. Anna had always been very proud of her ability to read, being, to her knowledge, the first member of her family to be at all literate. She was a little shaky, especially on bigger words, but she could read and write well enough to get by. It had helped her to secure this job at Havisham hall, in fact, and she employed the skill now, for a letter addressed exclusively to her:

*My dear Anna,*

*I must confess I enjoyed our earlier interaction a great deal. It would be pleasant to see more of you, and converse further, if your duties permit it. If you possibly can, meet me in the grounds in one hour, at six o'clock. I will be by the entrance to the maze.*

*Yours, B.*

He had given away little, but it was more than enough to pique her interest. So he had enjoyed their earlier interaction! She was overwhelmed by the thought. It had been her fear, that she had tried to push to the back of her mind but which was large and persistent enough to worry her considerably in the hours since, that he had simply used her as an easy-going, immediately to hand, relief for his masculine desires, as she knew many hot-headed young gentlemen, who were yet to settle down with a bride, often did with serving girls.

He had said that she was pretty, and she had heard it often enough in the past to suspect that he meant it, but for him to take an interest in more than just her body was deeply flattering and filled her with hope and joy. She thought back to their earlier closeness, to the touch of his skin and his firm, muscular frame, his erect manhood and clean-cut jaw. The thought of him filled her and she overflowed with happiness, and with desire.

She forced herself into caution however. They had not fully consummated their earlier interaction, and Anna knew enough of such matters to suspect that he would desire more of her. In his mind, most likely, it would be her who would be revealing her naked body and most intimate anatomical features to him, and, despite her attraction, this filled her with wariness. She knew (indeed, Lady Duckington had been at great pains to remind her not ten minutes ago) that she was lowly, a country girl working in domestic service. If the Viscount did have feelings towards her he would know, even more clearly than she, that any sort of match between them would be out of the question.

And then of course, there was that other thing, her secret, which she did not dare to impart to him, or to anyone else for that matter. "I must be cautious" she thought, before looking up at the clock to see that she had already spent more than ten minutes pacing the room, in feverish contemplation of the note, and of Richard Maitland, Viscount Bellham.

She hurried from the storage room, hoping that Mrs Cartwright would not find anything more for her to do right now.  She looked up as she hurried through the entrance hall, to check on the time on the grand old clock that stood there.  She should not really be here at this time, but it was the most accurate clock in the house, and she wanted to be sure of the time. It was already twenty-five minutes to six, there would be no time to get ready, even had she had any other clothes or anything she wanted to do.

Anna slipped briefly into her little room in the servants' quarters. There was a little time to kill, and she knew she would have to avoid getting pulled into any more work for the present time. She sat down and had a little sip of water. As hard as she tried, she could not seem to take her mind off the situation, the impending encounter, the body of the Viscount. At last she could bear it no longer, and she hurried up a servant's passageway and out into the grounds via the gamekeeper's door, panting from her hurry, and her excitement.

The maze loomed dark and complex on the horizon. Anna picked her way hurriedly across the grounds, around the rose garden where she knew her new mistress Catherine liked to walk in the day-time, past a few stout trees, one of which Miss Theodora, the Earl's niece, had fallen from and broken her arm under last summer, towards her intended destination.

As a fairly junior servant of the household, she rarely had the leisure to walk in the grounds, and was grateful for any opportunity to do so. Having grown up amongst farmers, she had a certain affinity with nature, with trees and grass and streams, although she was not used to seeing them laid out in such a neat and meticulously planned manner as they were in the grounds of great houses.

Everything conformed to some plan; it was all planted and laid out, not for profit and practicality, but for decoration. The gardens were so serene and luxuriant she could not help herself but be deeply impressed.

At first she was worried that he had not come after all. She could not see him at the entrance to the maze or on any of the benches that sat around it. This filled her with dread; what if he wasn't serious? Could this all be some kind of strange prank, the like of which she had heard upper-class young gentlemen liked to play on simple serving girls for sport? Oh what a dreadful world it was, in which men could court the affection of women beneath their station, for no reason other than the apparent pleasure of deceiving!

She had started to blame herself, lapsing into familiar but very unhelpful and negative cycles of thought. *'Silly girl'*, she, said to herself, *'to think that a man like that could be interested in you'*. The doubts built to a climax and she knew not what to think, other than to be filled with shame, until finally, she saw that it had all been for nothing, for there he was. Emerging from behind one of the hedges that formed the maze was the Viscount, smiling at her and chuckling to himself.

"You look quite startled, Miss Perkins" he said with a grin.

"Do I, sir?" Her breathing was still fast and a little ragged from having hurried. She transferred her worry momentarily over to the notion that she might have been seen from the house. If word got up to Mrs. Cartwright that she had been running about the grounds there'd be hell to pay, especially if anyone suspected what her reason for doing so was.

"Well, I suppose I am in a most hard-pressed occupation, especially on occasions like this." He looked at her contemplatively "if you don't mind me saying as much, sir."

"Not a bit, I appreciate your honesty. My own servants are constantly pretending to be entirely content with the world, even when it is clear that they are not. But come now; let us not speak of such tiresome things. I should like to see that harried look on your face replaced with a smile."

This, accompanied by the twinkle in Richard's dark eyes was enough to immediately draw a smile out of Anna. She felt at ease, all her earlier worries about serving and status, and whether or not this was all a cruel deception, floated away into nothingness. The Viscount offered his hand and she took it, and they strode into the maze with confidence, looking happily into each other's faces.

"I don't suppose you might have explored this maze before, and unlocked its secrets for yourself?" he asked.

"Oh no sir, I have never had the time. I have only been employed here less than two years, and duty rarely permits us the time to stroll about the grounds for leisure." She winced inwardly. She was still talking about domestic concerns, even though he had explicitly said she should not!

A new anxiety started to grow on her; what if she had nothing to say to this fellow? Their backgrounds were so utterly different!

"Tis a pity" he said, still in a jocular tone of voice. "If we are to find ourselves lost at the centre of Havisham maze, we shall have no idea of how to get out." she laughed nervously.

He might have a point. She had never been in a maze before.

"We have a labyrinth of this type back at the house I grew up in, at Tewkesbury" he went on.

He seemed to have a great gift for making her feel comfortable, and she felt a desire to lean into him and be held.

"I fear it is not as extensive as your Lord Stanningfield's, but it is a most amusing way to pass an afternoon." He looked at her, and seemed to tighten his grip on her hand.

Her heart beat faster at his look, and she knew that her rapid breathing made her bosom heave in a way that would draw a man's eye. She tried to make her sigh quiet "- especially in good company."

Her body stirred once more, responding to him as she had to no-one since John, and the ache of need between her legs intensified, making her whole lower body tense in awareness.

She was opening herself up to him, whether she willed it or not.

"One summer, when I was still only a boy, I ran into it alone, playing at soldiers or some other such silliness. I had confidence that having grown up walking around it with senior members of my family I would know it well, but I quickly found myself lost. I ran around frantically, tears filling my eyes, worrying, thinking awful thoughts, what if I never get out, what if I die here, things like that. I was desperate. And do you know what I did, to get out?"

"What did you do sir?"

"It seems silly really, it was so obvious, and yet it took a situation like that, and what felt like hours of worry, for the notion to even come to me; all I did was I clambered up to the top of one of the hedges and looked around. It was easy enough for a spritely young fellow, I tore my shirt a little and stained it green, but by that stage I didn't care for such concerns, I just wanted to get out. And you know, from up there" he indicated the summit of the hedges, which stood seven foot tall about their heads on all sides. "- it really is rather easy to work out where you are, and where you need to go. I remember laughing when I realised I was right by the entrance all along, I'd merely panicked and missed a simple turning. I got out and never spoke of the whole sorry affair again. Until today."

He looked at her, his face close to hers. She felt him pressing close to her, their hearts beating along as one. She knew now where she stood. She had drawn an intimate admission from him, and now it felt like there was a bond between them, of things shared only together.

"There is always a solution, Anna." The sound of her name from his lips brought a little shiver to her. "No matter what our predicament, there is always a way out, to better things." As if compelled by some force greater than either of them, they had moved closer and closer together as he spoke, until his lips brushed hers and words disappeared in a kiss.

Many of the same sensations as had assailed her that morning in his chamber came over Anna, only now, away from her duties and the possibility of being seen by onlookers, she allowed herself to embrace them.

His tongue was hot and fluid in her mouth, and she did not hesitate to meet it head on, with movements of her own, bringing the two muscles together as if in a dance. He pulled her close to him, tight against his body, her breasts pressed against his hard chest, her heart pounding against his, and they lost themselves in the kiss, consumed for a few moments by wild passion. She clung to his shirt, her fingers scraping against his finely-toned body, his arms around her, one of his legs curled past hers, bringing her to him, willing her to submit to his desires. She was all too happy to do so, feeling the truth of his desire for her in the hard ridge of his cock pressed against her, feeling her own desire spiralling through her whole body, pulsing along with her heart and with him.

A modest marble bench was just to their left. They spotted it in unison, it seemed to have been placed there just for their use, for the communion of lovers lost in the maze and in each other's contemplation. He pulled her to it, lowering himself onto the marble surface, so that she found herself suddenly atop him, with her legs spread across his hips, her skirts riding up around her, and his manhood, the splendid rod she had seen and briefly touched earlier, pressed up against her, in exactly the place that she wanted it most. The sensation of it, and of their wild kissing, was almost too much, after so long without giving herself to a man. She felt it consuming her, sending warm flushes and cold shivers to all parts of her body, narrowing her vision until all she could see were rapid glimpses of her lover, his handsome face, his well-cut coat, his strong, hard shoulders. Her head was awash with feeling and she was all too happy for it to be so.

Suddenly changing pace from the initial outpouring of feeling, in a single practised motion, he lifted her from him, and laid her back on the bench , leaning over her to kiss her again as he did so. She leaned back, her cap falling from her head, and her tangle of dark red curls escaping their pins to tangle about her shoulders.  She was panting in anticipation, knowing what was to come. She was no maid or virgin, she had some idea of the affairs of the heart and body, knew what her body was capable of in circumstances such as this.

Expecting him to undo his falls, and immediately press into her, as John had always been all too keen to do, she was surprised when she felt a different sensation.  This was not something she had ever felt - her petticoats and drawers had been moved aside, her skirt was at her waist, but it was not Richard's manhood that was now approaching her most intimate area, but his mouth and tongue, and she gasped at this new sensation. Her breasts hardened, as if plumped up by his lapping motions, and her moistness, that had been slowly building since they had first met at the entrance to the maze, was multiplied tenfold by the sensations that his skilled tongue was creating.

Her breath quickened to a staccato pace, keeping time with his dextrous motions and with the feeling of building ecstasy that she could not suppress. She wanted to cry out, to scream affirmatives to high heaven, to keep making love to this man forever more. And yet it was almost too much, she had no knowledge of how to cope with this intensity, nothing in her experience had prepared her for this moment.

Her eyes sealed themselves firmly off from the world, the better to enable her to drink in these incredible sensations. At some point his fingers replaced his tongue, continuing to work against her flesh, driving her desire to an ever greater pitch. She barely noticed his movement as he shifted himself back up her body, and undid the buttons at her neck.

He pulled her dress open, and exposed her breasts to his tongue, kissing down the slope of her neck, to the curves of her breasts and then around each nipple.  Somehow, she realised, he had undone his falls, and she felt the brush of the velvety skin of his cock against her moistness.

The sensation was exquisite, delicious, she moaned in response, her body arching up to him, thrusting her nipple further into his mouth as her hips pushed up to welcome him in.

The moment she had been waiting for, needing so desperately, came as he entered her, hard and throbbing, so defined that she could feel every inch of his length and every subtle variation in the shape of his shaft.

He slid in, slowly, but with an elemental force, and she gasped, not frantically this time, as when he had attended to her with his tongue, but in a drawn-out breath of pleasure.

She felt how wet she was, how much her body wanted for him, as he shifted and moved, drawing gasps and little moans from her, that were ever more frequent and electrified. He thrust his full length into her and she was entirely overwhelmed.

There was so much innate sensitivity in her vital areas that every touch was a rapturous new feeling, every gyration of their hips together a fraction closer to glorious climax.

He thrust into her, at first smooth and controlled, but rapidly becoming harder and faster, as the pleasure overtook his control, until, with a cry of "sir, oh Richard, sir!" her pleasure was unleashed, harder than she had ever felt it in her life, and she was momentarily lost in the sensation, and unaware of her surroundings.

He continued, slowing a little after that moment of shared intensity, savouring his own pleasure and enjoying watching her pleasure, so unrestrained, so different from the noble ladies that he had bedded.

She was warm and welcoming around his cock, wet and tight in all the right ways and he continued languidly stimulating her with every thrust. Reaching up, she ran her fingers down his body, revelling in how it felt, as his muscles moved in time to his thrusts.

She closed her eyes firmly again and allowed feeling to ebb and flow through her, from the top of her head right into her tingling, wriggling toes. That she was lying in the dirt on the bench in the maze, covered in dust, and with a menial job to return to, all seemed irrelevant now.

This was life, being loved in a way that she had never experienced before. After a short while, he began to move faster, to thrust into her harder again, as his climax came upon him, pushing him past any care for control.

She clung to him, riding his movement until at last, with a deep cry, he pulled out of her at the last moment, spilling his seed to the ground beside them.

Languidly, she considered again, how different this man was. How much care he gave to her – to choose to make sure that there would be no unplanned child from their pleasure.

They lay there in the warm air, regaining their breath under the darkening skies, watching evening creep in beyond the clouds.

"You know, I have entirely forgotten the way out of the maze. I fear I have been rather distracted." Richard said at last, still a little breathless. She laughed, and leaned over to kiss him warmly.

"It does not matter sir, I'm sure we will find a way, as you yourself said."

"You are right of course. I could always shimmy up to the top of the hedges if needs be, I just hope a passing groundsman doesn't see me" they laughed, and shared another kiss, the movements of his tongue in her mouth a delicious warm wet echo of his cock in her body just moments before.

"There is no need to call me sir, Anna" he breathed against her mouth, his teeth nibbling her bottom lip for a lingering moment. "My name is Richard, and though my family might have titles and monies, I am but a person, an Englishman and a human, like you."

"Oh sir" she said, cradling him to her bosom. "You are too kind to me, but you know that we cannot continue as equals, it is impossible."

"I know what you say, but I hate it all the same. It is absurd, these divisions we erect between people. To think that in the eyes of many, a clever, pretty and decent young woman like you is lower than a hussy like Lady Duckington, there is no justice."

"It is not my place to comment on such concerns" said Anna, modestly. She knew that, even now, after their moment of passion, she could not risk acting in any way outside what was acceptable for her station in life.

"And therein lies so much of the problem" replied Richard, tutting.

"I am brim full of desire for you, Anna, and with affection. I sense from the nature of our encounter that you are not entirely unversed in the affairs of the flesh. This pleases me, I would not wish to have robbed a young maid of her honour. And yet, my desire for you is so strong, I did not pause to ask, to check, and I am sorry that I did not do you that courtesy."

"You are correct, sir" Anna felt suddenly embarrassed at this scrutiny of her own past. "I have lain with a man in the past. I have also..." she paused, pondered. Her feelings for him were such a powerful tide that she knew that she could not hope to resist them, and she must tell him the whole truth. It might be agony, but there was no question in her mind of deceiving him.

"- also I must confess, I have been wed before, to my childhood sweetheart, down in Harteston Parish. His name was John Perkins, and we had a child." Richard sat up, a serious look suddenly crossing his face.

Anna knew that this was a difficult admission, for him as much as for her, but she did not regret her frankness.

"Good grief Anna, I had no idea."

"Well no, I do try not to bring it up in polite conversation, and I don't wear the ring neither, the memory of it all pains me too much. He died, I'm said to say, before Sam, our little one was even born. That was over two and a half years ago now, I was barely twenty years old when he passed. He went to war, like so many others, and never came home."

Tears swelled inside her, displacing all the carnal pleasure of only moments ago. She picked herself up, put her clothing to rights, and dusted herself down.

'*Oh John!*' she thought. She'd believed at the time that she'd really loved him, the sandy haired ploughman with strong arms and bluff humour, but the Lord (and war) had taken him from her, and she had not lain with a man since, until now.

"My ma and pa take care of little Sam for the present, down in their cottage. They're still young and energetic enough to care for an infant, and they have more means than I. I help them support him with the money I make working for Lord Stanningfield, and go down to see them whenever I have a spare day."

Richard came over to her, and placed his arm about her. He was clearly taken aback by this admission, but Anna was pleased by his caring reaction. A real gentleman he was, to cradle a young widow and unwed mother to him like this, laying a little kiss on her cheek.

"I fear sir that there can never be anything more between us than a little rollicking in the dust. And as enjoyable as that of course can be, there's no good or honest future in it, as my ma might say. I am of low birth and humble profession, and I have my little Sam to look after. I would not wish to burden you with such. It would be much of a burden to any farm lad, let alone a man of your station and breeding." She had a tiny hope that he might contradict her, fling himself down on one knee and declare his desire to help her, to help Sam, to be with her and ease the pain that had encased her heart these past two years.

But she knew of course, that he would not, could not, that he had his rank and inheritance to consider, and the matches that his family were no doubt planning in high society for their eligible bachelor.

"It pains me to say this, but I fear that you are correct in your analysis of our position" he said at last, gravely. "I admit to feeling strongly for you Anna, else I would not have invited you out here with me and lain with you as I did. You inner strength and concern for your child and family moves my heart and does you great credit, but I regretfully concur, we cannot go on. Over time, our relationship would come to be no more than my use of you, exploitation of you and your body, and I will not inflict that upon you."

She sobbed, and he held her for a few moments. He was a good man the Viscount, and yet she could not help but feel that it had been a mistake, after all, to come out here and lie with him as they just had. No good could ever have come of it, she could see that now.

"Now come" he said, in a softer tone. "Let us endeavour to find a way out of this infernal maze." They shared a little chuckle, and walked arm in arm to the edge of the yew-tree maze with little difficulty. As soon as they reached the boundary they uncoupled their arms and parted, he towards the grand entrance to Havisham Hall, she back towards the little passage that led to the servants' quarters, each of them alone.

Sadness at the situation between her and Richard took a while to creep up on Anna.

Over the next two days she distracted herself from her worries and pains as she had for two years, by throwing herself into her work, keeping her head down and trying to focus on other things.

All of the members of staff at Havisham were still immensely busy catering to the many esteemed guests of Lord Stanningfield, serving them meals, drinks, and rounds of tea to accompany their polite conversation and various efforts at aristocratic match-making.

With so many people of wealth and taste about as well, the demands of keeping the house clean and in perfect running order were greater than ever before, and so Anna filled her days, carrying trays of cakes and sandwiches here and there, dusting and polishing the surfaces and keeping the sheen on the Stanningfield family silver and crystal ornaments.

It certainly helped her to not think of Richard too much, though she did inevitably see him around the house. They exchanged polite, and highly charged, smiles and nods, but no words were said between them.

She had a brief conversation with her employer the Earl, who cornered her in the main entrance hall as she was dusting the great clock.

"Ah, Miss Perkins" he said in his rakish brogue. Anna had always considered her lord to be a rather attractive man, despite herself, and he had frequently flirted with her in the past. "Keeping busy I see. I hear that something of an unlikely friendship has developed between you and Viscount Bellham? Something to do with a platter of spilled jellies?"

"Yes, My Lord" she said at once, concerned that he was going to reprimand her for her clumsiness, or worse, that he knew about their encounter in the maze. Would she be dismissed in disgrace? Would she have to face the notorious Stanningfield rage?

"Regrettably word has got out, but I care little for such trifles. Jelly has never been worth making any great fuss over; and Bellham has claimed sole responsibility for the incident. Decent chap, Bellham, been a good friend to me over the years."

Anna bowed and nodded, not having anything to say in response.

"Just as long as you don't make a habit of depositing confectionary on my guests, I think I can turn a blind eye to this one."

 He gave her a little wink, demonstrating that he was only joking.

"Between you and me, I can think of a few other guests at this seemingly never-ending party of mine who might benefit from having something spilled upon them, but do not interpret that as encouragement. I've enough gossip to cope with as it is…" he rolled his eyes, alluding to his rather unusual love marriage, and with a friendly smile he left, leaving Anna feeling quite relieved.

Later the same day she had an even stranger encounter with Professor Greenidge, who was just hurrying out of his beloved library with a very purposeful look upon his face.

"Ah!" he had exclaimed, giving her a momentary turn. "Miss Perkins wasn't it?" she nodded assent, still slightly disturbed by the scholar's knowledge of her family.

"I had been hoping to er, er, er, bump into you, as it, were in er, one of these er, er, passageways that you servants make such diligent use of. I can see that you are er, er, attending to your, er, duties, with a consummate professionalism, excellent to er, er, see, what, what?"

Anna was quite struck dumb by this stammering outburst. He was an odd fellow to be sure.

"Thank'ee sir" she said in reply, after a moments hesitation.

"I have been looking as I er, had er, alluded to er, er, into your family, and a possible connection to several er, er, medieval houses. Franklin Perkins, your husband's father's name was, wasn't it?" his voice suddenly picked up on mentioning her husband's name, until he was almost shouting, despite standing only a couple of paces from her.

"Yes, professor, that is true."

His voice dropped, and he muttered a moment, something that sounded like "finally, finally, the trail of the de Montforts!" before turning back to her, as if he had not paused in their conversation at all.

"Now tell me girl, this is er, er, er, very, very important, I cannot stress that enough, the fates of ancestors and descendants present may depend upon it, what was his father's name, this Franklin, your beloved, er, *husband's father* as it er, were?"

"His father's name was Geoffrey, sir."

"Excellent! And his father before him?"

"His name was Obadiah, sir, a strange name, John told me about it, I never made his acquaintance, him having passed and been buried in the grounds of Harteston Parish Church afore I were brought into this world."

"Splendid! And are there are any others of the Perkins line buried in this er, Harteston Parish, as you say?"

"There are sir, a score or more stretching some way back, and many more before that, I'll wager, though their older graves don't be marked any more. The vicar likes to keep the history where he can, I am sure that he can show you where the graves are, for each of the families buried there."

"I don't believe it! This is remarkable news!" Anna thought maybe she ought to call a doctor. Professor Greenidge did not seem to be in his right mind.

"One final er, er, query if you don't mind, Miss Perkins, did he have a brother, your husband's father? Did your husband have a brother? Or do you know of any other male issue from the loins of goodly, er, Mr. Franklin Perkins, your er, husband's father? Did you have your husband's child perchance?"

"No sir, neither my husband nor his father had brothers.  His father had a sister, but no brother. My John, he was the only child of his father and mother I'm afraid. Though, yes I do have a son of my own, born to my late husband."

"A son! Oh, you have a son! Oh this is remarkable, remarkable news, thank you kindly, Miss Perkins! Our paths will no doubt cross again!"

Professor Greenidge shook her hand forcefully, and fairly ran back into the library, leaving Anna feeling more than a little confused.

The next day Anna could not stop herself from thinking about the professor's words. She had initially ignored and dismissed it as a lot of strange, academic babble, but having slept on it, and pondered further what he was trying to express, she could not get away from her internal questions.

What did he mean? Why on earth could he be so interested in her humble family of farmers down in Harteston?

Why did he keep mentioning them in the same breath as this great medieval family, the de Montforts?

It was certainly an enigma, and one that seemed unlikely to reach any resolution until Professor Greenidge had cleared up his research and explained himself to her in plain English.

There was no light that she could bring to the topic that was for sure.

All day she served drinks and refreshments to the noble guests in the ballroom and drawing room, listening, as ever, to their conversations.

She was concerned that she might overhear some rumour of Viscount Bellham having a tumble with a serving girl, but was pleased that no such hearsay reached her ears.

The noble ladies and gentlemen didn't seem especially interested in the servants at all, as one might expect, but rather spoke endlessly of their own concerns, of balls and parties and matches between people of their own rank.

"I hear that the daughter of the Earl of Derbyshire is to be wed to a Captain of the Guards, heir to a Marquess", said one lady, sipping her tea conspiratorially.

"Yes, I too had heard such rumours, although I had heard as well of some connection to James Blackwood? Evidently there was some complication there"

"There always is with Blackwood" said the first lady, sourly. She pronounced the name with a fierce contempt, tinged with fascination.

Anna had no idea who they were talking about, but knew at once that he sounded like a cad.

"There is speculation that he means to flee the country. No doubt he has disgraced himself by seducing someone he should not, once again."

"No doubt whatsoever! He simply cannot help himself, it is probably best for all of English society if he finds his way into a long exile."

Moving away from this conversation, which it was not her place to either participate in, or even understand, Anna noted that the Viscount did not seem to be present. Indeed, she had not laid eyes on him all day, or exchanged one of their silent smiles and nods. She found she was missing that, rather intensely.

Still, in a way she was relieved - every time she caught sight of him she was filled with swelling, fluttering notions and sensations, that were entirely inconvenient to her ability to carry out her duties, and had to go away and collect herself in private, back in the pantry or kitchens.

Yet, at the same time, she had been sustained by those lingering moments, and reassured that she had not made a terrible mistake.

She needed that confirmation of her place in the man's affections, even though they had regretfully agreed not to be together. It was difficult, she knew deep down that she still yearned for him, and would most likely continue to do so.

She still had not seen him all day when she headed into the billiard room to polish a little silver. There was a selection of old ornaments in there which Lord Stanningfield largely neglected, but which required polishing all the same, for the sake of making a good impression on the guests, if nothing else.

She did not expect to find anyone in the room at this time of day, though it was often occupied by bored young gentlemen come the evening, who would come in for a round of billiards on Lord Stanningfield's great table, or perhaps a round of cards and some drinks, away from the prying eyes of hopeful unwed ladies, their mothers and chaperones.

It was a room apparently without purpose during the daytime, the cues and balls sitting solemnly, like an army formed up in ranks just for the parade square, so Anna was shocked when she walked in and saw Lady Duckington, her skirts pulled up and her petticoats all atumble, being rather roughly 'served', up against the billiard table, by a bare-bottomed young gentleman.

She could not see his face, and the low grunts the pair were producing were indistinguishable from any others, but she knew at once that it was Richard. Lady Duckington spotted her at once and let out a little shriek.

"Aargh! Get out of here at once girl, begone! Can you not see that this room is in use?" she had quickly restored some modesty by pulling her skirt back down, and had a look of horror spread across her face, which was red and slightly sweaty.

The man fiddled with his breeches and turned around, and she saw in an instant that her suspicions were correct. It was Richard, looking at the floor, clearly embarrassed and ashamed.

"You ought to be ashamed of yourself girl, creeping around unannounced in that manner! I shall inform your employer of your insolence at once!"

"Begging your pardon, My Lady, I shan't disturb you any further…" Anna edged back towards the door, horrified at what she had just witnessed. Nevertheless, she was cut off and compelled to stand her ground by a warm, familiar voice, which immediately eased her panic with its surety.

"Now, now, Lady Duckington" Richard said, looking up at them both for the first time.

"It is not for Miss Perkins to feel shame at this encounter, but us. She was merely attending to her duties - we were, in a sense, entirely neglecting ours. I should think it best if we left now, and never spoke of this again."

Lady Duckington made to formulate a reply, but could think of nothing, and with a harrumphing "tut, tut", she swept from the room, followed by Richard.

As he shut the door behind him, he threw Anna a little nod, and a half-smile. It was a small gesture it was true, but one that, despite his indiscretions and the vast social gulf between them, which they were both all too aware of, set her heart racing at the same rate as it had back in the maze.

She was utterly conflicted in her emotions – she felt at once betrayed and cheapened that he could so lightly forget her and turn to that horrible woman for his pleasure, and yet heartened that he had, once again, seen fit to defend her from attack.

Little did she know that Richard was also conflicted, and felt more ashamed of himself than he had for many years.

The look on Anna's face had struck him like a knife to the heart, and Lady Duckington no longer looked so appealing.

There had been nothing caring in their coupling, and he was left with a sense that she had been using him, as much as he was using her, in a desperate attempt to forget his interlude with Anna.

That evening, Anna was quietly picking her way along the main corridor on the top floor, feeling deeply saddened. Her earlier encounter had made her feel a deep sense of shame and regret. It seemed to reflect rather poorly on the character of Viscount Bellham that a mere three days since their love-making in the maze he could be pursuing an illicit affair with another woman, under the nose of her husband, as well as his host, family and friends.

That he could do so with a woman as obnoxious and haughty as Lady Duckington made it doubly distressing. Perhaps her earlier assessment of the man's character had been wrong, maybe he was just a cad and seducer, using pretty ladies of all classes to pursue his own gratification, and then saying fine words afterwards to ease their heart-break.

She felt very foolish and very alone.

Looking up at the portraits of Lord Stanningfield's ancestors she felt herself calling out to them. Had they faced agonies and anxieties of this sort, these great men of history who had founded the house she depended on for employment? They must have done, she thought, they were only as human as I, or as Viscount Bellham.

When they had posed to have their portraits painted they had done all in their power to project a sense of strength, of confidence and right, but inwardly they too must have doubted everything, feared their own tendency to misjudge or make mistakes, and hankered after attractive ladies who seemed to be beyond their grasp.

It was strange, given her lowly birth and station, and her being a woman, but she found herself relating her feeling and her position to these men, and feeling a little better for it. If only, like them, she always had wealth and titles, and protective outer shells like the 15$^{th}$ century suit of armour displayed on the third floor.

 All of those privileges of the upper classes must make life a lot easier to endure, she thought.

Rounding a corner she suddenly found herself face to face, not with another portrait of the Stanningfield family, but with a living, breathing member of it, her friend, the former governess and now wife to the Earl, Lady Catherine.

They had established a friendship some time before her unexpected marriage, and remained on good terms.

"Anna!" Lady Catherine exclaimed, pleasantly surprised. "I have not seen you for days! I trust you are keeping well?"

"Very well, yes Miss" Anna replied, before quickly amending, "That is My Lady, I should say, please accept my apology."

"There is no need for such an apology, Miss Perkins, I am only just getting used to the title myself. It feels rather silly really, this suddenly becoming a Lady. I wonder if I shall ever feel at home in the title."

"I am certain you will, Miss, er, sorry, My Lady, why you undoubtedly have the blood for it, and the education, as you yourself have said."

"All that is true, but if I am to be perfectly frank with you Anna, as I should hope you would be with me, I grow tired of all this aristocratic conversation. It is all so formal, so stuffy! These old Lords and Ladies are obsessed with the most absurd and trifling notions, you'd think they have no idea of the affairs and tribulations of ordinary folk! I've been trying to slip away whenever I can, and I'm sure none of them care a jot. I don't think they'll ever entirely accept me but I don't care much for them either."

"I can imagine Miss" said Anna, feeling herself lapse back into the mode of their earlier friendship.

Catherine was so honest with her, she could not help but realise the absurdity of the situation. She was still the same old Miss Thornberry, even if she had now married into the upper ranks of the gentry, and though she was pleased that her friend had gone up in the world, she was also glad that she had kept her head grounded.

"I have quite enough difficulty conversing with the folk from grand old families myself, being but a humble country girl."

"Then neither of us are alone in that" said Catherine, beaming at her. "I am aware Anna, that you have entered into something of a correspondence with Viscount Bellham."

Anna quickly repressed the look of intense shock that suddenly came over her face. Was there anyone at this party who had not heard some rumour or other about her?

"Do not look so surprised, or ask me how I know, I just know, and that suffices between young women. We know the affairs of the heart intuitively."

"Oh, My Lady", Anna replied, "I am so sorry, I pray I have not brought dishonour to your name and house..."

"Don't be silly, Anna, of course you have not. He is a very charming fellow, and very handsome, and from what I know, I suspect he feels as strongly for you as you do for him."

"But My Lady, how could you possibly know anything of it?"

"As I say Anna, a woman's intuition, never underestimate it." Anna was consumed by affection for her friend, but also assailed by questions. What about Lady Duckington? What about her rank?

"Are you aware at all My Lady, of his relations with Lady Duckington?"

"I have witnessed a little of their affair it is true." Catherine's tone was grave. "She is an attractive woman to any young man, though I personally find her conversation very difficult to endure." They shared a smile at this allusion.

"She is, herself, trapped in a loveless marriage against her will, and eager to grab any means of escape, no matter how irresponsible or un-Christian. I would not interpret their interactions as being of much import, it is likely a passing fancy."

"But Miss, how can I possibly hope for more between myself and the Viscount than a passing encounter? I am only a ploughman's daughter, and he is heir to the Earl of Wiltshire. I am nothing next to him, I feel it most profoundly!" she gasped, choking back tears.

She was expressing her deepest fears and anxieties, and it was good to have this sympathetic ear to unload them into.

"It is not unknown for members of the gentry to fish outside of the conventional pond, where affairs of the heart are concerned" Catherine replied, grinning.

"There are one or two recent precedents one could cite. Who knows what stirs within Bellham? It is merely for you to carry on as you were, and exercise the attraction he clearly has towards you as best you can."

"Oh Miss!" Anna burst out of all formality, and gave Catherine a big hug.

They held each other for a few moments, the two Harteston girls, and both felt better for the open continuity of their friendship.

They parted amicably, and Anna allowed herself a moment of optimism.

Maybe one day, she too would find herself the Lady of a great house, swept up in the arms of a man she loved.

# Chapter Ten

Anna's mind was far too preoccupied for her to sleep that night. She found her way back to her modest room in the servant's quarters, with its bare-board floor and crumbling, white-washed walls. Curling up in bed with her candle extinguished did no good whatsoever for her efforts at sleep, all she could think about was Richard, her Viscount, and her Lady's words of insight and wisdom from a few hours before. Her brain was pulsing, racing ahead of itself and then doubling back.

What did he really feel? Was an affair between them at all possible? And what on earth, if any, was the significance in all this of Professor Greenidge, and his obsession with her family?

Was it possible that it might come to something, that there might be something important about John's family, or was he just an eccentric quack with too much time on his hands?

None of these lines of enquiry seemed to head towards any conclusions.

She did not know enough, and she had had no opportunity to talk to Richard about his feelings in all of this, beyond their sad conversation as they left the maze. Indeed, she realised with a heavy heart, she might never actually have the chance to speak to him, ever again.

He, with his household staff in tow, would soon be heading back to Wiltshire, and might not grace Havisham Hall with their presence again, or at least, not for years, by which time he might have found a more suitable bride, or simply forgotten the humble serving girl he'd once rolled about with in a maze when he still had wild oats to sow.

Perhaps Lady Duckington's frail old husband would die, and he would end up with her, absorbing, over time, the sneering, arrogant attitude she seemed to have towards everything. It was all too horrible, a shivering anxiety grew inside her, and became a physical sensation that she could not ignore.

Sleep eluded her, and she was overwhelmed by twin desires; an urge to run about frantically and a strong urge to cry. In the end, she found she was too distracted to manage either.

And then, entirely without either expectation or prior warning there came a knock at her door.

A jolt ran through her, a strange blend of excitement and panic and she sat up sharply.

She sat in stunned silence for what felt like the passing of an age, entirely unused to being disturbed late at night, aghast at the potential of who might be there - who on earth could possibly want to see her at this hour.

Assuming it was probably Mrs. Cartwright, come to chastise her, or give her some egregious new duty for the morrow, she tremblingly clutched the bedclothes to her and called out.

"Who is it? Come in?" the door creaked as it always did, swinging on its hinge. It swung slowly, and she braced herself for the Housekeeper's thumping Suffolk accent, lathered in decades of experience and a servant's manner. Instead she was startled, astounded, and incredibly pleased all at once to see Viscount Bellham, dressed more simply than usual, and creeping forward cautiously, offering up a tentative smile.

"I really hope I'm not disturbing you too much" he said, almost whispering, closing the door gently behind him. He seemed less confident than usual, clearly in unfamiliar territory, and aware that she might quite rightly not receive him gladly. "I know that you servants need your rest if you are to fulfil your duties."

"Not at all sir" she said. "Why, I was struggling to sleep, and would be glad of a little company." It was not what she had intended to say, but the ingrained habit of not arguing with the nobility, of accepting their wishes and complying, had taken hold, and she found herself welcoming him.

The part of her that was unbearably hurt by his behaviour with Lady Duckington retreated into the background, and she showed him nothing but her polite servant's face.

"It warms my heart to hear this" he said, sighing as he seemed to relax a little. "- and I share your desire for human contact, my bed grows cold on these chilly nights, despite the approach of summer."

He stepped forward, seeming almost to grow in stature as she met his eyes and did not turn away.

She contemplated him, his upright posture, his lush hair, his robust features and compelling, dark eyes, and she could not help but feel the full force of her attraction, the same force that had led her into the maze only three nights ago.

It felt like an eternity had passed since that evening, and yet, at the same time, she knew that it was so recent as to be fresh and clear at the front of both of their minds.

"I wanted to apologise to you properly for what you had to witness earlier, in the billiard room. It was unseemly, and improper, and I regret it immensely. I'm afraid I have been tempted in the past by the advances of Lady Duckington, I am but a weak-willed mortal man, and capable of exercising less control over my baser instincts than perhaps I would like. I pray that you can forgive me."

She smiled at him. This was the first time he had truly let her see the man, not the aristocrat, and she was impressed by it.

His vulnerability made him more endearing, as, in a very different way, it had when she had spilled the jellies onto his coat when they had first met. It was this willingness to be seen as he really was, and his remarkable honesty of speech and thought, that made him so intriguing - that and his devilish good looks.

"Are you going to stand there looking hesitant all night, sir?" she said, playfully, ignoring his plea for forgiveness for the time being. "- there is nowhere to sit but this bed, humble as it is, but I wouldn't want you to catch cold on my account."

He smiled at her, and nodded, and then moved forward with singular purpose towards her. He sank to sit on the bed beside her, drinking in her tumbled hair, no longer hidden by a servant's cap, her deep brown eyes and fresh skin.

Without conscious intent from either of them, they found themselves drawn together, until he kissed her with a softness of touch, but more depth of feeling than she had ever before known, not with him or any other man. Their lips met lightly, not with the vigorous passion of the other evening in the maze, but with an elemental inevitability, like the creeping approach of spring blossom, or the gentle babbling of a mountain spring.

As his mouth caressed hers she felt a slow but very discernible growth of passion within her, a shivering at his touch and flashes of desire in every part of her. Longing flowed into her and she thrust all thought of status, or impossibilities aside, and chose to simply take pleasure in the moment.  After all, she might never see him again, painful as that thought was.

"You shall have to make room" he said against her lips, and she shunted over so that he could lie on the bed with her. He wrapped her firmly in his arms and a safe, warm feeling came over her, mingling easily with the newly aroused desire. Her fingers slowly wrapped themselves about his shirt and she dug in, tactile and dextrous, feeling him, expressing her innermost urges with every lingering touch.

The fabric of his shirt and the rippling of his muscles beneath it all seemed to say something unutterably profound, without the need for a single word to be said. She pulled him closer, and he pulled closer to her, they pressed themselves together and were locked at the lips in silent, sensual communion.

Anna was used to desire being somewhat forced upon her, to the simple and rough love-making of a farmer. This was something new, something that felt, though she knew that she was foolish to think it, deep and serious.

She felt herself expand up and out to new dimensions, felt a new sureness in herself and in this act. Her nipples hardened, their sensitive peaks teased by the coarse fabric of her night rail and every hair on her body seemed to stand up with her tingling awareness of his body and her own. She accepted his kisses, and gave back her own in turn.

He responded to her touch as she desired, touching her in return. First he gently brushed the curls of her rich burgundy hair, where it tumbled against her neck, his touch electrifying as his fingers drifted sensually across her skin, to open the top of her night rail to the air.

She shivered as the cool night air touched her heated nipples, and he lifted her breasts firmly, gently sucked at her nipples and licked the delicate skin surrounding them.

She arched back and let feeling take over, her fingers tangling in his hair and pulling to encourage him, to accept what he offered gladly.

Need was rising in her with every touch of his lips, and she could feel his hardness growing against her hip.

Her breathing was ragged now and she cried out as he slid his fingers across that most sensitive bud of flesh, teasing her until her hips pushed against him with her helpless need, and finally, he took pity on her and, lightly at first, then with greater speed and dextrous skill, began to pleasure her with his fingers.

Starting in a slow circling motion, he progressed to a steady rhythm, brushing his fingers across her bud again and again, then sliding them into her, repeatedly, skilfully driving her to a new energy in her movements that forced her to snap her head up and forwards gasping his name. Fingers still thrusting, he arched himself and brought his tongue to work with his fingers, until she spasmed against him, crying out her pleasure as she peaked.

She reached for him, as he slid himself up her body, kissing her breasts, and up her neck, to find her lips again. She welcomed his kiss, tasting herself on his lips, amazed at what he could do to her.

For all the sensations that had run through her, she felt larger, more whole, more complete and able to move with confidence and pride towards this man, her Richard, heir to the Earl of Wiltshire or not.

Their eyes met, and she was suddenly drowning in the passion that she saw there, the slow certainty of pleasure, of much more pleasure to come.

Moving back from her a moment, he slid out of his breeches, and pulled his shirt off, standing magnificent in his nakedness for a moment before reaching for her again.

He pulled her up, pulled the night rail over her head, and stood back again to admire her, strong and slim and beautiful, rounded in all the right places, bountiful breasts and rich mahogany hair tumbling down to her waist. She sat, drinking him in with her eyes, awaiting him. He came back into the bed and they came together with ease, feeling every tiny part of each other's intimacy, connecting deeply, communicating on a whole new level.

He watched her face, as he lifted her hips and pushed into her, in one long hard thrust, and paused, revelling in the sensation, the feel of her around him, the perfection of their joining. Movement began slowly, with steady, rhythmic thrusts, perfectly synchronised in their movements, their bodies becoming a singular whole. Anna had never felt so completely at one with anyone.

Time seemed not to matter. Space did not constrain them. Any concerns of status or work or the world beyond this bed drifted into the ether.

They pivoted as one body, she now on top of him, gradually taking her fill of his manhood with her hips and thighs, moving fluidly with him as support. She went at her own speed, creeping at first, but then picking up, gyrating more fluently and rapidly with every move she made.

He lay still a moment, watching her move above him, enjoying the sensation, then began to move again, arching his body beneath her to thrust up into her, holding her hips in his strong grip and gasping as his pleasure mounted. He curled himself up, catching her nipple in his mouth and she redoubled her efforts as intense pleasure pulsed through her.

Finally, he almost shrieked in a pleasure she knew that she had drawn out of him, and the sound and feeling of his pleasure tipped her over the edge into her own. After a shared moment of pulsing ecstasy, they reluctantly released each other, separate bodies now, and slid down again to lie in each other's arms.

"Thank you, Anna" he spoke softly, his breathing still fast and uneven.

"For what?"

"For giving me sensations I never thought possible." She smiled, and kissed him strongly. Her lips parted, her tongue sought his, and he returned her passion, with more kisses, and gentle nips of her lower lip.

"Well what can I say" she said, some hot little devil moving through her still "- we country girls know a thing or two."

She made him laugh, then gently slapped his firm body teasingly. He seemed to have surrendered himself to her this time. It had been the other way around in the maze.

"This can't go on though, can it sir?" she added, seriously now.

"You must return to your estates, and I to my feather-duster. It's been nice, but I think…" she stammered. She was unused to this level of forthrightness, certainly in her own mouth. It was clear though, that this was impossible. "… I think you'd best leave."

He let out an odd sound, almost like a groan of pain, and turned swiftly to face her.

"Anna…" he said "I know that it is true what you say, yet it grieves me so acutely to have to hear it. Oh if only you had some name my idiotic family would find acceptable, then perhaps we could find some way." It was his turn now to stop, unfamiliar with the ideas and notions coursing through him.

A strange mixture of utter joy and deep sadness had come over him. For perhaps the first time in his life he had no idea how to get what he wanted, even though it was the one thing that he wanted more than anything.

"Some way to make this feeling last forever, for the rest of our lives. But, I do not know, you may be right…"

"I am right sir, though I say it myself. My name is not great, it is only Perkins, and I have nothing to offer you by way of a dowry save a little homespun wisdom and a talent for baking cakes. Do not worry…" hearing her practical tone, which conveyed resignation and acceptance of the situation, she suddenly stopped herself.

This was not what she truly felt and she knew it.

She too yearned desperately for a solution to their predicament, for a prolongation of their affair, for a way to make moments like this permanent.

It was only because she knew that it was impossible, that, no matter what Catherine had said, there was no happy ending here, that she was trying so hard to be sensible and grounded. She wanted to cry, but stopped herself, knowing it would do no good. She clung to him, unable to speak, knowing suddenly that she would not see him again, not like this, ever.

"If only..." she said at last, whispering in his ear, gently kissing his neck. "If only" and they fell asleep there, bittersweet in each other's arms.

81

# Chapter Eleven

Tomorrow arrived, and with it, what both Anna and Richard knew had to be the end of their affair. Anna rose early to attend to her duties, whilst her lover was still asleep. She planted a little kiss on his cheek and then left him, unsure whether or not she would see him again. Her heart was heavy but, as ever, she found solace in distracting herself with practical concerns. Since she had heard of John's death, she had many times only got through the day by thinking of Sam, and just doing what was needed to survive. This day was no different. She would survive.

At about half past eleven in the morning, she sat in the drawing room, polishing silver. The house was slowly beginning to empty, as some guests departed for their homes, and there were no guests in the room to be disturbed by her working.

She scrubbed and polished vigorously, taking her work very seriously, grateful for it, for it helped her to forget about Richard, and last night's indescribable pleasures. Looking out of the great windows, she saw horses being hitched to carriages, and footmen in various liveries running around with many trunks and cases of luggage. The house party of Lord and Lady Stanningfield was coming to an end, normal life was returning to Havisham Hall.

Out in the distance, beyond the business of the guests and their staff, the grounds stood still, as serene as they ever would be, tall oak trees unbending in the May breeze which disturbed the roses and brought their beautiful scent to her nostrils. Anna sighed, a heavy but happy sigh. If she could not have the man that she loved, for she did love him, she had come to realise, at least she had known his touch, and could hold the memories dear. It was not such an awful life this, when it really came down to it.

She was busy polishing up a serving spoon when she heard a noise behind her, as the door creaked open and somebody came in. Assuming it would be another servant, she did not bother to stand up or turn around to greet the newcomer, but continued in her duty wordlessly. Nevertheless, she was compelled to look up when a familiar voice stammered:

"Er, Miss Perkins, er, er, was it?" it was Professor Greenidge, looking a little sheepish and peering at her from behind his pince-nez spectacles.

"Yes sir, it was" she spoke a little sharply, surprised and unsure of his purpose. "And what might I be able to do for you, Professor?"

"Well, not a lot, er really" he said, fidgeting uncomfortably "- it was more, er, that there was er, er, something I wished to communicate to you. The results in fact, of some of my, er, er, er, research, as it were, er…"

"Yes sir?" Anna was unsure what to think. She had little formal education, and feared that Professor Greenidge wished to engage her in discussion of some deeply academic topic, of which she had no knowledge. Reading came easier to her than to the typical country housemaid, but that was about all that could be said of her education.  She had not had the chance to indulge in intellectual pursuits, and feared greatly that she would not understand anything that he might wish to tell her.

"Well, it's like this you see" Greenidge continued "- I'm afraid I may have startled you a little with my er, oddly extensive knowledge of your own family, and er, er, considerable interest in your er, husband's lineage. I must profusely apologise for any er, unnecessary, er, er, consternation this may have caused you, but I er, er, feel that the result of my enquiries will be most to your er, er, pleasant surprise, and er, satisfaction?"

"Whatever can you mean Professor?"

"The de Montforts. That is to say, you are, of the de Montforts, you are er, er, a de Montfort, by marriage, one of the few remaining, er, your husband, was er the rightful inheritor of the de Montfort title, of er, er, Duke of Dorchester, and your little son Samuel is er, er, now the bearer of that title, your husband being sadly, er, deceased, which makes you the Duchess and, er, er, once Samuel marries, that will become Dowager Duchess, of course."

Anna was more than startled. She was momentarily beyond speaking, and sat, frozen in place, as she considered what she had heard.  She had really heard that, had she not? It was not just her wishful thinking? Was this really true? Was this a joke? How on earth could it be possible?

"But sir…" she said, getting to her feet, shaking, her mouth wide open in shock. "Professor, how can this even be possible?"

"I presumed you might ask that!" Greenidge was newly animated, as he always seemed to be when discussing his favourite subject. He produced, from the bundle clutched under his arm, a huge document, covered in an intricate web of names, dates and marital connections. "Which is why I took the liberty of drawing this er, er, fairly straightforward and considerably simplified er, chart of the lineage, to demonstrate, the path of descent of the title."

"Simplified?" Anna wanted to say, but thought better of it. She'd not like to see the complicated version, the chart was impenetrable!

"But er, put simply this is your husband's family tree, tracing his lineage all the way back to Simon de Montfort, the renowned, er, Lord and Knight, of the Middle Ages. His line has become somewhat er, confused over the years, you will note the complex web of marital arrangement in the mid-15th century in particular, but your son, or that is to say, your husband's father, er, Franklin Perkins, and therefore your son, now, is the rightful heir to the title, via this chap." He pointed firmly at a name on the chart, a man called Cecil de Montfort-Perkin, in the late 1600s.

"That was a good, er, one hundred and sixty years or so ago, and the rightful heir has not been known until now. I am most pleased, most pleased, to be the one to have finally found a true heir!" Professor Greenidge beamed at her, obviously more pleased for himself than for her.

"I regret to say, there is only a small fortune to come with the title. Little of the family's money has been traced, and much has been used up on er, er, legal fees and such like. What remains is stored in a London safe deposit. Then there are the estates of course – the entailed properties remain, but need upkeep. Anything not entailed was sold or otherwise passed out of the control of the family's men of business long ago."

"How much sir?  What do you mean when you say a small fortune?" Anna asked feverishly, assailed by another wave of shock.

"Oh, very little as I say, around three and half thousand guineas, give or take a few, er, er, shillings here and there, with the bankers.  And I believe that the estates still produce an income of five thousand pounds a year, but most all of that goes on just barely maintaining the entailed properties. I'm sorry that it isn't more, er, but I suppose it would be enough to restore at least one estate to a modest condition and a pay a few er, critical staff, what?"

Anna was amazed, stunned. Three and a half thousand guineas! And then an income of five thousand pounds a year! She had no idea what great houses cost to run, but surely that was enough. That was more money than she could ever have dreamed of, more than the whole village combined could ever have earned in a lifetime!

And now it was theirs, well, Sam's, along with the title and name of an ancient and noble family. She was noble by marriage – it seemed overwhelmingly improbable…. Yet…. This was incredible.

In that moment she realised that there was one thing that she had to do, right now. She had to tell Richard!

"Come with me Professor!" said Anna purposefully, fairly grabbing Greenidge by the hand and hauling him out of the drawing room. "There's someone who needs to know all this and quickly!"

They ran, Anna as quickly as her legs could carry her, Professor Greenidge stumbling and stuttering behind, his precious family tree diagram billowing in his grasp, holding on to his pince-nez in a most ridiculous manner.

They tore down corridors and into the various rooms, surprising and disturbing those guests who were still taking tea and cakes and discussing aristocratic concerns. It seemed that Richard was nowhere to be found.

Anna's panic rose the further they went without finding him.

"Begging your pardon!" Anna said, after bursting in on a few old ladies gossiping in an anteroom.

"I should think so too!" one of them said sourly as the exasperated girl rushed out.

"Awfully sorry!" Greenidge saw fit to add, on his way out, as if it excused any kind of mad behaviour. "She's a de Montfort don't you know!"

They hurtled through the main hallway, weaving a path through footmen who were carrying cases and valises outside, barely avoiding old Featherstone the Steward on the stairs (at which point Greenidge, by way of apology, could only manage a short cry of "de Montfort!" which confused all and sundry) up to the guest suites. Anna sprinted to Richard's bedchamber, but only his valet was present.

"Where's Richard, er, that is to say, where might I find Viscount Bellham, good sir?" she panted desperately.

"My master is already at his carriage. I am just bringing down the last of his things. He is to leave Havisham on the hour." Anna looked up at the nearest clock. There were less than five minutes to go until twelve o'clock! She had to find him, as quickly as she could, so she turned around, barged past Greenidge shouting "come on!" into the professor's bemused face, risked her neck dashing down the stairs four at a time and hurtled out of the front door, knocking a large leather valise over as she did so.

There were four carriages assembled outside, but she immediately knew which one was her intended target, for there, giving instructions to a footman and looking splendid in the same light blue coat she had selected for him only five days ago, stood Richard Maitland, Viscount Bellham, the man who she now knew, with certainty, that she loved.

"Viscount Bellham! Viscount Bellham!" she dashed over in a manner unbefitting a lady of her recently discovered rank, but she did not care. She had but one purpose, and she was going to see it out.

"Anna!" Richard said, his eyes gleaming the moment he turned to face her. "It is good to see you, but what is it? Is there something wrong?"

"Professor Greenidge…" she panted, trying as hard as her lungs could manage to take in air and catch her breath "… has discovered… I am… title… what is it er, professor?"

"Well…" said Greenidge, equally exasperated and holding up his family tree "- simplifying tremendously of course, and taking into account several years of dedicated er, er, research, I can confirm that Miss Perkins here is in fact, the widow of er, John, son of, er, er, Franklin, er de Montfort-Perkin, rightful heir to the title Duke of Dorchester via er, er, his descent from the de Montfort family line, making Miss Perkins the Duchess of Dorchester and her young son Samuel, Duke of Dorchester. Delightful discovery, don't you think?"

The Professor beamed at the Viscount, thrilled to have such an attentive audience.

Richard was as shocked as Anna. He looked almost pale with awe at the notion, his eyes and mouth wide open. He stared at her, his mind racing, here he was, having spent the morning desperately trying to find a way that he could marry Anna, even penniless as she was, without being completely disinherited, his heart breaking at their predicament, and now this. It was a miracle, an absolute miracle!

He looked from the professor to Anna, and as they shared a moment of eye contact, the whole situation was just too much and they both broke out into uncontrollable fits of laughter.

"You're a Duchess!" he exclaimed, jubilantly. "You're a bloody Duchess, I don't believe it!"

The professor had begun to sputter his explanations again at these words, but Richard hastily put his mind at rest

"Well, actually, I do believe it, and it's wonderful!  There's only one thing for it…" and then suddenly, solemnly, romantically, he dropped to one knee.

"Anna De Montfort-Perkins, will you be my bride?"

"Yes sir! Yes of course I will!" she all but shouted. Richard rose to his feet, pulled her into his arms and embraced her with feelings of utter joy, and kissed her in a way she wanted to last forever more.

Here is your preview of

Book Four

The Counts Impetuous

Seduction

by Arietta Richmond

The Derbyshire Set - Book 4
Regency Historical Romance
The Count's
Impetuous
Seduction
Arietta Richmond

# The Derbyshire Set – Book 4

## Regency Historical Romance

# The Count's Impetuous Seduction

# Arietta Richmond

Charlotte cast her eyes around the church, looking for Don Diego. With a dismayed sigh she realised that he did not appear to be among the guests, here for her sister's wedding. She stifled her sigh so as not to alert the other guests to her desperation.

For weeks this had been the only date on her mind, the only day that she could focus on, whenever she looked at a calendar or glanced ahead in her diary.

It was today, the twelfth of June 1817, the day that she would be reunited with her Don, yet it had come and he did not seem to be here.

It was almost too much. This might be the greatest day of her sister's life, but she was not sure she could bear it. Risking ruination, she thought about getting up and running out, finding a quiet spot in the shadow of a yew tree, or beside a grave, in which to cry her eyes out.

Despite all of the affection that she had towards her older sister, who was marrying her handsome captain, the joy of the occasion dissipated. It seemed as if all she could imagine of life from here on was struggle and pain.

She had poured over Diego's short note obsessively, ever since it was delivered to her, shortly after he had left for London.. Every word had been scrutinized, every syllable picked apart, ever stroke of his pen analysed for signs of his true feelings. He had addressed her as 'My Lady' but then signed off as 'ever yours', a strange clash of formality that could probably be attributed to him being a foreigner.

Likewise, he had said that he was 'eagerly awaiting the chance to see you again', but in her infatuated haze she could not allow herself to believe that this was an entirely sincere expression. Did he mean it, or was he merely being polite?

Was he really eager about her, or merely about another occasion in the social calendar? It was impossible, trying to start a love affair with a letter, yet in her head it was almost as if she had done everything in her power to do so. She closed her eyes to go to sleep every night and he was there, holding out his hand to her, smiling at her on the dance floor, his flamboyant Latin attire glistening in the candlelight. But he was not here, and that seemed to be all that mattered for the present.

Charlotte, trying very hard to look demure and entirely focused on the wedding proceedings, still desperately craned her neck, trying to get a look around the columns of the church.

It was possible, if unlikely, that she had not seem him entering, and that he was in one of the many nooks and crannies around Tideswell Parish Church that was not visible from where she was sitting, in pride of place beside her mother and father, in the first rank of pews. As her eyes darted around the room they met the gaze of many strangers, and many more relations and friends of the family. There was Lady Staveley, looking fatter by the year, and Miss Henrietta Elmton, still without a husband even after her thirtieth year.

They all looked back at her curiously, presumably wondering why on earth Blanchette's sister was behaving in such a distracted and unseemly fashion on the day of her sister's wedding. All the faces seemed familiar to her, until suddenly, her eye settled on one face, handsome, distinct, masculine, that she had never seen before but immediately wanted to go on seeing, for as long as she dared.

He was seated near the back of the modestly sized church, and seemed to be alone, or as good as.

The moment she spotted him she was surprised that she had not noticed him earlier, owing to the fact that he seemed almost to dominate his entire pew, so bright was his shock of red-brown hair. He seemed, from his bearing, his ferociously intense gaze and the half smile that curled the corner of his lip, to be in command of all his surrounds, with that easy swagger that comes to many sons of the nobility.

He wore a dark green coat and a richly embroidered waistcoat, topped by a crisp white cravat, all finely tailored, all enhancing his appearance of nobility and confidence.

Charlotte was seated some distance from him, but she could see that he had the most incredible green eyes, of a brighter green than she had ever before seen, looking intently forward, towards the ceremony going on at the front of the church.

She could not quite understand it, but she was for a few moments at least, distracted from thoughts of Don Diego, and focussed instead on this mysterious, dashing young man whom she had never seen before. Ignoring all laws of etiquette and sisterly decency, she turned to her mother.

'Mother' she whispered, as loudly as she dared '-who is that fellow near the back of the church with the reddish brown hair? I don't believe I have ever laid eyes on him…'

'Shush girl!' her mother hissed back '- have you no notion of decency? This is your sister's wedding!' and Charlotte noticed Captain Westbury, looking remarkably handsome in his full parade uniform of the guards, twitch slightly at the sound of muttering behind him.

The threat of the soldier's fury, and the prospect of her shame-faced apologies to Blanche at the reception party, was enough to silence her. Her mother however, to her immense surprise, had turned around to follow up her interest, despite her earlier recrimination.

She saw her look carefully behind, scouring the banks of seats for a sight of the man her daughter had just mentioned.

'I see who you mean' Lady Derbyshire said, directly into Charlotte's ear, with practised discretion. 'I believe that is the Marquess Hemsbridge, from down in Somerset. You'll have to ask your father if you want more detail; he invited the fellow'. Charlotte's interest was piqued.

A Marquess? And yet he looked so young and full of life and energy, to have already come into possession of a great estate and title was most impressive to the impressionable young girl of twenty. Charlotte leaned in towards her mother, and almost as privately, whispered:

'He's rather handsome isn't he?'

'Coarse girl!' came the immediate response, Lady Derbyshire's shock barely contained by her whisper. '- to speak of such things on an occasion like this!' Then however, her mother glanced around for another quick peak at Hemsbridge.

'Between you and me however...' Charlotte barely repressed a giggle at her mother's tone, which would have been especially embarrassing had it escaped. At the front of the church, the Bishop of Derby was just working his way towards the vows. '... I should have to say I echo your sentiment. Don't you dare disclose that to your father however!' They shared a second's grin, and returned to facing the front.

'If any person present...' the Bishop droned on in his reedy, pious voice '... knows of any reason why these two may not be joined together in Holy Matrimony, may he speak now, or else, forever hold his peace.' An awestruck silence descended on the room. Many here had been present at Blanche's abortive wedding a few short months ago, and instinctively, they feared a repeat performance.

This time, however, (perhaps owing in part to the absence of one Mr. James Blackwood) nobody spoke up, Captain Westbury held his ground, and Blanche was able to quickly turn the fearful expression with which she had regarded the room into one of happiness and security.

'Lady Blanchette Cavendish, do you take this man, Captain Henry Westbury…' the bishop carried on, and for the first time that day, with her sister finally tying the knot, Don Diego somewhere in England, hopefully pining after her, and that handsome stranger Hemsbridge seated at the back of the church, Charlotte Cavendish felt nothing but happiness at being alive.

Outside, the congregation greeted the happy couple with cheers, a few tears, and showers of confetti. Bells pealed, and despite their friendly rivalry for the attentions of desirable men like Henry Westbury, which had persisted throughout their adolescence, Charlotte was swept along in all the good feeling, and felt overjoyed for her sister. Captain Westbury turned to face the crowd for a moment, with Blanche in his arms, and cried out in his commanding, military voice:

'My Lords, Ladies and Gentlemen! To Amfield!' the guests cheered once again at this, and all at once set about the rather arduous process of each collecting their maids and footmen and making for their carriages. There was to be a great ball this evening, in celebration of the wedding, at a cost which Lord Derbyshire had winced at on principle and then happily paid.

The servants at Amfield had been in a frenzy of preparation to ensure that only the best was provided. Tomorrow, after the celebration was complete, Blanche and her Henry would set off for Italy, for a leisurely and protracted honeymoon which would presumably involve the delicate business of producing an heir…

In the press of bodies that had assembled along the small churchyard path, Charlotte found herself suddenly and unexpectedly separated from her parents, with whom she would be riding back to her house. Momentarily panicked, she tried to raise her small frame upwards to spot them amongst the crowds, but could not.

She was considering calling out when suddenly, as she turned, looking for them, she found herself face to face with Lord Hemsbridge, the man whose eye she had met inside the church, looking even more impressive seen close up, as he strode assertively towards his carriage.

'I beg your pardon, my Lord!' Charlotte could not help but cry out at once. Fixed by his powerful, green gaze, she was suddenly frozen in place, her awareness of the crowd around her fading away, and felt an unfortunate blush creeping up the back of her neck.

He was undoubtedly handsome; she only hoped that he would not notice her sudden redness, or if he did, that he would be enough of a gentleman to pretend he had not, and therefore not embarrass her completely.

'Please, the fault was entirely mine' he said in a crisp voice that did not sound used to waiting around or indulging in idle chit chat.

He gazed at her for a moment, as if he were looking for something in her face, in the depths of her pale blue eyes or the slight kink in her fair hair.

His eyes narrowed contemplatively, and they shared a silent moment of communication, seeming to say all that needed to be said of the attraction that instantly existed between them with their eyes and faces.

'Forgive me' he said, injecting a little more warmth into his tone of voice '- I don't believe we've been introduced' he placed his hand on his broad, toned breast, and offered a slight bow. 'I am Lord Hemsbridge; I have journeyed up from Somerset at the behest of the Earl of Derbyshire. My attendance had been a mere formality but now that I see that with such fair company...' he maintained his piercing gaze, even as he stopped to kiss Charlotte's hand.

She felt a little flutter, somewhere deep inside her. Once again Don Diego seemed for a moment to be but a passing fancy. '- I can see that the trip was not in vain. What is your name, my Lady?'

'I am Lady Charlotte Cavendish' Charlotte replied, trying to be coy and reserved, as Blanche would be when confronted by a handsome gentleman. 'I am the younger daughter of the aforementioned Earl, and also have the privilege of being sister to the bride.'

'You are Lady Blanchette's sister?' Hemsbridge said, promptly. '- and there was I convinced that the fairest of the famous Cavendish sisters had already been wed. It is a bounteous pleasure to make your acquaintance.'

'The pleasure is undoubtedly mutual, sir' said Charlotte, with a pleasantly flirtatious nod that concealed the complex and powerful feelings bubbling up inside of her.

She still felt for her Don, yearned for him even, and yet this man had stirred something in her as well, something irrepressible, and impossible to ignore.

Was love always this difficult, she felt like exclaiming? '- I trust you shall be joining us at Amfield House for the subsequent celebrations?'

'Undoubtedly' he replied, not wasting a single breath. 'I had wondered whether such an attendance would be worth my while, but I can see now...' he regarded her conspiratorially.

She knew that dark look some gentlemen liked to throw out. Charlotte was used to watching other girls receive it, bat their eyelashes and glance away from it tenderly, and it was quite a thrill to finally be on the receiving end. What great mysteries those green eyes concealed!

'... that it would be quite a pleasure.'

'Indeed, my Lord. I must now re-join my carriage; however, I trust you shall have a safe and comfortable passage through the Peaks.'

'As do I' he replied. 'Safe and comfortable indeed.'

They looked at each other, the one contemplating the other, imagining all manner of carnal possibilities in the silent and private parts of their minds.

And then without another word, Charlotte turned, and hurried to re-join her family for the ride back to Amfield House.


Read the rest……

Get

# "The Count's Impetuous Seduction"

as soon as it's released – go to
http://www.ariettarichmond.com

and make sure that you are signed up for news and release notices !

Arietta Richmond has been a compulsive reader and writer all her life. Whilst her reading is broad, history has always fascinated her, and historical novels are amongst her favourite reading.

She has written a wide range of work, including non-fiction works (published under a pen name), but fiction has always been a major part of her life. Now, her Regency Historical Romance series is finally being released. The Derbyshire set is comprised of 9 shorter novels.

She also has a standalone longer novel shortly to be released, and two longer series of novels in development.

She lives in Australia, and when not reading or writing, likes to travel, and to see in person the places where history happened.

Be the first to know about it when Arietta's next book is released!

Sign up to Arietta's newsletter at

http://www.ariettarichmond.com

When you do, you will receive a free copy of the <u>subscriber exclusive</u> prequel novella **'A Gift of Love'** which ends on the day that 'The Earl's Unexpected Bride' begins

This story is not for sale anywhere – it is absolutely exclusive to newsletter subscribers!

# Other Books in 'The Derbyshire Set'

Available at all good book stores and for ebook readers too!

Coming Soon!

# Books in the 'His Majesty's Hounds' Series

Enchanting the Duke (coming soon)

Redeeming the Marquess (coming soon)

Healing Lord Barton (coming soon)

Winning the Merchant Earl (coming soon)

Loving the Bitter Baron (coming soon)

Rescuing the Countess (coming soon)

Attracting the Spymaster (coming soon)

# Other Books from Dreamstone Publishing

Dreamstone publishes books in a wide variety of categories – here are some of our other bestselling books:-

We have books in many categories, ranging from Erotica and Romance to Kids Books, Business Books, Photography, Cook Books, Diaries, Coloring books and much more.  New books released each month.

Be the first to know when our next books are coming out

Be first to get all the news – sign up for our newsletter at

http://www.dreamstonepublishing.com

www.ingramcontent.com/pod-product-compliance
Lightning Source LLC
Chambersburg PA
CBHW070733190726
48292CB00002B/243